**"Were you spying on us?" she said, part question, part accusation.**

Jason looked over his shoulder at her. Those soft brown eyes had always melted her heart, but they'd have to burrow through the frost that had developed in the past few minutes. "You've been in my field of vision forever."

"That's screwed up. I believed in you, and now I don't know what to believe." She'd dreamed of having him back for years, but not like this. Her traitorous eyes teared up.

"You need to trust me." He reached for her hand. The heat of his touch scrambled her thoughts, and for a brief second, she wanted him in the most indecent way possible.

She pulled away and let out a gruff laugh. "That would work if you hadn't lied to me for the past five years."

Dear Reader,

I'm so glad you're here for the first book in the Fresh Pond Security series. I love writing underestimated heroines, women who are far more capable than they first appear.

Fiona Stirling, a petite novelist, learns that her deceased husband did not die in an overseas military assignment. Not only is she furious he lied to her, but his reappearance puts her and their son in jeopardy. Jason, on the other hand, learns his wife had once been a government assassin, taking down government targets across the globe. Thrown back together in the middle of chaos, they have to learn to trust each other again while dodging bullets and rescuing their son.

This book is dedicated to my father, who died only a few days ago. He embodied the best kind of hero, one who valued his partnership with my mother and parented my brother, Steve, and I as a mentor, not an authoritarian. He allowed me to find my confidence and strength while always having my back. The novel's hero, Jason, learns to embrace those same qualities as the story unfolds.

Grab your favorite beverage, give a quick toast to the hero in your life and enjoy the story.

Best wishes,

*Veronica Forand*

# PROTECTOR IN DISGUISE

## VERONICA FORAND

**Harlequin**

## ROMANTIC SUSPENSE

**Harlequin®**
# ROMANTIC SUSPENSE™

Recycling programs
for this product may
not exist in your area.

ISBN-13: 978-1-335-50256-8

Protector in Disguise

Copyright © 2024 by Deborah Evans

 Harlequin Enterprises ULC
22 Adelaide St. West, 41st Floor
Toronto, Ontario M5H 4E3, Canada
www.Harlequin.com

**Printed in Lithuania**

MIX
Paper | Supporting
responsible forestry
FSC® C021394

**Veronica Forand** is the award-winning author of romantic thrillers, winning both the Booksellers' Best and the Golden Pen Award for the novels in her True Lies series.

When she's not writing, she's a search and rescue canine handler with her dog, Max.

A lover of education but a hater of tests, she attended Smith College and Boston College Law School. She studied in Paris and Geneva, worked in London and spent several glorious months in Ripon, England.

She currently divides her time living between Philadelphia, Vermont and Cape Cod.

### Books by Veronica Forand

### Harlequin Romantic Suspense

#### *Fresh Pond Security*

*Protector in Disguise*

Visit the Author Profile page
at Harlequin.com for more titles.

## For Dad

**A man who preferred history and political books
but read every one of my romances.**

# Chapter 1

Fiona Stirling's first blind date in the five years since becoming a widow would be the death of her. Death by boredom. The elegant restaurant overlooked Boston Harbor with its seagulls and sailboats and a steady stream of aircraft landing across the water. While the intoxicating aromas from the kitchen encouraged diners to try some of the best seafood in the city, her companion, George, preferred roasted chicken and a beer, and had berated the waiter for not allowing him to order from the lunch menu. Fiona asked for the roasted sea bream and a glass of Sauvignon Blanc from South Africa. Based on the first few minutes, she might need an entire bottle. For an appetizer, they agreed on an order of artichoke dip. She was starving when it arrived. The scent of melted cheese with a touch of white wine filled her with a dozen memories of meals with friends and family. Before she had a chance to taste it, George bit into the French bread, toasted to a perfect warm tan, and spit the bite into his napkin. He waved down the waiter and sent the whole dish back to the kitchen before Fiona could say a word.

"Are you okay?" she asked, her patience evaporating each minute she sat across this man who would never measure up to her dead husband.

He gestured with his hand while he found his voice. "I expect a certain level of quality while dining. This isn't it. The bread is stale."

Fiona bit back the remark burning on her tongue. The Oceanside Grill was her favorite restaurant. She ate there at least once a month with friends or her son or her literary agent, Janet, when she was in town. The bread was never stale. "Was the bread stale or toasted?" she asked.

His expression froze, then he straightened his back and resumed his focus on all the other patrons of the restaurant. "Toast can be stale."

Fiona had a very low tolerance for rudeness. If George acted like a recalcitrant toddler with a piece of bread, how would he deal with more serious issues in life?

Her phone vibrated. She glanced at the text from her son, Matt.

I'm home. Found the lasagna. Thanks.

Although thirteen years old, Matt conducted himself like a seventy-year-old man. He was the kid most mothers wanted their own children to hang out with. Solid grades, a skilled athlete, mild-mannered, preferring an at-home movie or game night to wild parties. Despite all that, Fiona worried about him every second of every day. After already losing one man in her life, she would do everything in her power to keep her son safe.

The waiter brought over a bread basket and placed it on her side of the table. He returned with another glass of wine only moments later. She owed him a very large tip for reading her mind.

As the dinner dragged on, two other guests came

over to the table to ask for an autograph. She smiled, signed a napkin and posed for a selfie. George nodded toward the other guests as though he were harassed by fans all the time. Perhaps he was. A college professor in molecular genetics, he had an impressive résumé and bragged about his soon-to-be promotion to department chair. Fiona asked him about his work, but he dismissed her as though she would never understand such complex issues. Her platinum blond hair and 34D chest precluded intelligence for many people who had imbibed the stereotypes thrown at them for decades. Fiona's deceased husband, Jason, had been the exception. He'd been her biggest champion and a perfect husband in looks and everything else that mattered. To be fair, George was attractive, in a lawyerly sort of way, with his blond hair swooping over his blue eyes like a Wall Street Ken doll. Quite the opposite from her *type*. Jason had sported a permanent three-day beard on his chiseled jawline. His dark hair, dark eyes and intensity had sent Fiona into a sexual meltdown every time he looked into her eyes. In the sixteen years she'd been with him, he'd never said a mean word to her or to anyone around him. He'd been her anchor. Even five years after his death while on a military assignment in Colombia, the grief bowled through her, sending her mind into a glum and restless place.

"…sex on a train?" George was talking about something Fiona wasn't sure she wanted to hear.

To avoid being rude, she snapped out of her memories. "What?"

"The sex scenes you write. Where do you get your ideas?" George lifted his second beer and winked at her.

"Oh." She forced a smile. Her thriller novels often

had one or two sex scenes in them. It spoke volumes that those scenes would be George's focus. She now saw how the rest of the evening would go if she didn't separate him from his assumptions. She leaned forward on her elbows, her arms pressing her breasts together and causing George's attention to drop in anticipation of the rest of the night. "I make up the sex scenes from things I read in books or watched in movies," she said in a low purr. "The murder scenes, however, are carefully orchestrated and practiced. I can slit a throat without breaking a nail." She was a bit rusty, but she was sure she could still handle the task with a three-and-a-half-inch Bench-made blade.

He choked on his beer. It was the first time she laughed all evening.

Her phone rang. Matt. He never called. Ever. "Sorry. I need to take this. It's my son." She pressed Answer. "Hey, honey, what's up?"

"Someone is sneaking around the back of the house." Matt whispered the words. "I saw him by the back hedge after the motion light turned on."

Everything inside her went still. "Where are you?"

"In my room." His nerves traveled to her phone like a high-voltage surge. She always told him to always trust his instincts and she would too.

A wave of panic crashed over her. Nothing mattered to her more than Matt.

She checked the cameras she'd installed around the house. In the backyard by the hydrangeas, a shadowy figure tried to hide, but his solid dark pants and shirt didn't blend into the nuances in the background. "If you hear a window or a door break, run to Meaghan's house.

Otherwise, don't come out until I get home. I'm on my way. Call the police and stay on the phone with them." She stood up and grabbed her purse. "I need to get home. My son needs me."

George finished eating a bite of chicken, then stood too. "Rushing off every time your son has a problem won't prepare him for the real world."

"Fuck off, George." She threw down three twenties to pay for her half of the bill. Her best friend, Meaghan, would be hearing from her about her insistence that George was her *perfect match*.

Once in the parking garage, she scanned the parking lot full of Mercedes, BMWs and Teslas for her ten-year-old Jetta. It may have been smaller and not as luxurious as the cars surrounding her, but it was cheaper to run and could move surprisingly fast. The tires squealed as she circled down three stories of concrete and exited onto the street. As usual, the Saturday-night traffic shuffled along State Street. Fiona couldn't wait. She swerved around several cars and managed to slip through a light as it flickered orange, keeping everyone behind her stalled at red.

Matt's voice pushed her to maneuver like a Formula One driver. He tended to remain calm in most situations, like his father. Tonight she heard apprehension.

She used Alexa to call Meaghan so she wouldn't have to slow down.

Meaghan answered on the second ring. "You better be calling to tell me you just had the best sex of your life."

"Not even close. George is an ass."

"He can be, but he's gorgeous. Couldn't you just ignore everything he said and enjoy the ride?" Meaghan said with a chuckle.

"No. My mind has to be as seduced as my body for me to enjoy sex."

"That must lead to some pretty lonely nights."

"George is not why I'm calling." Fiona wasn't in the mood to discuss her sex life when her son was in danger.

"What's wrong?"

Meaghan was a no-nonsense kind of friend, the only kind of friend Fiona could tolerate, so she just burst right out with it. "Someone is trying to break into my house, right now."

"Oh. My. God. Are you okay? Is Matt okay?" Meaghan, a person who never showed a wide range of emotion, sounded stressed.

"Can you get over there?"

"I wish I could. I'm with a client in Rockport, but I'll tell them I have to go."

"Don't bother. I'll be there before you find your car."

Fifteen minutes later—after a lot of near misses and some angry exchanges with annoyed drivers—Fiona arrived home without a speeding ticket. Their simple one-story ranch house had no lights on, not one. Her neighbors had power and the streetlights still cast a bright ring on the road every hundred yards or so. Fiona rushed to the side door, her eyes scanning her surroundings as she unlocked it. The kitchen was dark with only the external lights casting enough of a glow to make out objects on the counters. The large glass casserole of lasagna she'd made for his dinner sat uncovered on the stove, half-eaten.

"Matt?" She stepped inside, her only defense the keys

in her hand and her small leather purse. She'd never been so unprepared for something in her life.

Before she could call out again, a large arm wrapped around her and covered her mouth. She fought to get free, but another arm locked her body tight against a brick wall of a chest. Her assailant had the physique of a bodybuilder. A burglar? Where were the police? Where was Matt?

The man pushed her forward toward the family room. Fiona twisted and tried to slam the back of her head into his face. No such luck.

They passed the edge of the counter. The darkness hid the colors and details of the interior, but this was her space. She reached behind her and took the ballpoint pen she'd left by her grocery list. One stab to the neck and he'd not only loosen his hold on her, he'd be headed to the morgue, but she'd promised herself she wouldn't kill unless absolutely necessary. So she hesitated, and his grip on her tightened. Before the bastard could crush her ribs, she smashed the pen into his thigh. He stepped back, and she slipped through his arms. Clasping both hands together, she rammed a double fist straight up into the man's groin. He fell forward in pain, but recovered faster than she expected. He grabbed a stool from the table and swung it into her. The hit launched her against the oven, and she dropped to the floor.

Headlights outside the house brought some light into room. The man, his large form coming into focus, wavered. Fiona scrambled back from him. Without a better weapon she stood no chance. But he surprised her. Instead of rushing toward her, he sprinted out of the house into the backyard. Fiona pulled herself up, swallowed her nerves and raced down the hall.

"Matt?" she called out, pushing open his bedroom door. Turning the flashlight on her phone on, she scanned the room. No sign of him. He could have escaped through the window and been safe at her neighbor's, but she paused and waited.

A muffled sound came from under the bed. She dropped to her knees and looked underneath. Behind two flat sweater bins, her son's beautiful brown eyes peeked out.

He pushed his way out of his barricade and stood—he was already a few inches taller than Fiona. She wrapped her arms around him and held him tight as her heartbeat slowed. Having someone invade her space in such a violent manner while her only living relative was home alone shattered the sense of security she'd built around them.

"Are you okay?" She examined his face, his arms, until he pulled away, annoyed enough at her actions to decrease some of her tension. She never should have left him alone. There were too many things that could have gone wrong.

"I'm fine," he replied, "but your nose is bleeding."

She turned away from him and wiped her nose with her sleeve. "Let's get out of here before the beast returns."

"He's still in the house?"

"He escaped out the back door, but I have no idea why he was here so I have no idea if he's coming back." She pointed to the door. "We'll wait out front until the police arrive."

He remained silent as he followed her to the front yard. They stood next to the streetlight, but remained partially hidden by an oak tree on the Murphy's front lawn. Just in case.

It took over ten minutes to hear the sirens. Matt waited with his hands in his pockets, slouched against the tree trunk. He'd always been a calm, levelheaded kid. He had to be deeply processing everything that had happened. In the dark, he looked like a thinner version of his father. If only Jason was still with them. She shook her head. This wasn't the time to be drawn into what-ifs. The *what-is* was too pressing. Someone had broken into their house while her son was there alone. Fiona had never for a moment felt unsafe in this neighborhood, but now, the house where she'd lived these past five years had a shadow over it, one that wouldn't lift. The police arrived, and two officers came out of their car, hands on their revolvers. She announced herself before moving around the large tree in case she surprised them. Matt followed behind her.

The police officers looked past her to Matt, and the older one, about forty-five years old, spoke first. "I'm Officer Dunlop. Did you call 9-1-1?"

He nodded and turned to his mother. Fiona squeezed his arm and stepped forward. "Someone broke into the house and attacked me."

"Where is he?" Dunlop glanced over her shoulder toward the house.

"I don't know. He ran away after I stabbed him with a pen. His blood should be on the floor."

He sent his partner, about ten or so years younger, toward the house. Fiona gave the officer as complete a description of what happened as she could. Matt offered little help as he'd hidden immediately and remained hidden while the man rummaged through several rooms.

She was proud of him. Had he tried to stop the man, he would have been seriously injured or worse. The man who had attacked her was not playing around.

A second police car arrived. The additional blue lights swirling through the neighborhood brought out several neighbors.

The lights flickered on inside the house, which meant her tormentor had only flicked a switch. She'd been so concerned about Matt that she hadn't checked the circuit breaker. Several minutes later, the younger officer returned alone. He strode over to Dunlop and Fiona. "The scene is clear. The circuit breaker was switched off."

Several officers present spread out and searched the neighborhood for "A male suspect, approximately twenty-five years of age, over six feet, black T-shirt, Caucasian, dark hair," as Dunlop had reiterated what Fiona told him.

She looked around. A maze of streets created an easy escape for someone who had left a car one or two blocks over. "You should be able to get his DNA off the blood on the floor."

Dunlop's partner shook his head. "There's no sign of any forced entry and nothing in your house looks disturbed."

"I stabbed him in the leg. There had to be blood on the floor or on the pen. I dropped it after he hit me with the stool."

"Can you show me inside?" Dunlop asked.

Fiona hesitated. She didn't want to be ambushed again, and despite the police officer's presence, something felt off. She told Matt to remain outside with the other officers as she reentered the premises with an armed guard.

The entire scene appeared quite mundane under the five cool-toned track lights illuminating every surface in the kitchen. After her eyes adjusted from the dark, she scanned the room. Not a drop of blood anywhere. It was as though her brain had malfunctioned and now everything was back in order. Even the stool had been placed back next to the island. Officer Dunlop remained beside her, watching over her shoulder, glancing in every direction she looked.

The kitchen floor was cleaner than it had been when she'd left for her dinner date. The man who had assaulted her didn't do this. It would have been too much detail work for someone with an injury. The first officer didn't have time to turn the room over in the five minutes he was in the kitchen before coming outside. Someone else?

"Where's the lasagna?" she asked.

"Lasagna?" Officer Dunlop shook his head as though he were being baited.

"There was a half pan of lasagna on the stove. Right there." She pointed to where she'd seen it when she walked into the room. It wasn't in the sink or the refrigerator. Her stomach twisted as she opened the trash can. Not there either. Even more than having a stranger in her house trying to harm her and her son, the loss of the lasagna scared the hell out of her.

# Chapter 2

Jason spent years setting up a perimeter around his wife and child to protect them in case someone from his past came looking for revenge. He wiped the sweat from his brow. Even with every safeguard he could think of, someone came close enough to kill them. The thought of what could have happened tonight burned. For five years, his family had lived unaffected by his past, and he'd let his guard down. He never would again.

For now, Fiona and Matt were safe. He took a deep breath and leaned back against the passenger seat of the delivery van he'd repurposed for surveillance. Regret never fixed anything. He'd take the information learned and up the security around them. He'd also have to face the consequences of withholding the truth from his team.

After returning to the States from a military deployment in Colombia, he'd been permanently removed from his military position—not really discharged since it had been agreed that his family would be safer if he died on the mission. Awarded a small stipend and new identification to start an alternative life, he created Fresh Pond Security, a security firm specializing in the protection of individuals at risk who were entitled to little or no protection from regular law enforcement units. The company started as a front to keep his own family protected, but the enterprise expanded into something fairly profitable. He only employed the best of the best. Men and women who were highly skilled and unable or unwilling to continue their work for the government. They risked their lives to protect their clients and they had the right and the need to know and understand Jason's past in order to provide the best protection possible for Fiona and Matt.

He rubbed the place where his wedding band had once been. The cool fall air reminded him of the first time he'd met his wife. A graduate student in Global Affairs at the Fletcher School of Diplomacy, Fiona had a parade of admirers following her about like pathetic ducklings. She dismissed most of the men who wanted a place in her orbit with an apologetic smile and the excuse of a schedule too busy for dating. Jason, however, saw obstacles as opportunities. After watching her from a distance for a week or so, he came across her in the library, trying to study, her blond hair twisted at the nape of her neck, her focus on a twenty-pound geopolitics textbook. Two aspiring diplomats sat across from her, peppering her with questions about her time in Belarus. Her frown at their constant interruptions gave Jason an excuse to finally meet her.

"Guys, I would appreciate you annoying someone other than my girlfriend." He sat in the empty chair next to her, pulled out his laptop and proceeded to ignore her while he finished a term paper in his Contemporary Spanish Literature course. Her classmates left, leaving Fiona and Jason to study in companionable silence. If she didn't have any interest in him, she had the option of packing up her things and leaving, no explanation necessary. Instead, she remained. After an hour, she invited him for coffee. They had remained together ever since...until the day he "died."

He carried three other memories of her with him everywhere he went, anchors to a past he never wanted to lose. The first was the moment Fiona stepped out to walk down the aisle on their wedding day. Dressed in a stunning black gown with her blond hair curled into a 1950s siren's bob, she dazzled. Despite protests from her parents, she'd refused to dress as a virgin and pretend an innocence that wasn't there. Instead, she radiated confidence, sex appeal and an independence that kept him happily caught in her web.

The second memory involved the thirteen hours of labor and physical exertion Fiona went through at Matt's birth. She had ten pounds and three ounces of complaints to use against him and she did curse quite a lot, but not once at Jason. They were a team even in the worst of times.

Then there was her lasagna. Double the ricotta and beef, and half the tomato sauce of a regular recipe, but enough sauce to fill each bite with a perfect tang. She always broiled it for five minutes at the end to turn the mozzarella golden brown. She could easily seduce a man into her bed with that dish. He shouldn't have taken it, but he was a man starving for a taste of his past. If he couldn't have a relationship with Fiona or Matt, the lasagna would have to do.

"You could have shared." Steve, Jason's business partner, stared at the empty pan.

"Not a chance. You almost blew the whole operation with your insistence on running into the bathroom."

"You pulled us into this assignment at the last minute. I didn't have time before I was shoved into the van."

"Always prepared?" Jason echoed his partner's favorite catchphrase.

"Sure. I even cleaned the blood off the pen. I have to give Ms. Fiona Stirling a lot of credit. She looks like Marilyn Monroe and fights like Ali. She nailed that guy. Almost took him down without a hair out of place. Now that's what I call a mother bear."

Fiona always drew attention with her movie star looks, light blond hair veiled over one of her bright blue eyes. Her appearance was a weapon, disarming everyone around her. That's what had made her so exceptional at her job at the State Department negotiating international trade agreements.

The intruder stirred and tumbled forward on the van floor. Steve pushed him back toward his seat. The man fell against the side of the van—not that he'd be going anywhere. They'd put handcuffs on him before they cut the phone cords and pulled him into the van in the street behind the house just as the sight of the police lights caught the neighborhood's attention.

Jason called up to the driver, Finn. "Any word on our passenger's identity?"

"The photo you took of him wasn't the best quality since his eyes were closed and his nose was broken."

Steve bent over to look closer at their passenger's face. "He had a gash in his forehead and his leg was bloody from the pen, but his nose was fine when I caught up to him."

"My fist must have accidentally hit him while I was moving him to the van," Jason said, feeling the impact on his knuckles. He would have done far worse to the person who had threatened his family, but the information in the asshole's head was more important than letting his rage fly.

They turned the corner into a garage under a storage facility one town over from Fiona's house. The proximity allowed them to arrive and disappear before the police pulled up. Jason had monitored her house from the moment she'd moved in.

He went to his office to wait for the suspect to wake up. The asshole had better be willing to speak or he'd have a very uncomfortable night.

Two hours later, Finn, one of his best security consultants, contacted him with an update on his family. Jason had pulled him off an assignment protecting the CEO of a pharmaceutical company, leaving only Sam protecting him. Sam could handle the job while Finn watched over Jason's family. Although they'd been too late to prevent the break-in in the first place. Despite all his preparation for just such an event, he'd failed. He shuddered to think what would have happened if she hadn't been able to fight off the intruder. She'd been so lucky to have gotten away with only a bloody nose.

"Hey, boss."

"What's their status?" Jason didn't have time for pleasantries.

"They packed up and headed to the Seagull Hotel."

"You're kidding me." They were sitting ducks if someone was truly after them and not anything in the house. The Seagull Hotel was so named not from a view of the ocean, but for the throngs of birds circling the local Walmart parking lot next door.

"Wish I was. The police think she's safer there for the night, but don't have the resources to watch over them. They're calling it a bungled burglary."

"It doesn't matter what the police do. We're going to keep them secure." An absence of actual police presence was for the best. Jason wanted to limit their involvement until he understood the exact risk. Any press would place a spotlight on Fiona and Matt. She'd already brought too much attention to herself with her skyrocketing book career.

"I agree. I checked into the room next door and have been keeping an eye out for anything unusual, but I've been working on both assignments for over twenty-two hours combined. I'm ready for a replacement." Finn prided himself on his eagle eye and sniper-perfect shot, which meant he demanded rest when he needed rest.

"Noah's on the way. Thanks for keeping an eye on them. Can you send me the room numbers?"

"Sure."

"And Finn?"

"Yes."

"Thanks for switching assignments so quickly."

"That's my job."

Jason closed his eyes when he hung up. Part of him wanted to drive down there and tell Fiona she had to go into hiding to protect herself and Matt from his past, but he knew she wouldn't listen. Her stubbornness was her biggest asset and most annoying quality. She'd survived his *death* and raised their son into a strong and competent soul. She left her government job because of its heavy travel schedule and her need to be closer to Matt. Then she published a whole series of thriller books and made a name for herself. She deserved the recognition and the income helped her where his life insurance couldn't, but it also brought attention from the wrong people. Hiding her would be near impossible unless she agreed to tamp down her personality and become average. Fiona was anything but average.

His phone rang. He picked it up on the first ring as he always did for Kennedy, an analyst in the NSA who assisted him.

"DJ?" she always asked, as though someone might have compromised his phone. Jason used DJ as his alias to keep his name as buried as his former life.

"Go ahead."

"Great news. My sources identified the guy's mug as a Robert Harper." Her sources were unmatched in the field.

"That name means nothing. Who is he?"

"A hired gun for Federated Security. They have many clients, some not so aboveboard. They have a reputation in the field as being outside the law and are more than willing to do anything if the money is right." The constant tapping on her keyboard was her official soundtrack, digging down under layers and layers of security walls to find out what they needed.

"Thanks. Let me know if you learn anything else."

"Will do." She hung up, leaving him staring in silence at the wall.

The news reinforced the urgency to find a safe place for Fiona and Matt until Jason could eradicate the risk. His past might have finally come for his family.

He strolled into the back room, a place with no windows, one door and a whole lot of safeguards. Mr. Harper was on the floor gaining consciousness. He'd be remaining here until Jason figured out what he wanted with Fiona.

Although Jason had lost his wife's companionship five years ago when he'd faked his own death, he'd never given up looking after her. His love hadn't faded one bit. If anything, by watching her from a distance, he'd only fallen in love with her more. She aged like a fine wine, more complex but in a mellow way.

And Matt? He couldn't imagine loving a person more. He looked out for his mother, received good grades, used his strength to protect people from bullies in school and broke enough rules to make Jason assured that he'd never be a pawn for anyone. Not like his father had been.

The memories sent a surge of regret through him. He leaned back in his black leather chair and squeezed his eyes shut. It wasn't enough to orchestrate their safety— he longed to pull them into his arms for as long as he could.

Steve walked in without knocking, eating one of the energy bars he always seemed to have in his pockets.

"I'm going to replace Noah in a few minutes," Jason said. "He was pulled from another assignment like Finn, and I want them both to have a break."

"I can do it if you want."

When he started this business, Jason didn't trust anyone. Money and power could transform someone from loyal to backstabbing. Yet, over the years, the team showed more commitment and reliability than any group he'd ever known. His deception, if they knew about it, could burn the entire operation to the ground. But it was time to come clean.

"I've got this," Jason said. "Before I go, we need to talk about Fiona Stirling."

Steve nodded. "Sure. What's up?" He sat down in the chair across the desk.

Jason took a deep breath and told him everything.

# *Chapter 3*

The sound of cars rushing down Route One outside her window did nothing to ease the stress hammering through Fiona. At three in the morning, both she and Matt should be asleep. They weren't. Back-to-back-to-back reruns of *Law and Order: SVU* allowed them to sit in their respective beds without speaking to each other. Her duffel bag and Matt's backpack with his homework in it rested on the table.

Her mind ran over everything they'd done in the week and month prior to the break-in. She'd had her share of readers targeting her after something she wrote, but all the harassment came in the form of social media bullying. She'd never experienced anyone physically threatening her as an author. Matt had no known enemies, especially men who probably had ten to twenty years on him. Her writer's brain had all sorts of reasons they were attacked. An obsessed fan, an everyday burglar, someone from her husband's world or maybe someone from her own sordid past.

While Jason had thought she had a respectable job at the State Department, she actually worked as a specialized skill officer in the CIA's Special Activities Division. She acted as an employee of the State Department in order to move in normal diplomatic channels, a deadly weapon dressed in navy suits and carrying a briefcase. She enjoyed acting as a diplomat who wined and dined business executives all over the world, but her actual assignments had more sinister ends. She had handed over a piece of her soul for a large sum of money to pay off her student loans. It was a decision that took her outlook from sunny and optimistic to stormy and destructive. They trained her to take out the most villainous men with the most minimal fanfare. Her techniques had become so refined that her targets often didn't die until long after she departed whatever country in which she had delivered her death sentence. Only she and a few higher-ups knew her actual objectives. Even Jason had been excluded from her inner circle. After giving birth to Matt, she could no longer handle the work. She wanted out. Jason's death gave her the perfect excuse. She had to raise her son alone. She couldn't travel anymore. She had lost her touch. It was for the best that she left the government all together. An old friend from college encouraged her to write a book based on her past. She couldn't, but she could make things up. Her first novel had no plot and no character development. Her next one? Better. Three attempts later, she was a published novelist making up stories for a living. She never wrote about or looked back at her former occupation.

If her past had been outed, they'd never be safe.

After another hour of television, Matt fell asleep, to the drama of the night. With him sleeping soundly, she had a chance to think about everything that had occurred. She pulled out her notebook and looked at the notes she'd jotted down. The names of the police officers who had responded to the call, the assistant district attorney who wanted to meet with her the following Monday, and the phone number for a victim assistance agency. One page had a hastily drawn sketch of her assailant. The police took a picture of it to compare to databases. Regrettably, the blood all over her clothes was her own.

When she had gone back into the house to pack, she had examined every nook in the cabinets and on the floor. Not a drop of blood found. She had even picked up the pen and opened it up. The inside was damp as though someone had taken the time to rinse the blood away, but didn't have time to thoroughly dry it.

Questions raced through her head. Wiping away the evidence of a crime scene was the stuff a hit team would do or someone in organized crime. It didn't make sense. If someone wanted her dead, they could have waited for her to get home, taken a perfect shot with a .22 and a silencer to keep the sound to a minimum and driven away, changed cars a few streets over and have been long gone by now. Heading into the house added risk. From what she'd seen, nothing besides the lasagna had been taken. Which meant they were after people, not things.

She shook her head at her detailed assessment of the best way to kidnap or kill her. Old habits never died. It bothered her that such an analysis was necessary. She hid in the bathroom and called Meaghan. They'd left text messages back and forth, but hadn't connected otherwise.

Meaghan answered on the first ring. "Are you okay? Is Matt okay?"

"We're both fine. Matt hid under a bed and only came

out when I went looking for him. I might have a black eye from the assailant's punch to my face, but he's worse off. I stabbed him with a ballpoint pen in the leg before he escaped."

"That's insane. Were you in heels?"

"Seriously? That's what you want to know?" She shook her head,

"It would be wicked hard to take out a guy in heels and if you did—damn, girl." She paused, then said more seriously, "Who was he?"

"No idea. But that's not the weird thing. I'm sure there was blood on the kitchen floor when I left. When I entered again with the police, the whole kitchen was immaculate. Like someone had scrubbed the scene. There's no way he cleaned up the kitchen on his way out the door, but someone did. I looked like an idiot to the police."

"Sounds like one of your novels. Do you want to come over?" The offer was wonderful, but someone might want to hurt her, and she couldn't drag Meaghan into it too.

"Thanks, but we're okay for right now. Matt's already asleep. I might stop at your house tomorrow morning for some coffee or maybe a Bloody Mary. You can help me pick out an outfit for the book signing next Saturday."

"You're not going after all of this."

"I've planned this for months. I won't let my fans down."

"Your fans? What about your stalkers?" Meaghan asked.

"I'll be better off doing something to keep my mind from obsessing over this, and I'll bring Matt with me so he isn't at the house alone."

"Fine. I couldn't change your mind anyway. If you're

going to be stubborn, I'll go to keep an eye on your son while your fans worship you."

Fiona laughed. "I bet he'd love your company." Matt enjoyed hanging out at Meaghan's house. She was the only person Fiona knew who could kick Matt's ass in *Call of Duty*. She'd been lucky to find a neighbor like Meaghan. A person she could share her parenting worries with even though Meaghan wasn't a parent. She'd also made an awesome babysitter when Matt had been younger.

Fiona hung up and sat on the toilet, staring at her reflection in the mirror. Remnants of her date makeup had smeared together, giving her face an impressionistic look. The wave in her hair had flattened into something that looked as though she'd woken from a ten-year nap. Not her best look. The whole evening had been one disaster after another.

Dressing up to meet her readers had always brought her joy, but going out on dates? Not so fun. Especially when that date had been George. At thirty-eight-years-old, she preferred nights at home reading to going out to meet new people. She could hear George's voice in her head snickering over the sex scenes she'd written. The life of a spinster seemed far preferable to having the companionship of the wrong man. *Spinster* had once been a pejorative word, but now, it was more of a badge of honor. When a woman happy in her own existence chose to spend time with someone else, that someone else had to be extremely special. George was not special. He was more the kind of guy who expected a single woman to be grateful for whatever crappy treatment he was willing to give her. Fiona didn't have the desire or the ability to kiss the ass of an ass.

It was all Jason's fault. He'd been too perfect, and truth be told, he became more perfect with each passing year. His flaws diminished and his personality took on superhero attributes. If he walked into her room at that exact moment, she would be putty in his hands. Hands that were large and strong, but so gentle when they needed to be. Her body heated up at the thought of his touch. She stood up and rinsed her face with cool water. This was not the time to get all hot and bothered over the ghost that haunted her dreams.

She found a nip of Bombay Sapphire in the minibar. A bit of ice would make this the perfect nightcap to an otherwise crappy day. She grabbed the key to her room and slipped into the hall. On her way back from the ice dispenser, the door next to hers opened and a man stepped out in a tweed coat. He seemed like a young professor who spent his free time competing with the football team for time in the weight room. Lost in thought, he barely acknowledged her.

Fiona glanced into the man's room, never one to ignore her surroundings. Another man, tall, dark, muscular, calmly stood up and disappeared into the bathroom as the professor type closed the door. She dropped the ice bucket. Ice scattered across the hall. She didn't care. The man in the room looked exactly like Jason.

It was impossible. Jason was dead. She remained frozen staring at the closed door.

"Are you all right?" the other man asked, kicking the scattered ice to the side of the hallway. His demeanor softened as he picked up the ice bucket and handed it back to her.

"This has been a long day. I should just go to bed." She waved and turned back to her own door. It had been a very long day.

She had to stop her obsession with her husband. She'd thought she'd seen him a hundred times since his death. But he was dead. And the man next door wore his hair in a long ponytail, not the crew cut from his last family photo. That sliver of his profile, however, displayed Jason's best features, the nose, broken only slightly from a college football incident that never healed quite right, and intensely alluring lips. Lips that fit hers so perfectly, they could kiss for hours, all night long, and never be sated.

Shutting the door, she sat on the edge of her bed. If Jason had been home, the pen in the intruder's leg wouldn't have been the worst thing that happened to him—he'd probably be dead at the hands of a very competent army captain. But Jason had died in Colombia. The military claimed it was an accident, although her research through her government connections revealed questions that no one could answer about the incident. The military handed her son a folded American flag at his service. His ashes were over her fireplace mantel in a wooden box inlaid with black onyx.

She'd made her peace with his death years ago. Yet, seeing his doppelgänger threw her memories back to the last time they'd seen each other. He'd been playing soccer in the backyard with Matt, never letting him win, because in Jason's opinion, Matt had to fight to beat him or what was the point. He hugged her and their son before he grabbed his gear and headed to his car. Matt didn't cry. His dad left all the time. For him, this was another goodbye with a reunion guaranteed in a few weeks. But he never returned. Matt had waited by the window for months, just staring. Fiona restored Jason's car, a 2000 red Mustang convertible, adding a few more safety features like a back-up camera and integration with Matt's phone. They drove it around town and on brief trips to the mountains. Eventually, she wanted to give it to Matt. It wouldn't bring his father back, but might provide a connection to a man who would have been such an amazing influence in his life.

She took a sip of gin and savored the taste. As of tonight, she had to step up her security. There were too many loose ends from her past that she'd taken for granted. Trying to hide from what she'd done only placed Matt more at risk. She downed the rest of the glass and poured herself some Jack Daniel's, staring at the wall to the next room as though she could see through it. Without seeing his entire face, she no idea who that man was. She took a sip, then another. She had to scrub any thought of Jason's potential resurrection from her brain.

Her obsession with seeing Jason again had led her to create his resurrection in her last book. For months she'd written about a beautiful world where a military mission gone wrong had left her heroine's husband unable to remember who he was. Although they thought he was dead, he was very much alive. When his memory returned, he rushed home to be with his family. It was a complete fiction, more of a fairy tale. She wanted to understand why her husband never returned home. Her government contact had shared classified details on Jason's death that the military had left out of the story they'd given her. He'd been delivering military aid to the Colombian government, the truck was ambushed, everyone died. She rewrote that story, changing some details, but having her hero survive an ambush and eventually reunite with his family. The hardest part of the story was typing "The End" and leaving her hero behind to begin a new book.

Yet, this entire line of thought was ridiculous. Obsessing about Jason coming back to her only exacerbated the heartbreak she couldn't escape. Her son needed a strong presence in his life, not a grief-stricken parent who couldn't get out of bed in the morning. Perhaps a few more dates with men who weren't George would provide some solace to her broken heart. Doubtful, but why turn down an orgasm from some handsome and generous soul? She smiled. Maybe a five-year dry spell was long enough.

Matt stretched his arms over his head and turned his face toward the pillow, his arm resting over his ear. She was so proud of the way he'd handled the whole situation. He'd remained calm, found a safe place and called the police. At the police station, Matt had recapped the entire incident step-by-step three times to three different officers. He had a good mind for details, like his dad.

Swallowing the last of the whiskey, she leaned against the pillow, grateful he'd come out of this unharmed and that she had a mere bump on her nose and the beginning of a black eye. Now if she could only figure out the identity of the intruder and what he wanted with them.

Jason clenched his fists to keep from slamming them into a wall. Of all the bad moments for Fiona to leave her room, she had to choose the exact time when Noah left theirs. This whole situation was a nightmare. He'd spent the last five years hiding himself as close as he could to Fiona and Matt. Too close and he would trap them inside his nightmare. Too far and he'd have missed the attempt on Fiona's life. Now he needed to find out why she was a target and if it was related to the ambush in Colombia.

He should have had Steve keep an eye on his family at the hotel, but it was Jason's family. While Steve had been understanding of why he'd hidden his identity, that didn't stop his anger toward Jason for placing the rest of the team in a dangerous situation by not giving all the facts of the assignment. It would take time to earn his trust again, if ever. So far, however, Steve remained on the job. Jason didn't know how he'd make it up to him, but he would. Jason had met Steve when some loser at a restaurant had hit on his wife and wouldn't back down. Jason stepped in and blocked the idiot from ruining Steve and Olivia's anniversary dinner. They invited him to join them for a drink to thank him. They'd been friends since, which made the deception even worse.

They didn't have the chance to tell the rest of the team that the secret client who paid to keep Fiona and Matt safe was Jason himself. By withholding that key information, he had placed his team at a disadvantage protecting them. That one omission could implode the whole organization. Trust was the keystone of everything they did, and Jason had blown that right open.

He called Noah, who answered on the first ring.

"Did Fiona say anything to you?" Jason asked.

"Nothing of importance, but at one point, she stared past the door into our room. From the look on her face, something spooked her, and it wasn't me. Maybe if you stopped dressing as one of the Hell's Angels, you wouldn't get such a drastic reaction from women. She'd just fended off an attack by a thug in a black T-shirt. It would make sense that she'd fear another guy in a black T-shirt in the room next to her."

"Are you sure she saw me?" he asked, but knew damn well she had.

"I'm sure of it. You were on the bed, then walked over to the bathroom."

If Jason was lucky, it wasn't his identity that concerned her but the black T-shirt, as the intruder was wearing black as well. He returned to the exact spot he'd sat on the bed when the ice bucket went down. An image of his face in the window reflected back at him, not super clear, but enough to give a good indication of his facial features. And she'd have seen his profile when he walked to the bathroom. What the hell was he thinking? He should never have come over here.

"Next time, I'll wear a golf shirt."

"Something with color to bring out that sparkling personality of yours." Noah's voice dripped with sarcasm, which was fine. Jason gained more insight into their cases when everyone could speak freely. Ass-kissing only led to unimaginative teams and lots of conflict between employees. The team was a family, trusting each other in life-and-death situations. Except Jason hadn't done his part to protect them. Once they found out he'd hidden his identity from them, the trust and camaraderie he'd built up over the years would disappear.

"Point taken. See you back at the office in the morning. Ask Steve if he can replace me. I need to get out of here."

"On it," Noah replied and hung up.

After a few minutes of beating himself up, he had to shut down the urge to go to Fiona and comfort her after such a long, hard day. She'd remained so strong over the past five years and here she was caught up in the middle of a nightmare. If the attacks continued, he'd gladly sacrifice himself to keep Fiona and Matt safe. For now, he had to understand exactly why she'd become a target. He opened the hotel door, standing half in the hall, half in his doorway. If someone approached their room, he'd be there. If she opened her door again, he could step inside before she saw him. Steve had better get his ass over here soon.

Fiona woke to the television blaring across the room. "What the..."

"Sorry, I didn't know the volume was so loud." Matt turned the television off and sat on the bed. Half his hair stood straight up and the other half pressed into his skull.

"Don't worry about it." She stretched but didn't sit up. The sun was already awake, offering a sliver of light from behind the curtain. "What time is it?"

"Nine o'clock."

"I never sleep this late."

"You were up late talking on the phone."

"How do you know that?"

"I heard you."

"You did?"

"You aren't exactly quiet when you talk to Meaghan."

He was right. Meaghan and Fiona got on so well, their voices increased with the enthusiasm for whatever topic they were on. Meaghan was the sister Fiona never had and the family she needed after her tiny family unit had broken apart. She also provided Matt with an adult in his life who didn't carry parental expectations. She loved him exactly as he was and didn't care what he did with his life as long as he was happy. Fiona was different. She wanted him safe, financially secure and able to find a partner who would care for him the way Jason had cared for her.

"We should head out. I want to make sure the police closed up and locked the house after they left. Then I need to get some work done."

"We have time." Matt tended not to worry about anything, although after last night, his brows remained furrowed as he packed up his things. Should she take the day off and let them rest on a mental health day, or should she plow on with her schedule? The slightest smile appeared on his face as he texted a friend. It would be okay. Maybe it would be best to carry on without focusing on what had happened.

She headed to the bathroom. "Let me wash my face, and we can eat breakfast at Meaghan's." She paused and before she shut the door, she turned to him. "Is that okay?"

"I guess. Am I going with you?"

"I would prefer it. Last night freaked me out."

He nodded. "Me too. Okay, I'll go."

"That's what I love about you. You're the best kid ever." She ruffled his hair until he pulled away. The furrow over his eyes disappeared during their interaction, and mild amusement took its place.

An hour later, they sat in Meaghan's kitchen enjoying

freshly baked blueberry muffins and omelets. Meaghan, all five feet ten of her, had dressed in cargo pants and a white tank top. Not her usual wardrobe. She typically wore tailored pantsuits and had her hair just so. Not this morning. Her hair was up in a ponytail and if Fiona didn't know better, she'd think Meaghan was headed into battle. She bustled around the kitchen, looking at her phone, her watch and even scanning the windows now and then. No doubt the break-in next door also upset Meaghan's sense of security.

"You spoil us," Fiona said to break the tension.

"It's nothing. Besides, I feel bad I wasn't here last night."

"Why would you feel bad for working? It's not like you're paid to wait by the phone for my panic calls."

Meaghan sighed and took a sip of her coffee. "Do you want me to go with you to your house?"

Fiona waved her request away. "You have a million things to do today—you told me yesterday before I went on the date from hell. Go. We'll be fine, won't we, sport? It's broad daylight. I doubt someone's waiting in the closet for us." She brushed back Matt's hair.

He shrugged, still looking at his phone. "Can I go over to Sarah's house for the afternoon?"

"Absolutely. First, let's get the bad vibes out of the house so I can lock myself in my office for the day without looking over my shoulder."

He thought about it and then nodded. "Deal."

When they got to their front door, Matt hesitated.

"Everything okay?" she asked.

"Are we sure there's no one in the closet?"

"No, but I'll do a quick sweep to make sure. You wait here."

She went inside and looked around. This time, she expected someone to come from behind her and was mentally ready. Just to be safe, she also grabbed one of the fillet knives from the kitchen counter. She checked the coat closet in the foyer. Clear. The living room and bedrooms were untouched. When she returned to the kitchen, the spotless floors annoyed her. Someone was hiding something. She wasn't sure whether to blame the police, the intruder or someone from her past, but she knew a cleanup job when she saw one. Looking around, she didn't see anything else out of place.

"All clear," she called out to her son as she placed the knife back into the wood holder.

Matt came in and looked around. "Will I ever feel safe in here again?"

"I think so. I'm going to install some extra security cameras this afternoon, including ones inside the house. Maybe you can help me. We'll link them up to both of our phones. If anyone comes close to the house, we'll see them. Nothing is foolproof, but a security camera might have caught the man sneaking in."

"That works. What time do you want me home?"

"Two?"

He nodded and headed back out the door.

"Also, can you answer the phone whenever I call just for today?" she called out to him. "Just so I know you're safe."

He turned around. "Okay. You do the same."

She pulled him in for a hug and watched him take off for Sarah's, only six houses away.

After he left, she walked the perimeter of the property and found where the man entered the yard. The damp grass showed footprints under her hedges. She followed them back into her neighbor's yard to the edge of his garden and found one nicely preserved footprint caught in the damp soil. She placed her hand next to it and took a photo from two different directions to get the shading of the large imprint better, which was more like a sneaker than the shoes and boots most police officers wore.

She searched closer to her house to find his exit point, but the police had added significant traffic under all the windows and out the doors. It would be nearly impossible to track him under so much visual noise.

In need of more coffee, she went back into the house, poured a hot cup of black coffee and retreated to her office. With the help of her computer and a credit card, Fiona located and bought several security cameras for the house, the kind that ran off batteries and recorded video both wirelessly and with a copy saved on the camera. She also contacted her closest ally at her former agency for any potential leaks that had occurred recently. Nothing. That was expected as the agency had a near flawless record of getting their jobs done and leaving without a trace. But it only took one mole to bring a whole organization down.

When done trying everything in her power to protect her son, she went to put her cup into the dishwasher and nearly dropped it on the floor. Taking up the entire bottom rack was the lasagna pan, rinsed clean.

Assembled in the conference room at a round table that could seat ten comfortably, five members of the team waited for DJ, the founding partner, to go over what had happened with Fiona's case. There were a few team members, including Meaghan, still out on assignment. Jason would follow up with them later. Steve sat next to him, looking every bit as uncomfortable as his partner. After Jason had told him the truth earlier, Steve shook his head and told him he'd expected more from him, especially since his lie had directly affected the team. While Jason believed Steve would have done the same to save his own family, he probably would have come clean eventually. Jason should have opened up about it. Coming clean now, after Fiona was attacked, was too late as far as he was concerned.

The trust Steve had placed in him years before didn't fall to the wayside easily. But Jason assured him that he would do everything in his power to earn his full trust again. Steve had slapped him on the back and reminded him of the Maxwell case, where Jason pushed Steve out of the way when someone began shooting at them. As far as Steve was concerned, he owed Jason his life after that, and the least he could do was forgive him for this omission. Jason wouldn't argue with him although Steve had saved his ass in many situations as well. The gesture kept their partnership and friendship intact.

He looked over the team, all waiting for what might seem to them a normal group meeting to go over what had happened and to plan for the future. While that was true, what had happened would take a lot of explaining. He hated the prospect of losing anyone. Each person employed by Fresh Pond Security deserved a seat at this table. The only one who didn't was Jason himself. Finn and Noah chatted about their weekend plans, while

Sam and Calvin, their computer expert, focused on coffee and the doughnuts Jason had brought in to keep the mood lighter. Not that his bombshell would land softly.

Jason hesitated, so Steve broke the ice. "We're meeting together because the Fiona Stirling case has issues that have come to light that need to be clarified and understood before we can carry on as an organization."

Steve's words had the team members, all former members of the military or law enforcement, sitting up straighter and turning toward Jason. This was going to be so much harder than he'd anticipated, yet he also blamed himself for not having had the guts to come clean to them years ago. Whatever happened from this point forward, he would never leave out information that could hurt the team.

He looked over the group. Steve Wilson, his partner, stood out with his red hair and scattering of freckles more noticeable after years of weekend boating trips. He'd been FBI, not the sleek gun-toting type who rescued kidnapped children but more a bean counter who could track down missing funds in tax havens and other financial black holes around the world.

Sam Dempsey sat as though he were still a first lieutenant in the US Marines. With his bronze skin, crew cut and a wrinkle-free button-down shirt and khakis, he could blend in as a billionaire's bodyguard or a country club tennis pro. He'd been dishonorably discharged from the Marines for ignoring his command and rescuing a civilian. He had more integrity than the whole group combined.

Across the table sat Finn Maguire, dressed in a pair of well-worn jeans and a comfortable sweater. His light brown hair, carefully brushed back in a style that appeared to have demanded an excessive amount of time and effort, failed to hide the reddish scar slashed across his pale cheek. He left the military in disgrace as well, a pawn in a powerful game that protected leaders and let the smaller guy take the fall. His issue was trust. But despite his casual appearance, he rarely cracked a smile while at work. The scar on his face symbolized the price he had paid for his misplaced trust in a system that had ultimately let him down.

Mild-mannered Noah Montgomery seemed more prep school teacher than bodyguard—a former intelligence analyst who could handle himself in most any situation. His clean-cut look gave him an advantage when doing surveillance. Calvin Beckett came from the NSA. He could create magic with computers and what information he couldn't obtain from certain secure systems, Kennedy could, as she was still inside the government. She was more of a shadow member of the team and never came to meetings.

They each brought their own special skill set that supported everyone else. They also called bullshit when they saw it. Jason braced himself to receive the blowback from his omission. Whatever happened, he deserved it.

After a tension-ridden sigh, he spelled out what had happened to him years before. Being the sole survivor of a military operation gone wrong, where the cartel leader Andres Porras lost his son. How Jason's "death" had prevented anyone from taking revenge on his family. And how he created this group to both help other people in his situation who had to work one step outside the law and to protect his own family. After Fiona's house was compromised, he was terrified that Porras had learned he was alive and was trying to flush him out, although he had no proof. When he finished telling his story, there wasn't a friendly set of eyes at the table, except for Steve's.

His partner took a sip of coffee and shook his head. "I was as much in the dark about this as all of you were, but after almost five years working side by side with DJ, I still trust him with my life."

"Easy for you to say. You get fifty percent of the profits," Sam replied.

"Is it about the money or his deception or both?" Calvin asked. "Because I can make more money elsewhere. Here I thought I was part of something bigger, helping the little guy, protecting those who needed assistance but couldn't receive it anywhere else." He put his hand up toward Jason. "I need a few moments to think."

Finn stood. "I don't need anything else to make up my mind. It doesn't matter what you say. I'm done. I can't work for someone I don't trust. DJ had five years to establish whether he could trust us with his secrets. Five years. And now that the shit's hit the fan with his wife, he's decided to come clean. That means if Fiona Stirling hadn't been attacked, we'd still be in the dark and our own lives would be at risk from a danger we couldn't anticipate."

Jason understood where he was coming from. Finn had been framed for a murder on a military base to protect someone pretty high up. With no ability to prove his case since the government controlled the evidence, he ended up pleading to manslaughter and getting a dishonorable discharge. His honor meant everything to him and so did loyalty. Losing all of that in the service destroyed him until DJ came along and offered him a fresh start. Since then, he'd spent every day proving himself to those around him. Jason's deception had erased all those years of trust between them.

Jason acknowledged it. "I was wrong. I wanted to protect my family and in the process I hurt you, my new family."

"Save your words." Finn pulled the weapon from his belt and placed it on the table. "I don't have it in me to pull a knife out of my back again." His anger burned behind his eyes, but he held himself under control. He looked over at Noah, his closest friend in the group, the strain on his face evident. "Stay if you want. I won't hold it against you, so don't hold this against me." He shook his head. "Wait until Meaghan hears how all of this has been a one huge lie."

With that, he left the room. The sound of a slamming door echoed down the hall.

Everyone remaining sat in silence. Jason didn't want to believe he'd lost Finn, one of the best things to happen to Fresh Pond Security. Not only would he miss him as a colleague, but he'd miss him as a friend. A friend he'd deceived. It was no use racing down the hall and begging for his forgiveness. Jason respected Finn and understood he had to live in alignment with his morals. Perhaps someday Jason could prove to him that he hadn't meant any harm by hiding his background, but until that day, he had to let him go.

He scanned those remaining at the table. "Anyone else?"

Noah stared at the door Finn had stepped through moments before. "You let us all down. If you can't trust us, what are we doing here? We're not just hired guns. We'd had an understanding that we had each other's backs."

"I agree. And I do have your backs."

"But your wife and kid take priority."

"That's not fair."

"Isn't it?" he asked.

"If you want to know if I'd lay my life down for you, I would without hesitation. I also want to keep Fiona and Matt safe, yes. I owe it to them as they never did anything to put themselves in the line of fire."

Noah's frown remained in place. "It's a lot to take in."

Sam and Calvin nodded in agreement.

The fact that they remained at the table boded well for the future of the group, but someone had to break through the distrust and get everyone one step closer. Jason had no idea how to breach that gap.

Steve leaned back in his chair. "That went better and worse than I thought it would. We still have important details to work out. Number one, should I be with you when you tell the rest of the team?"

"No. It might go better one-on-one. And if they want to kill me, you couldn't save me anyway."

Steve shrugged at the insult. "Okay then. Second, should we call you Jason or stick to DJ?"

Danger was at his door, and he had nowhere to go but through the middle of hell to get out. He regretted not trusting the team with the truth and losing one of his best people because of it. "I don't give a damn what anyone calls me."

"Good enough," Steve replied. "We'll stick to Dickhead for now until this is over."

# *Chapter 4*

The Grasshopper and Gopher Bookstore took up an entire brownstone on Beacon Street. Three floors of perfection. The first floor contained rows and rows of nonfiction books and a cute coffee bar that served the best chocolate brownies in the world. Matt sat in a window seat with his laptop, a chocolate chip cookie and a large hot chocolate with a mountain of whipped cream. He seemed perfectly happy. Fiona sat with him for a few minutes, nibbling on the final corner of the brownie she insisted she needed to calm her nerves. She could handle a lot of things in the world. A violent encounter with a terrorist was child's play, but standing before a large crowd and reading her own words made her sick to her stomach. Sugar and chocolate helped.

"Are you all set?" she asked her son.

"I have been for the past ten minutes."

"Just checking."

He tilted his head in the way teenagers did when they were merely tolerating a person until they left.

"Fine. I'm leaving." She then told him for the tenth time to not leave the bookstore, to keep his laptop with him and to call Janet, her agent, or Meaghan, who should arrive any minute, if he needed anything during the signing. He agreed.

Janet was in town to celebrate the impressive sales of Fiona's newest book and to coordinate Fiona's press tour. She'd dressed in a beige Chanel skirt and white silk blouse—every inch of her announced success. Her three-inch Jimmy Choo platform sandals alone cost more than all the shoes in Fiona's wardrobe. Fiona dressed a bit more casually in a white peasant blouse and jeans. She let her hair and makeup do the heavy work with her image. Red lipstick, perfectly styled platinum blond hair, colored and highlighted two days before, and red leather ankle boots to match her lipstick and nail polish.

Fiona continued to linger next to Matt until Janet tapped her on the shoulder and waved her along. "It's time." She paused and stared at Fiona's face. "Are you nervous? I've never seen you so distracted."

"I'm fine." Fiona didn't tell Janet about the break-in. Janet had a tendency to be overprotective and might have pulled the signing, disappointing both Fiona and her fans. For all her focus on making money, the woman never let a dollar come between her client's mental and physical well-being.

They headed to the back stairs and climbed. The children's section was on the second floor. A noisy place, but bright-colored and very nurturing. They headed up to the third floor where fiction in every genre was located along with seating for about fifty people. Early in Fiona's career, she'd done book readings to either empty rooms, bookstore staff or an occasional shopper. Her sudden success shocked her as much as it did her publisher. As she climbed higher up the stairs, a line of people twisted around the stairwell, blocking access to the third floor.

"These can't all be for me?"

Janet put her arm around her. "You're a hit. Not only are your readers loving your latest book, but they're discovering your earlier books as well."

Someone in line reached out to her and shouted, "Love your book. Bradley is the hottest hero you've ever written."

"Thanks." She waved and received a bunch more comments from people in line.

When she arrived at the top of the stairs, the room had so many people milling about, she could barely see a path to the microphone. One of the staff of the bookstore waved and directed customers into empty seats. Within minutes, the event was standing room only. For an undercover asset who had always worked behind the scenes, the attention was overwhelming—even more so considering the events a few nights ago. Someone had invaded her space and put her child at risk. She didn't take that threat lightly, but trying to corral Matt into this room and keeping him from leaving in the middle of her reading would be impossible. The best she could do was keep him in the same building in a public place where others could keep an eye on him.

The what-ifs dominated her thoughts again and a thousand scenarios interrupted her focus. The man who had been in her home had not been located. With zero idea about what he was specifically after, she had no idea about the threat level. A botched burglary tended to end at the house with no second attempt since the residents of the invaded space would increase their security. The burglar would just go on to another house. If she were the target, the intruder could show up here in the bookstore. Although that was unlikely with so many witnesses, she had to take everything into consideration.

She'd called Meaghan, who was already in downtown Boston, and would be there in under ten minutes. Fiona took a deep breath. It would all be okay.

The store manager walked to the microphone situated in front of a cozy armchair. "Welcome. We love having you all. Before we get started, can the people standing in front of the stairwell please move. Safety first. If there isn't enough room to see well, we have set up a simulcast in the coffee shop downstairs. I assure you, the author will stay until the last book is signed, so there's no need to worry about missing anything. So let's get started. Our guest today is the bestselling author of international thrillers with a touch of romance—Fiona Stirling. Her newest book, *Wake the Dead*, involves a sexy army officer who is presumed dead after a botched operation in South America. His wife has no idea that she's not a widow, and their second-chance romance melted my heart." The woman placed a hand on her chest and sighed deeply.

"In her former life, Fiona worked for the State Department and helped negotiate several international trade deals. Let's give a big welcome to Fiona Stirling."

The crowd cheered. Fiona waved. Instinctively, she scanned the crowd for anyone suspicious. Mostly women sat in the crowd, mostly relaxed, except for an intense woman talking on the phone in the northwest corner, but she seemed more likely annoyed with a spouse or a child. The manager went over to the woman and asked her to take her conversation outside. After a rolling of the eyes without receiving an ounce of support from the other customers, she finally left.

Fiona took a deep breath, thanked everyone for coming out and introduced her new novel. She read the opening pages with as much personality as she could muster, stopping at the point in the story where an older woman in a bar walks up to the hero and points a gun to his head. The audience visibly reacted to the abrupt ending, exactly as she wanted. They'd be more apt to buy the book if they couldn't wait to learn what happened next.

When she was done, she received a standing ovation. Janet stood to the side and gave her two thumbs-up.

Two staff members brought her to the table where she would conduct the book signing. A line formed in front of it. The signing was going to take hours to complete but she wanted to do it because she appreciated every last reader, despite her hostility toward small talk. Janet went to the back of the table and placed some decadent-looking drink in front of Fiona.

"I thought you could use an iced mocha latte."

"You thought right. Thanks." Fiona took a sip and let the sugar and caffeine motivate her to meet the roomful of readers. "If I've never told you before, I love you."

"Everyone does." She laughed. "You're doing great. Keep up your energy. There's just over a hundred people lined up, some with multiple books."

Fiona glanced at the first woman in line, a thirty-something-year-old holding her newest release and waiting patiently. When Fiona had started writing, her audience was mainly women who were forty and up, but as her books became more popular, her audience changed, or perhaps it expanded, to include a whole variety of new readers.

The exhaustion of the past week hit Fiona like a truck, but she would never let her fans down. She owed everything to them. She took another sip and waved to the woman. "Hi, what's your name?"

Two-and-a-half hours later, she was still smiling and still signing. There were only about a dozen people left. A young woman in a pink crop top and ripped jeans approached. She held a copy of *Wake the Dead* and an envelope.

"Can you sign my book *To Jessie*?" she asked.

"Sure." She signed the book and slid it back to her.

The woman handed her the envelope. Fiona had received lovely gifts from readers over the years so didn't think anything of it.

"Thank you."

"Oh, that's not from me. Some rando told me to give it to you. He said he couldn't wait." She thanked Fiona again and left with the signed novel.

Every nerve in Fiona's body fired. Without inviting the next reader over, she opened the envelope and read the note.

*If you want to see your son again, leave right now and meet me at the Mercedes at the front door.*

Jason couldn't risk being seen again, but he wanted to remain close enough to help. He'd rather blow his cover and save his wife and son than remain anonymous and not lift a finger to help them. Sure, he had a solid team—although one man short—that was on the job, and he trusted them, but the guilt that filled him over that bastard breaking into her house ran on repeat over and over in his head. He remained in the Expedition illegally parked a block from the bookstore. Inside the bookstore, Meaghan was watching over Matt, while Noah stood guard at the front door. Steve wandered about making sure nothing was out of the ordinary. No one would expect Steve to be anything other than a typical middle-aged Bostonian drinking Dunkin' and hanging out waiting for his wife to get her book signed inside. In reality, Steve's wife worked at city hall and helped the team get out of a lot of hot water as they protected their clients. He also had more skills than anyone gave him credit for. If something went down, Steve would jump in and handle it.

Fiona's book signing had passed the two-hour mark and Jason's patience faded. While part of him felt pride in what Fiona had done with her life, another part wanted the old Fiona back. The one who focused on two things: her work and her family. The work with the State Department offered her the ability to truly affect change in the world. Writing books would be satisfying, but being in the action had always been Jason's preferred place in the world, even one step removed from the military. He took a sip of coffee and froze. Fiona was walking outside. Her expression aloof.

"Noah, this is DJ. Is the signing over?" Jason radioed.

"There's only a few people left in line."

"Fiona is on the move. Do you see her?"

"I have her in my sight now. Damn, she's moving fast."

Fiona pushed through the glass front door, clutching

what looked like a card. Her hair so bright in the sun, it was impossible to miss her. Matt wasn't with her.

"Meaghan, do you have Matt?" Tall, elegant Meaghan Knight had been in law enforcement before joining Fresh Pond Security. After five years of watching guys getting promoted over her, she decided to step into a field where her skills would be better compensated. Her competence made every task better.

"Affirmative."

"Keep him with you. Something's up."

Had Fiona paused for a bit of fresh air after such a stressful event, Jason would have remained exactly where he was, but she strode over to a dark gray Mercedes and yanked open the back door as though she intended to rip the door off the hinges. A man who looked more like an overgrown teenager grabbed her arm and tried to pull her into the car. Her foot braced on the door frame, stopping him from an abduction. Jason jumped out of the Expedition and rushed to the car. Fiona wrestled back and forth trying to free her arm, until someone rushed up from behind her and kicked at her leg until it slid off the door frame, then they pushed her inside. The engine roared to life. When Jason arrived at the car, the door was locked. He could see Fiona struggling, so he punched out the window with his elbow and pulled his wife out through the broken glass, knowing she was getting cut up in the process. There was no other choice. Once the car was out of sight, he couldn't protect her from a much worse experience. He lifted her into his arms, blood dripping from her exposed skin.

Steve rushed to the car and pointed his gun to slow the car reversing, but it spun around, smashing into an

Outback parked on the side of the road. There were too many people in the area to take a chance with a stray bullet, so he lowered the weapon.

Son of a bitch. Jason had let her down again with a whole team surrounding her. Someone had targeted her and would be back, as guys this brazen did not give up. Jason had to gather his family and take them to safety as he should have done before. Not thinking, he carried her to the Expedition and then lowered her to her feet. In the rush to save her, he'd blown his cover wide open. She stared at him, her mouth open, her body frozen in place.

He'd imagined reuniting with her again, a scene filled with tears and warm embraces. Under these circumstances, however, there would be no warm embrace.

They had to leave. Once the police arrived, there'd be too many questions and more exposure for all of them.

"We need to get out of here." He held her by his side.

She pulled back. No tears either. Just laser beams coming from her eyes. "Not without Matt."

He glanced over at Noah, standing next to them. He gave Jason a thumbs-up and pointed inside. Matt was safe. "He's fine. Get in the car."

Twisting her shoulders, she fought for release. "No."

Noah made the mistake of trying to "save" her by shoving her into the back seat. She twisted his arm and flipped him onto his back on the hard asphalt. Steve took the easier way, pointing his weapon at her. His finger wasn't close to the trigger, but Jason wanted to rip his head off anyway for threatening her. His tactic worked, however. She slid into the back seat as he got behind the wheel. Before she could figure out that Steve and Noah weren't going with them, Jason drove off without turning around to look at her. He wasn't sure if they were being followed, so he headed to the Callahan Tunnel, circled around the airport twice, slipped through a secure area and then headed to one of the team's safe houses, the most secure place he could think of.

"Jason? What the hell is going on?" she said, her voice strained.

"I'm here to protect you."

# Chapter 5

The whole world tumbled inside out, leaving Fiona unsure of the exact point reality twisted into her dreams. Her arm hurt from the man in the Mercedes yanking it so hard he nearly dislocated her shoulder. She would have worked herself free if the person behind her hadn't slammed her leg. Then there were the slivers of glass in her arm and back and a head wound where she hit the top of the door on the way in or out, she wasn't sure. She reached back and felt a decent-size welt. When she looked at her fingers, they were covered in blood.

"We can look at your injuries when we get you somewhere safe. You might have internal injuries, but the gash doesn't seem large. Head wounds bleed like stink generally."

"I know." She wasn't in the mood for her dead husband to mansplain combat wounds to her.

The self-defense moves she hadn't practiced in years were not exactly there when she needed them. So much for muscle memory. She blamed her pregnancy for twisting her muscles into new forms. One thing for certain, she'd never let those skills go stale again. Despite the possible head wound, the rescue injured her more than the initial kidnapping. Her blood leeched through the outfit she'd carefully picked out for the book signing. Being yanked through broken glass shredded her arms, her back and her blouse. Not that her own safety mattered. All she could think of was Matt. Perhaps he was still with Meaghan. She prayed he was.

She took in her situation. The note, the man in the car dressed in jeans and a gray hoodie and the man who kicked out her legs dressed in jeans and a T-shirt. Then there were the two men fighting off the kidnappers. And Jason.

Her husband.

Her dead husband.

Janet was a great agent, but even she couldn't manage this kind of a publicity stunt. Yet, what were the chances of Fiona writing about a husband coming back from the dead and here he was?

He turned his face partly toward her. There was scarring on his neck and up to his ear—his skin red and white and imperfect—that appeared to have occurred years ago. Her mind analyzed possible situations that would have caused such devastation, and her heart ached over his pain. The tight buzz cut he wore in the military had grown out, but that strong chin, chiseled cheekbones and square jawline in need of a shave were all Jason. She had not one moment of doubt. He was also the same man she'd seen in the hotel room next to hers only days before. The sight should have been a comfort, but something in his reappearance burned away her elation. For years, she'd been alone, caring for their child, holding Jason's love inside her heart. Yet, if this was indeed Jason, he hadn't been lost to her—he'd abandoned her. Left her alone. All the love in the world couldn't sweeten that fact.

She couldn't look at him anymore, giving her attention to the blur of city out the window instead. She'd missed him, cried over him and had memorialized him. His return should overload her with love and compassion, but she felt nothing but a burning pain in her body.

"Are you okay?" he asked, all business.

She stared at him. Was she okay? That was one stupid question. "Sure. I'm perfectly fine. My child is... I don't know where my son is or if he's safe and my dead husband has not only kidnapped me, but has decided to yank me through broken glass and had his friends force me into this SUV at gunpoint. It's a banner day. Oh, and let's not forget someone breaking into my home last week. Were you involved in that?"

"We arrived too late to help you."

"We?"

"My associates."

"There's a descriptive word. Let me guess, you found the redhead with the gun in South Boston hanging out with Whitey Bulger?"

Jason laughed, a sound that almost knocked Fiona from the seat. She'd heard him in her dreams, but over the years she must have changed his laugh a bit, because this laugh hit at her deepest memory of him. Strong, confident and fearless. "Steve's my partner. He's a bit rough around the edges, but he always gets the job done," he answered.

"And the younger guy?"

"Noah."

Noah. The name was too normal for her to hate him

entirely. A normal person with a normal life hanging out with her dead husband.

"He's a former intelligence analyst with some pretty solid surveillance and defense skills." Jason listed his qualities as though he were selling her a car.

"He looks like he lives in a coffee shop, trying to write the next Gatsby."

Jason laughed again. "His appearance lets him get inside places someone less refined wouldn't be able to go."

"Like my book signing." She reached down and pulled off her boots. If she needed to run, she had a better chance in bare feet.

"Why did you leave the bookstore?" Jason asked, his laughter gone, his expression serious.

She buried her emotions and fell back in time, when she was the investigator. Information was power and right now she was powerless. Perhaps he could fill in the gaps. "I received a note."

"What did it say?"

She read it out loud.

*If you want to see your son again, leave right now and meet me at the Mercedes at the front door.*

The fear that had hit her when she first read the note washed over her. "Are you sure he's safe?" she asked.

Jason nodded. "He was sitting with your neighbor in the cafe."

"How do you know my neighbor?"

"I know everything about you, Fi."

That little statement annoyed her, so she ignored it. "Who wrote the note and why?"

"That's the big question. I promise I won't leave until I make sure you and Matt are safe." The implication was that he'd leave them again. For some reason that angered her even more.

She grabbed a napkin from his console, pressed it over the sore spot on her head and shut her eyes. Everything hurt, especially the memories of her perfect husband. Every word he'd spoken to her about love and their future together had been a lie. Fiona wished she could return to her date with George. He wasn't anything to write home about, but he'd probably never faked his death and abandoned his family. Maybe he had. She couldn't trust anyone right now. The biggest question was why Jason had returned now.

"Were you spying on us?" she said, part question, part accusation, her mind functioning on stress and the iced mocha latte from Janet.

Jason looked over his shoulder at her. Those soft brown eyes had always melted her heart, but they'd have to burrow through the frost that had developed in the past few minutes. "You've been in my field of vision forever."

"That's screwed up. I believed in you, and now I don't know what to believe." She'd dreamed of having him back for years, but not like this. Her traitorous eyes teared up.

"You need to trust me." He reached for her hand. The heat of his touch scrambled her thoughts and for a brief second, she wanted him in the most indecent way possible.

She pulled away and let out a gruff laugh. "That would work if you hadn't lied to me for the past five years."

Jason pulled off the turnpike and drove another few miles until they arrived in a secluded location south of Natick. Fiona didn't recognize anything around her. He drove down a dirt road and ended up at a broken-down wooden shack that appeared to have existed at the time of the Revolutionary War—stone foundation, weather-faded white paint, a red door partially off the hinges.

"Nice place. You've done well for yourself." She wanted the contempt to shoot from her words, yet she'd spent the past five years praying her husband would come back to her. As much as he'd betrayed her, she couldn't hate him.

A car driven by Noah pulled up next to them. Matt was in the passenger seat. The sight of him eased most of her stress. With him safe, she could breathe. For years, she'd tried to shield him from life's dangers, but she'd never envisioned having to physically fight to protect him from real and dangerous threats. The thought terrified her.

He jumped out when the car stopped. "Mom!"

He hugged her, until she couldn't handle the pain. She kissed him on the cheek instead.

Matt stepped back, taking in the blood and cuts and bruises. "You need a hospital."

He was right, but she wasn't sure her tormentors wouldn't wait outside the ER and take her out there. She wouldn't die from these injuries if she cleaned them and rested a bit, although she might need a few stitches for the worst cuts from the glass. She tried to hold it together, but her dead husband had been resurrected and how was she going to explain that to Matt?

"I'll be okay. Just a flesh wound."

"So not funny."

"I'm fine," Fiona repeated.

Jason said something to Noah, then walked over to them.

She didn't have to worry about Matt being devastated by the chaos. He had a serious expression on and took in everything around him, especially the man who had the same shape and color eyes.

"Who are you?" Matt asked Jason, but she could tell from his expression he knew exactly who he was speaking to.

"I'm from a company hired to protect you and your mother." The deep timbre of his voice vibrated through Fiona's heart.

"Who hired you?" he asked.

"Classified."

"Who broke into our house?" Matt was relentless when he wanted an answer.

"A thug from Houston."

The answer shocked Fiona. The police never caught the man. How did Jason have that information?

"Why?" Matt asked, his question exactly the question Fiona wanted answered. *Why?*

Jason shrugged. "I don't know yet."

Matt stood nearly as tall as Jason. He stared him down. "Why should we trust you?"

"Maybe you shouldn't. Don't trust anyone. Follow your gut. If it says you're okay, you might be. But not always. Life sucks that way."

"Seriously?" Fiona interrupted. "'Don't trust anyone,' and 'life sucks' are your answers? That makes sense. Your whole existence is a lie." Her anger accelerated, until her voice boomed across the front yard. For a woman who prided herself on self-control, this was a low point. "Don't you dare think you can return on a whim and offer our son advice as though you had the right."

"Mom?" Matt stared at her as though she'd gone off the deep end. She had.

Jason put his hand up to quiet Matt. "Her comment is valid."

"Dad?" Matt finally asked, but he stepped back from him and crossed his arms over his chest.

Jason sighed. "I can explain everything. I need to get you two inside to safety, then we can talk."

"I thought it was you, but you were dead. They told us you were dead. I was at your memorial. An honor guard handed me a flag. It's in my bedroom. You were dead," he repeated, his voice trembling on the last "dead."

Fiona's anger swelled upon hearing her son's pain. Her life had revolved around protecting Matt after the loss of his father. That his biggest heartache arrived not at Jason's death but at his resurrection stabbed at her more than the shards of glass still stinging her.

Then she noticed Noah, who stood nearby taking in the scene. From his expression, he seemed to know Jason was related to her and Matt, but wasn't prepared for a family showdown.

"Sorry about the body slam," she said to him.

He smiled. "I let my guard down. Totally deserved it."

"You body-slammed him?" Matt asked.

"More like I pushed him down."

Noah laughed. "Sure, make it less impressive than it was."

Jason strode over to him, whispered something in his

ear, something about speaking to Steve, then he slapped him on the shoulder. "We'll catch up later."

"Your friend isn't staying?" she asked.

Jason looked at Noah walking back to his car. "He has a laundry list of issues to deal with."

"All related to the note?"

"Among other things."

After Noah drove away, Jason led Fiona and Matt to the front door. She checked on Matt again, but he wasn't looking for care and affection from anyone. He stayed several arm's lengths away from her, but followed Jason. His father had become a hero to him over the years. One of the good guys, fighting the good fight, lost to evil forces. Now he was back. After the scare at the house and the bookstore, Matt's emotions would be all over the place.

And she had no ability to soothe him while he was focused on his father. She looked at Jason too. He had the same intensity he had whenever he returned from the field. Whatever he'd been doing the past few years, it involved weapons and some motley crew of *associates*.

She'd worked in the gray areas of international relations and from what she'd researched on her husband, so had he. She'd found various foreign news reports about his death. A drug cartel threatening civil war in Colombia attacked a diplomatic mission from the United States. The United States vowed support for the government. But Jason had never been involved in diplomacy, at least not that he'd told her. As far as she knew, he'd never been one for embassy dinners and military parades. He'd preferred the shadow side of the government where any battles he'd been involved in ended up buried in one of a thousand locked file cabinets in a warehouse in Maryland. She'd known he participated in dangerous missions, especially when she found new scars on him as they made love. He'd always acted as though they were minor scrapes. It was all part of being married to him, and she trusted him to keep her and Matt safe, which he was currently doing. At least that was what she thought he was doing, although bringing them to the middle of nowhere would be a perfect place to off the family he never wanted. But that didn't feel right. Even Matt had turned from frosty toward him to fascinated in the fifty feet they walked to the front door.

Jason unlocked the door and stepped aside to let them in.

Matt went inside first. "Damn, this is like Tony Stark's house," he exclaimed.

"Language," Fiona warned him, but couldn't help but agree when she entered a space of white concrete walls with beige leather sofas, and a white marble kitchen with appliances that seemed to have come straight out of *Architectural Digest*. "What the hell?"

"Language, Mom," Matt said, his lips curving into a smile for the first time all day.

Jason leaned against the countertop. "It's a quiet place to work."

Fiona didn't believe him. Had he gone to the dark side and he was in hiding? It was the only thing that made sense. Perhaps he chose money over his family and now worked for the very people he'd spent his earlier years fighting.

When she'd first met him, he'd been a senior ROTC candidate about to embark on a military career. She'd been a graduate student struggling to find a career in a world that preferred men with Ivy League diplomas. They both had big ambitions, and despite frequent absences, soon their lives were incomplete without the other. He'd always made her feel as though she were the most important person in the world, and she'd loved his charm, his clear set of morals and his eye-watering good looks.

Everything had been perfect until he went on that final mission. It should have lasted three weeks, but something went wrong. When he died, his absence destroyed her. If it hadn't been for Matt, she wouldn't have rallied as quickly as she had. Instead of wallowing, she pushed through her grief to raise Matt into a man his father would be proud of.

Jason called her over to a stool at the kitchen island. Now that the immediate danger had subsided, the pain of her injuries roared to life. Wrestling the man in her house, being pulled into a car and then pulled out again through a broken window, as well as the intensity of flipping Noah onto his back, had taken a huge toll on her. Her muscles ached, her head hurt and scrapes and cuts covered her.

Jason rummaged through a cabinet and handed Matt a bag of microwave popcorn. "Can you make this? I'm starving."

Matt nodded and crossed the kitchen to the microwave.

"Want a drink?" he asked.

Matt twisted to face him. "A beer?"

"How about something age appropriate. Look in the fridge. I think there are a few cans of soda there, and then you can watch television while I speak to your mother."

Matt stalled and looked over at her. He bit his lip as he always did when he was unsure of his next move. He stepped toward her, but she waved him away.

"I'll be fine." She nodded until Matt released himself from his indecision and went to the refrigerator.

His concern melted her heart. Fiona had never pushed him to take on the responsibilities of being the man of the house, first, because she was more than capable of handling whatever came along, and also because she never wanted to throw that burden on him. Despite that, he often kept an eye on her, as protective of his only living family member as she was of him. If he had his father back, she had no idea how their relationship would change.

She waved her arm toward the television. "I need to talk to Jason and clean myself up. Can we talk later?"

"Okay." Matt sat down on the couch and turned the television on, far enough out of listening range if she wanted to speak to Jason alone.

Jason placed a large first aid kit next to her on the island. "What hurts?" he asked.

"Everything." She watched him take out alcohol, tape and gauze pads.

He lifted her chin, his face so close that the intoxicating scent of his breath brought her back to their early days, kissing for hours, just because. "You have a scratch on your temple, but it doesn't seem to have broken through the skin." He wiped it with the alcohol anyway.

She pulled back from the burn. "Holy shit."

"Language," he whispered as his thumb caressed her

cheek. "Let me see the damage to your arms and shoulders. It looks like more scratches than actual glass in your arm. The benefits of punching through tempered glass."

She nodded as if in a trance or a dream or a nightmare—she couldn't decide. Shrugging her shoulders out of her ripped blouse, she could feel a few glass splinters catching on the fabric. Without the tempered glass, the injuries would have been deeper and more potentially life-threatening. Instead, she'd ended up with some minor cuts and bruising. She'd be fine. The pain kept her from caring that she was sitting in front of him wearing only a bloody beige bra until his eyes stopped their clinical evaluation and stared at her with a far more carnal assessment.

"I can do this alone in the bathroom," she said, feeling self-conscious. "Do you have tweezers?"

"If I help you, it won't take long at all." He was already picking off the larger pieces with his fingers, and Fiona didn't bother stopping him. There was no way she could reach all of them.

"Maybe I should sneak into a small community hospital, just to get cleaned up," she said, thinking out loud.

"It wouldn't be as safe as here. Relax. We have all night to fix you up."

She glanced around. "This place is a contradiction. Broke on the outside, sophisticated on the inside. Or is it a metaphor for you?"

"I have it for business reasons."

"Business must be profitable." The realization that he was alive was still clouded by her years of grief, but the idea that he'd been out in the world working while she had no idea if he was dead or alive grated on her every last nerve.

"I get by."

He got by living like some superspy in a villain's lair. He could be a villain. She had no idea. He could have lied about their entire relationship all the way back to the beginning of their relationship. Had he even been in the military? Had he been in Colombia when he *died*? She shook her head. She'd done extensive research through government back channels, and according to the classified documents her friend had unearthed, he had been a part of the military and in an operation that went bad in South America. "I won't ask." She wanted to know specifics but didn't want to beg.

His fingers brushed over her shoulder, scraping over several splinters of glass. She sucked back a curse. He continued picking out the pieces and looking for more glass with not so much as an "I'm sorry."

"Ask me anything you want. I owe you an explanation, although to be honest, I never anticipated having to explain anything to you. I thought I'd lost you forever."

"You lost me?" She recoiled from that magnetic pull. She'd been broken for years now, and he was the one grieving?

"Can I help you first? You can crucify me later."

She nodded. "I'm already planning on it." She remained next to him. Love and hate must be identical twins. Her emotions swirled hot and cold like a typhoon. She'd never believed them to be an average couple. They'd had secrets from each other, but they'd also shared love and trust. Without trust, there could be nothing.

He bandaged a fairly long cut on her shoulder. The

incision went deep enough to make her wish he had sutures in his bag.

She swore in a half scream.

"Mom?" Matt looked back over the couch from the other side of the room, staring at her shoulders. He made a face and flinched. "You look bad."

"I'll be fine." She could see blood on a cloth Jason had dabbed her skin with.

"Can you go into the cabinet by the window and grab the bottle of whiskey and two glasses?" Jason asked Matt.

Fiona shook her head. "I'm fine." She didn't want to become alcohol impaired, especially when someone was after them.

"Trust me, this will feel better after a shot or two."

Matt came back with the whiskey and poured the first glass half-full.

"Whoa. Not that much," Fiona said.

"It's fine. I'll drink it. A little less for your mother." Jason placed his own glass next to the first aid kit and handed her the smaller portion. "Bottoms up."

She took it, anticipating a very rough afternoon. She drank a sip and set down the glass.

"I remember you, you know." Matt stood staring at his father.

"You should. You were eight years old when I left. It wasn't so long ago, was it?" Jason spoke with his usual confidence, but there was a cloud over his emotions. Regret maybe, with a side of wistfulness?

"It seems like forever. But I remember playing soccer with you in the backyard. I wasn't very good, but you kept playing with me anyway. I made the traveling team the year after you died. I think they felt bad for me."

"Not true. You have natural speed. A coach can't train that. If the coach were strategic, he would have placed you as a wing and fed you balls from the midfield, balls no one else could catch." He spoke as though he'd been there. And then Fiona bit back more anger. Had he been there? Standing shoulder to shoulder with the other parents, a ghost in her son's life.

In spite of Fiona's turmoil, Matt smiled at his father's words. "Yeah. He did. Maybe it wasn't just because you were gone."

"Don't question your abilities. You have so much going for you. Don't think I haven't kept my eye on you over the years. I couldn't help it. You're my kid. I love you enough to blow up our lives to keep you and your mother safe," he admitted.

Matt's brows lifted. "What do you mean? Mom told me you died in an attack."

"That was what everyone believed. Some bad men wanted what I was delivering. During a fire fight, the cartel leader's son died, then everyone I was with. I only survived because I passed out in a bush and remained hidden until some really nice people took me to the hospital. The cartel leader wanted revenge for his son, but you can't get revenge on the dead. If he knew I was alive, he'd go after my family. I didn't want that to happen."

"Is that who broke into the house last night?" Matt asked.

"I'm not sure, but I'm trying to find out."

"If everyone thinks you're dead, why are they after Mom and me now?"

"I'm not sure about that either, but I hope to get some answers real soon."

Fiona sipped on the whiskey and took in all he said. Someone wanted him dead. And his family. The tension in her chest lifted. Not entirely, but enough to allow her to breathe easier and focus on the man next to her. Maybe he wasn't the monster she'd created in her mind over the past hour or so.

She glanced around the house. Sepia-toned landscapes framed on the walls gave nothing away about his personal life. Not one family photo, not one souvenir from his travels, not one reference to his military career. It was as if he'd stripped his life of any color or life and was merely existing.

"What happens after you fix me up?" she asked. She was asking about tonight and tomorrow and next week and next year.

"I leave you here while I figure out why someone is after you."

Staying here with him was one thing, but remaining in the middle of nowhere alone was not happening. "You're kidnapping us?"

He frowned. "You're more than free to return home and wait for the guys in the car to return with backup."

He had a point. This place had to be better than her house. She couldn't imagine sleeping there while people who had tried to hurt her and her son were still at large.

"What about the man who broke into my house?" she asked.

"He won't bother you anymore."

"You took him out?" Matt's voice rose in excitement.

"He's safely put away until I can figure out what he wanted with you." Jason stood and went to the refrigerator.

Fiona shook her head. "We'll need to inform the police of what's going on."

"No. That would get the press involved and that's the last thing you need. We took care to minimize the burglary and the attempted kidnapping last week. It's for the best."

"Awesome." Matt had those hero-worship eyes that might get betrayed someday.

"No, not awesome." She paused. Jason not only knew where she lived, but he'd been in her house before the police. "Did you take the rest of my lasagna?"

Despite his best effort, his eyes smiled back at her. "That's classified."

# *Chapter 6*

Jason set up an Epsom salt bath for Fiona to ease the smallest of the slivers out of her skin. He'd take care of his own injuries later.

Matt sat in the living room on the large leather couch, eating popcorn and drinking his way through all the soda in the refrigerator. Jason turned on *Die Hard* for him, a classic movie Fiona had never bothered to show him. Jason would never complain about her parenting skills since he'd left her to raise Matt on her own, despite her making helicopter parenting her chosen religion. No doubt he was half to blame. Her parents had both died within a few years of Matt's birth, and when he disappeared, she was completely alone. Losing so much family would set someone up to protect their remaining loved ones with everything they could.

Matt hadn't been allowed to play football like Jason had done in high school. Instead, he played soccer. Fiona had made the right decision. Matt had speed, but not a lot of bulk. He'd be flattened on a football field. Jason had shown up a few times to Matt's games, disguised, of course, to watch him. His son could outrun anyone on the field and had agility and a fantastic right cross.

Fiona would sit on the sidelines in a fold-up red chair with her designer travel mug steaming hot, no matter what the weather. Far too many of the fathers kept their eyes on the Marilyn Monroe of soccer moms. Yet, she never once flirted back. She'd remained focused on Matt and her career and the ghost of her husband. A shroud of guilt wafted through the room and threatened to obliterate him. If he'd found any other way to handle the mess he'd been thrust into, he might have been able to spend every morning at breakfast with his son and every night in bed with his wife. He drank a bit more, just to cut the pain of her not loving him now that he'd returned.

Fiona emerged from the bath an hour later. She came over to the couch dressed in Jason's oversize sweatpants and a T-shirt. Not since she'd dressed in a maid costume for one of their anniversaries had she ever looked so sexy. Perhaps it was five years without being close to a woman or his new proximity to her, but he downed the rest of his whiskey and tried to cool the intensity of his desire for her. His body didn't give a rat's ass about anything but feeling her in his arms again. His heart refused to get close to her when he'd have to disappear for their protection, but then wavered when she looked his way. His head warned him to keep his distance because his body and heart were way too untrustworthy in this situation.

She strode up to him, inches from his lips, her breath sweet and so inviting. After a long sigh that hypnotized him, she shook her head. "I honestly hate you right now. We needed rescuing because you couldn't be bothered to give me a heads-up on some lunatic who wanted to kill your family. I don't know whether to thank you for helping us from something you didn't prepare us for or slap you in the face." The words threw a bucket of ice water over his burning passion.

"Slap away," Jason replied, his chest aching. "I thought I was protecting you by keeping you from the reality of what had happened in Colombia. I was wrong. I should have trusted you."

Her expression fell as she shook her head, then she turned to Matt. "Do you need anything else to eat?"

"Pizza," he said, his eyes not leaving the screen as McClane watched his wife being taken hostage.

Fiona wasn't drawn into the movie at all. "Pizza? We shouldn't leave the house."

Jason's stomach growled. He respected McClane and his focus on doing the right thing no matter the cost. He'd lived the previous five years believing he was doing the right thing for the right reasons, but maybe it wasn't a matter of right and wrong. He did what he had to in order to protect his family and even if another way was better, it was the only path Jason had known to take. A simple solution to a complex problem.

The guilt of his absence in his son's life made him want to spoil Matt. He'd been through enough. "It's fine. I can arrange a delivery."

"You trust someone coming here?"

"I was going to ask Steve to come. He could bring pizza and we could strategize a solution."

"I guess," Matt said, pausing the television. "You trust him?"

Jason nodded.

"More than us?" The question was a valid one, but

he hadn't trusted Steve with his secrets either. He hadn't trusted anyone.

"The difference is that I can't live with the thought of you in harm's way. I care so much for you, I'm willing to sacrifice a perfect life with my family to keep you all safe. He's in a job that has inherent risk. It's what we do." Fiona and Matt shouldn't have to dodge bullets or run from kidnappers. Not because of him.

Matt stared at his father and pondered what he'd said for a minute and sighed. "I guess that makes sense," he said without any conviction.

Jason wanted his son to understand him, to respect him, but lying for five years wasn't a strong base for building such a relationship. They were strangers right now and their relationship wouldn't be repaired in the next few hours. In the middle of this chaos, he didn't have time to forge quality connections. Not if he wanted to keep Matt and Fiona alive. He had to figure out what was going on. He had to find out if Porras was involved.

Matt turned back to the television. *Yippee Ki Yay.*

Fiona waved Jason over to the bathroom. When he arrived, she closed the door for privacy. "Is this Steve guy really trustworthy?"

"He worked for the FBI as an undercover agent at a pharmaceutical company, then moved into the accounting department of an oil company. He left the service before his cover was blown. He seems like an open book but it's all a smokescreen to keep you from knowing anything about him." Steve was goofy enough to get under the skin of most people, which made people open up about things they shouldn't speak about with him. He was the best of the best in his former life and the FBI still used the information he acquired from his assignments.

"That's all well and good, but can he keep a group of bad guys away from us?"

"He's deadly serious when he needs to be. Matt will love him. You may want to kill him after a few hours. He's not your type."

"He isn't?"

"No." Jason was her type. After watching the disaster date she'd had a few nights before, he was even more sure of it. Another part of his subterfuge he'd done wrong was to overly monitor Fiona in her private life. She had every right to find someone new, someone with whom she could create a full life. He didn't have the right to limit her in any way, despite how much it killed him to see her with anyone else.

"You don't know anything about me anymore, even if you have been stalking my movements over the past five years. Now if you'll excuse me." She walked toward him, backing him out of the room.

He didn't move. She stopped when she reached his chest. The scent of the antiseptic he'd placed on her skin stung his nostrils, reminding him of the medical reasons for stepping back. But he'd been dreaming of being this close to her, and the temptation ached inside him. "You're more beautiful than ever."

She lifted her chin, her body leaning into him. "And you lied to me."

An emotional and physical torture he deserved. And until she believed he'd acted in their best interests, he had to keep his distance. "I didn't lie, I omitted."

"The memorial bench with your name on it says otherwise." She placed a hand on his shoulder and leaned towards him, her breath caressing his neck. "Why do you think these guys have something to do with the cartel?"

"Because you told my enemy exactly what he wanted to believe."

"What was that?"

"That I'm still alive."

She shoved him back into the hall. "What are you talking about? I didn't say a word."

But she had. The entire plot of her book was about a soldier on a secret mission in South America who pretended to be dead to protect his wife and two daughters. A bit too close to the facts of their situation to be a coincidence.

"How did you get details of the mission? It was all classified." He knew she had secrets of her own, connections in the government that rivaled his, but she'd never spoken about it.

Her face paled. "It was a story. I made it all up."

"You thought I was dead, and so did everyone else until you wrote a story so close to what happened that people who know something about this may now question if I am indeed alive or not. You still use your contacts, don't you?"

She kept her expression neutral. "That's classified... But I never suspected you were still alive. It was more like wishful thinking." After a moment, she looked at the floor. "I'm sorry, but I filled the holes with a story that healed my heart. There was nothing I learned from official records that gave me any hope you were still alive. Actually, you shouldn't be blaming me at all for something I couldn't have known without you confiding in me. And apparently, I wasn't trustworthy enough for you to give me the truth." She shifted around him and went into the bedroom.

The chance of them rekindling anything seemed like a long shot, so he had to get more serious about keeping them safe. He'd given away his right to a family when he'd decided to hide away.

He checked on Matt, fast asleep on the couch. He needed the rest after so much action. Jason turned the volume down and went to his office.

Finally alone, he cleaned up the abrasions he could reach on his shoulder and then called his team to update them. Steve, Meaghan and Noah appeared on the screen in front of him. Each one had worked extralong shifts over the past week, loyalty he didn't deserve for dragging them into this.

They'd all placed their lives in his hands to join him in a dangerous business. He'd broken their trust. Because of everything that had happened at the bookstore, Jason hadn't had time to tell Meaghan the truth in person. Steve had had to fill her in. From the look on her face, she hadn't taken it well, but at least she was still there and hadn't left like Finn had.

"Thanks to you guys for acting so fast. Fiona and Matt are at the safe house doing well. Fiona has some scratches but nothing life-threatening." Jason waited for a response, but none came. "You guys have every right to be annoyed with me. I was protecting my family, but by not sharing my secret with you, I put everyone at risk. I promise to make it up to you."

"I have so many issues with what you did," Meaghan said. "You need a course in leadership, because keeping such important facts from us hindered us at our job. You owe a huge apology to your family as well. Fiona has become more than an assignment. I value her as a friend. You should have trusted her too."

Jason nodded. "Hindsight is twenty-twenty." He wouldn't deny that he had to earn the trust of everyone at Fresh Pond Security all over again. "But if I had to do it all again, I would have trusted all of you."

Steve interrupted his apology. "Now that your *mea culpas* are done, I located the owner of the car at the bookstore. It was rented to a Federated Security corporate account. Hopefully, they paid for collision damage. Not that they couldn't afford paying for the window you smashed. Federated is one of the best-paying gigs in the field."

"Looking for a new job?" Jason asked, confident Steve would never leave Fresh Pond Security.

"To be fair, the pay here could be better," Steve said, always on the team's side. "We're practically a nonprofit. While we have some higher paying gigs, helping those who can't help themselves is not lucrative. Sure, I go home every night thinking I assisted someone who needed it, but is it enough? The hired thugs at Federated Security have a nice bank account and probably drive something like a Porsche 911. I'm just not sure how they sleep at night."

"Probably on really high-thread-count sheets," Meaghan said.

Steve agreed, but his smile fell as he added, "Once you enter into a job with someone as unscrupulous as Federated, you can never leave—and my freedom is not for sale."

"Exactly," Noah said. "My plan is to retire to the Caribbean in a few years and never pick up a snow shovel again."

"I hope that's a reality for all of us. It's that relentless show of violence and their unlimited resources that are our biggest problems. The question is whether we can keep Fiona and Matt safe until we cut the head off the cartel," Jason pondered out loud.

"Figuratively?" Meaghan asked, glancing back at the samurai sword mounted on the wall behind her.

"Whatever it takes." Jason needed to eat something and rest, as his mind had clouded over with everything that had happened. "Noah, you need a break. Take the next eight hours and get some sleep."

"Sounds good to me." He signed off, leaving Jason, Steve and Meaghan.

"What about me? Should I come over and speak with Fiona?" Meaghan asked.

Jason thought it over. At this point, he didn't want to upset Fiona over another betrayal until she had time to come to terms with her current situation. "Let's wait on that. She's already pissed off at me. Once she settles into her new reality, you can come in and throw me under the bus."

"You should have told both of us."

"I know, but I can only beat myself up so long. We have an active case and pointing fingers won't do a damn thing to keep any of us safer."

She leaned back in her chair and tented her fingers. "I deserve a raise."

"We'll talk about it after."

"That's a shitty negotiating tactic. I heard Finn left.

You're down a man. As the only female in this ensemble, I'm very much needed at this time."

Steve, a man who understood people better than Jason would, leaned toward the screen. "I think your bonus should go to the team."

Everyone on the team made a percentage of the profits at the year-end. This year was their biggest yet, and Jason and Steve would take the biggest share. "Agreed. I put everyone at risk—they deserve a piece of my skin. I'll even send Finn his percentage."

Meaghan smiled. "That seems more than fair, but that's not an increase in salary. So let's meet up after we make sure Fiona and Matt are safe and discuss how much more I'm worth."

He laughed. Meaghan knew her worth and had already negotiated one of the highest salaries of any of the employees, but she had a point. Without her, they wouldn't have a woman for assignments and that was bad business. "It's a deal."

She waved once and signed off.

Steve lingered, his chill disappearing. He'd never chewed Jason out over his bad decision, but he let him know that he had to be straight with everyone forever. Not that Jason planned on continuing his lies. For all his preparation and layers of security, his plan sucked. Had he worked on it with even one trusted colleague, he would have had a solution that didn't involve losing his wife and son.

"You look exhausted," he said.

Jason shrugged. Sleep wouldn't protect Fiona or Matt or the team. He had to understand what they were up against. "I'm good."

"Good to know. I just want it understood that it's your bonus we're talking about. I have to pay for two kids in college."

Jason couldn't argue. He'd put the whole firm's future at risk through his actions. "My secret, my responsibility."

"Agreed. Do you need me to relieve you?"

"That would be great. Can you pick up a few pizzas on the drive over?"

Steve nodded. "Sure, but I pick the toppings. What's your son like. I'll get his favorite too."

"Pepperoni."

"I'm on it."

Jason hung up the phone and rubbed a hand over his head. If Federated Security was somehow linked to Porras, it was only a matter of time before they located Jason and his family.

# *Chapter 7*

The salt bath helped to release most of the slivers of glass out of Fiona's skin and made her far more exhausted than she wanted to be. Although the time said one in the morning, it was still yesterday to her, a day that would not end. She wouldn't sleep for hours, not when danger pricked at her senses. The safeguards her resurrected husband had infused throughout this place only made her more aware of the people after her and her son.

She checked on Matt. He'd curled under a fleece blanket, his socks sticking out of the end. He'd always been tall, like his father, and was wearing one of Jason's old Bruins T-shirts. The yellow shirt fit him almost perfectly, although not entirely in the shoulders, not yet anyway. His breathing seemed steady enough, but the nightmare of that note saying they'd kidnapped him had burned into her memories. If this was all because of Jason, she might never be able to forgive him for placing them in such danger.

She rummaged through the kitchen to find a few crackers and a bottle of wine, but then changed her mind. More alcohol would muddle her thoughts. It wasn't the time to numb her senses. She filled a tall glass with water from the faucet and sat at the kitchen table to go over her situation.

Jason had always been involved in risky operations. Most of the time he couldn't tell her about his job except through vague references and murky descriptions, but surviving a massacre and then "killing himself" with government approval was something else.

A knock on the front door set her guard up again. She started toward the door wishing she had a weapon, but Jason appeared in clean clothes behind her, holding a handgun—from the look of it, some version of a Glock, most likely a 19 or 22. He waved her back and looked out the peephole. The barrel of the gun aimed toward the floor as he opened it wide.

Steve stood in the doorway, three large boxes of pizza in hand. "That will be sixty-five dollars, plus tip if you're feeling generous."

Jason waved him inside. "I'll Venmo you." He pointed to Matt. "It seems like Matt might eat it cold tomorrow."

"The best way." Steve walked to the kitchen island and placed the boxes down. Turning to Fiona, he put out his hand. "I'm Steve Wilson. Nice to meet you under calmer circumstances, Fiona."

She shook his hand, then laughed when Steve looked down for a monetary tip and feigned a frown. "Nice to meet you. I hear you had the luxury of sharing Jason's life these past years." She regretted the bitterness immediately, but the pain that scorched through her wasn't something she could put aside so easily.

Steve nodded, his silent acknowledgment making it easier to like him. "I swear, if I had known of his idiotic plan, I would have driven him to your house personally and thrown him onto your doorstep." He seemed like the type of person to do just that.

"I appreciate your unearned loyalty."

"It's not really about loyalty—it's about doing what's right. Jason took a shortcut, but shortcuts don't always have safeguards built in." Steve went over to the coffee maker to make a pot of coffee. "My recommendation for you two is to get a decent night's sleep so we can hit the ground hard tomorrow."

"I'm not really tired," she replied. Her mind spun through a thousand scenarios for the next day and none of them would create any peace of mind.

"Go ahead, take the bedroom. I'll sleep on a chair in the family room." Jason pointed to an overstuffed chair across from Matt's spot on the couch.

She trusted him, and she trusted Steve, but she wouldn't sleep unless she was near Matt. "I'll stay here. You go and rest in the bedroom."

Jason hesitated until Steve made a gesture for him to leave. So he did. At least he listened to someone. He went into the bedroom, but didn't close the door.

Steve sat at the island and grabbed a slice of pizza. "Want a piece? There's pineapple and green pepper, plain cheese, and pepperoni."

"The last one is Matt's favorite."

"That's what Jason said." Steve bit into a slice of the pineapple and green pepper.

His comment made her pause. What exactly did Jason know about them? Did he have them followed, did he break into their computers or stalk them on social media? The thought of having someone observe her so closely gave her the creeps, even if it had been someone she'd loved once. They'd kept the specifics of their jobs from each other, but then he hid the biggest part of him away from her—his entire existence. The strange thing was that until she saw him, she'd loved him so passionately no one came close to luring her into another relationship. Had she only hated him for a few hours?

"Has he been watching over us all these years?" she asked Steve.

"That's a conversation between the two of you, and if you don't receive satisfactory answers, I promise I'll fill in the gaps. Although I don't agree with the way he went about everything, I trust that he never wanted to hurt you. He deserves the chance to clear the air with you and Matt before someone like me stirs up trouble."

The way he spoke about Jason, Fiona could sense the affection he had for him. For some reason, that made her feel a bit more comfortable with him. Jason didn't trust many people—he never had—but if he trusted Steve, Fiona would too.

"I can say that I was very impressed with the way you handled yourself at both the break-in and the attempted kidnapping. You beat the hell out of Harper. Made our job all the easier."

"Harper?" Fiona asked.

"The man who attacked you in your house. Robert Harper."

More information not handed over to her. She had to treat this whole chaotic mess like an assignment gone wrong. Something she alone could fix, because without all the information, she and Matt continued to be at risk, and she didn't have confidence that anyone else could protect Matt and herself as well as she could. That said, she'd blown it at the bookstore. Unprepared and acting on emotion instead of logic. She replayed the events in her mind: the overwhelmingness of the crowds, the inability to watch Matt and the panic when she thought he'd been taken. Every decision she made was reactive, which put her at a disadvantage. She'd even set herself up to be kidnapped by the men at the car, because she panicked. That's something she'd never have done in her prior life.

Self-pity wouldn't solve her problems. Matt's safety had to be her priority. She took a deep breath and centered herself. Perhaps she should call in some favors from powerful players in the government, not relying so much on Jason. Steve admitted they were supposed to watch out for her family and had failed.

She shook her head. "I'm glad your job was easier because I was able to put my own life on the line to protect Matt."

"It's not like that at all. I regret arriving so late."

"Late, but before the police." She wasn't going to ask how they were monitoring her house. It would add to her annoyance and she had to rest. She could question her former husband in the morning. Or was he her current husband? Can a person come back from the dead and remain married? The circular thoughts gave her a headache.

The aroma of pizza—melted cheese, tangy sauce and a crust baked into a golden color—filled the kitchen. The atmosphere of the room, however, was far from relaxed.

From the living room, Matt's breathing was even and deep. Every so often, a muffled sigh would drift into the kitchen, hinting at the stress of the past few days.

She grabbed a slice of cheese pizza and pushed forward with her information-gathering. "So who is Robert Harper?"

Steve hesitated, but she could pull information out of anyone if she wanted to. In this case, she used simple guilt.

She picked up her water and took a sip. "Steve," she began, her voice low, "why was Harper inside my house?"

"We're still looking into it." He focused his attention on the pizza.

"Bullshit."

He met her piercing gaze with a wall of emotional barriers. "Look, Fiona, it's…complicated."

She had all night. She wasn't going to stop until she had some answers she could use to protect them. She leaned in. "Try me. Or was all that 'I'll fill in the gaps on what Jason doesn't say' just a means to placate me."

"The truth is, we know Harper is employed by Federated Security out of Texas. They're a private security team that works for people that prefer living under the radar. We don't know who hired them yet." He was telling the truth, but skipping over something large enough to make him avoid eye contact with her.

"Sounds like you're at a dead end. Or maybe you have a hunch, but it's not confirmed. I'd love to know what that is."

"A hunch? There are so many things to consider. The analysis could take weeks."

"Jason already gave me your background, so don't play dumb. Maybe you, Jason, and your team should explain your part in breaking into my house and cleaning up a crime scene to the police. Trespassing is not a

great look for a security guard, or are you a private investigator or are you as corrupt as Federated Security?"

Steve sighed. "You write too many thriller novels."

She'd heard every joke available about her writing.
He wanted her to back down. She wouldn't. "You have
more information. I need to know who you think is leading this operation." Her voice rose.

"It's no great secret. We don't know."

He needed a kick in the pants to get him talking. She
took a bite of the pizza and savored the flavor as she
thought through what she knew. This was all related to
Jason pretending to be dead. This was Jason protecting
them from an attack that not even his security firm could
anticipate. Then she walked Steve through it. "Let me try
to understand. If you had to guess where these attacks
are coming from, I bet your guess would relate to Jason's
time in Colombia. Which would mean it was related to
whatever happened there. Which would mean that some
large-scale drug cartel is involved. Which would mean
the resources available to kill me and Matt are endless."

Steve glanced at the open bedroom door. "We haven't
been able to connect the two."

"What do you know about the intruder?"

He shrugged. "The intruder is just a hired hand for a
bigger fish. From all the information we've gathered so
far, everything circles back to his employer, Federated Security. What we can't do yet is link him to Andres Porras."

Fiona frowned, searching her memory. "Why does
that name sound familiar?"

"Andres Porras runs a large cartel. Its influence
is global and he has the money to make anything he
wants happen. From what Jason told me—and it wasn't

much—five years ago, he was involved in an operation in Colombia. There was a skirmish, and in the chaos, Porras's son was killed."

Fiona's eyes widened in realization. "So, you're telling me that after all these years, Andres Porras, a man who caused the death of all those soldiers and a bunch of his own men because he's a greedy bastard, is back for revenge?"

"From what Jason told us, Porras lost his son on the day of the ambush. Even if Jason didn't pull the trigger, he's the only one left to blame. If we can link Federated Security to the cartel, we'd know the source of the threats."

The weight of the revelation bore down on Fiona. The loss of a child. A son he sent to battle at a far-too-young age to a fight he couldn't win. A cold fury simmered within her. "So my family might be the target for that man's twisted vendetta? A tiny detail Jason should have shared with me years ago."

"Nothing's proven yet. The intruder might be part of something completely unrelated." Jason came into the kitchen, his hair tousled, eyes a tempest of emotions, growing darker as he stepped closer to them. He stood next to Steve, but focused solely on Fiona. "And yes, I was wrong to keep everything from you. I was stupid. I should have come clean. But I'm here now, and I'm terrified that I've made the biggest mistake of my life. I promise I'll make it up to you. Somehow."

Seeing the only man she'd ever loved fall apart weakened her own anger toward him. She understood his reasoning, but under the same circumstances, she'd have trusted him with the information. "I'm not going to circle back to your deception. There's too much at stake to think about why you did what you did, but I will not be excluded from your plans anymore. Promise me."

Steve said nothing. He waited for Jason's response.

Jason, his eyes red and in need of sleep, nodded. "I promise."

Satisfied, she drank the rest of her water and stood. So many questions needed to be answered, so much preparation she had to do to protect Matt.

Steve pointed her to the bedroom. "Go. You need to be in top form tomorrow and sleeping half-upright won't be beneficial."

She didn't want to displace Jason. He seemed beyond exhausted. "I'll split the bed with you, but you stay on your side."

Jason brushed his fingers through his long hair. It might take a while to get used to his new look, but time together was something she'd wanted since he was declared missing. "I can do that."

She turned back to Steve. "Stay awake and don't blink longer than necessary. Matt needs someone alert enough to protect him."

This made Steve smile. "Yes, ma'am."

# *Chapter 8*

After five years apart from his wife, Jason woke up to her in his arms. Somehow, over the course of the night, their bodies merged into a single, comforting embrace. A position that was both familiar and felt a lifetime away. Jason lay behind her, his arm draped around her waist. His chest pressed gently against her back, their heartbeats syncing as though finally set to the perfect rhythm. Fiona, cradled within his body, leaned her head back slightly, finding a restful place tucked into his shoulder. Her hand rested atop his, fingers entwined. Jason loved how her long, elegant fingers curved toward his, linking herself to him. Their legs tangled gently, feet brushing against one another. The warmth of her body kept him frozen in place. He'd missed her so much.

The guilt threatened to wash over him again. He should let her go, so she could wake easier and not in such an intimate position. He should. In one more minute. Just a minute where he could remember all he'd lost. All of this warmth, trust and closeness; a shared moment of vulnerability and contentment.

He could feel her wake. She turned her head and blinked her eyes open. There was no fear or anger in their expression. She remained completely still, as though she too wanted to stay in this spot forever.

But he'd promised honesty and no deception. This felt deceptive, even if they'd unconsciously bonded in their sleep. He lifted his arm and turned away from her. The chill of the air made the emptiness inside him form into a larger void. "I'm sorry. I should have put pillows between us."

She stretched her arms over her head and turned toward him.

The room felt heavy with unsaid words as Jason looked into Fiona's eyes, seeking a glimpse into her thoughts.

She inhaled deeply. "My mind is a mess when it comes to you," she whispered, emotion evident in her voice. "It's haunted by the past, by memories, doubts and what-ifs. But my body? It recalls a simpler truth."

Jason's gaze held steady, absorbing every word. Each syllable echoed with the resonance of their shared history.

"Both of our bodies," she continued, her fingers tracing a faint scar on his cheek, "remember the connection, the intimacy, the feeling of being one. They don't dwell on the past mistakes and misunderstandings like our minds do."

A soft, rueful smile tugged at Jason's lips. "I feel that too, Fi, as if we're two pieces of a puzzle, perfectly fitting."

She leaned closer, the warmth of her breath caressing his face. "Perhaps we should listen to what our bodies have been trying to tell us. They crave that closeness, that unmistakable bond. I've been without love for such a long time."

He had too. Five years and countless hours staring at his wife mere yards away from him but untouchable.

Time stood still as they considered the implications of their shared longing. With a mutual, unspoken agreement, they both leaned in, guided by the visceral pull that their hearts and bodies never forgot.

His mouth covered hers in a hard kiss, five years of pent-up energy. His tongue caressed her lower lip, and she opened to him. The graduate student he'd kissed in the back of his Oldsmobile for the first time, the beauty he begged to marry him, the bride who took his breath away, the woman who kissed him the night their son was born, the mother who stood holding their young child on the night he left for the last time—he kissed every single one of them. She returned the kiss with the desire of a widow of five years finally back with the man she'd lost.

Their bodies remembered much more than their sleep position. As the sun crept into the spacious bedroom, Jason and Fiona explored old memories, new scars, and experienced feelings so intense they shattered the pain that had encased their hearts.

Fiona's eyelids fluttered open at the soft rays of the morning sun. The weight of the previous night's events pressed down on her chest, heavier than the toned arm that draped over her. Beside her, Jason breathed steadily, his chest rising and falling in a deep sleep. She traced the lines of his face with her index finger, her touch tentative. He was a ghost in her presence and she didn't want to either wake from this dream or have him vanish again.

Memories from the night before flooded her mind. The gentle caress of Jason's fingers, the passionate kisses, the entwining of their bodies. But the euphoria sat side by side with a pang of guilt. Although Jason had been gone—dead, she thought—he'd lied to her and placed her and Matt at risk. Instead of keeping him an arm's-length away from her, she fell into his arms without a moment's thought as to the repercussions for her and Matt. She had zero understanding of how he'd survived, how he hid his presence in the same city and the nature of his new business. For all Steve was a bundle of friendliness, she had no idea about his real background except for what Jason had told her.

Tears pricked her eyes as the most painful memories flooded back—the day she found out he had died, the agony of losing him and the years she had spent grieving, not to mention their son's pain. Yet, she couldn't deny that her attraction and love for him had never died. They had reconnected, reignited a passion that she thought was lost forever, a love she thought she had buried alongside her grief.

But even as the bittersweet reunion cast a warm light into her life, the reality of their situation set her more rational side into overdrive. Someone wanted to harm her family. If it was the Porras cartel, they would not stop until the leader found restitution for the death of his son. That could result in Jason's death or Matt's or her own. Or all of them. The danger they were in was very real.

The weight of Jason's arm now felt suffocating. She carefully slid out of bed, found her clothes and tiptoed to the window. Peering through the curtains, she scanned the surroundings. This place was isolated, but with her own knowledge of such organizations, she understood that no place on earth would be isolated enough to protect them. They had to leave and soon. A plan formed in her mind. They needed to disappear, change their identities and keep Matt safe.

Behind her, Jason stirred. "Fi?" he murmured, voice groggy with sleep, his piercing gaze meeting hers. There was a moment of unspoken understanding, a shared regret over lost time and stolen moments. Before either could speak, a loud banging sounded from the main living area.

"Mom? Dad?" Matt's voice called out, panic evident.

Jason reached for his weapon and was on his feet in seconds. His face darkened. "Steve?" he yelled as he rushed back into the kitchen, pulling his pants back on.

She followed him, her thoughts racing. She should never have left Matt alone.

Without a word, Steve reached for a remote, flipping on access to the security cameras surrounding the house. The living room's large screen displayed the outside. Bathed in the increasing light of the morning, Noah, the man she'd flipped to the ground at the bookstore, was at the door, carrying doughnuts, his car parked a few meters away.

"It's Noah," Steve said.

Jason dropped his gun to his side. Matt, however, remained standing and staring at the television.

The interruption to an otherwise quiet morning made Fiona's spine prickle with unease. Her eyes darted between Jason and Steve, the two men engrossed in whispered conversation. Again, she was an outsider and in this situation, she did not feel comfortable trusting anyone else in the room with Matt's safety, except maybe Jason, but full trust hadn't returned. There were too many questions that needed to be answered and one night of mind-blowing sex wasn't enough to get over that.

She cleared her throat, interrupting them. "We should leave. This place is too isolated."

Jason, her formerly dead husband, gave her a reassuring smile. "We chose this place precisely because it's isolated. We're safe here."

Steve, ever the mediator, nodded in agreement. "This farmhouse is secure, Fiona. It has a hundred fail-safes. No one gets on the property without us knowing."

"You didn't seem to know Noah had arrived."

He lifted his phone showing the same camera angles that were on the television screen. "I had prior knowledge, which was why I didn't come rushing around with a gun in my hand. I turned on the large screen for you."

Jason made a face, one that said a lot about where his head was. Terrified for Matt. He didn't think, because Fiona would bet all the money in her investment account that he had access to the same information on his own phone. That lack of focus would get them all killed.

"Trust us," Steve added. "We're not rookies."

Fiona clenched her fists, her former operative instincts flaring. "Trust? That's what got us here in the first place. You have no idea who we are up against. Until you do, we can't make an effective plan."

Jason opened the door.

Noah had dressed in a crisp white button-down and jeans. He seemed as though he'd just returned from a two-week beach vacation. He lifted the box of doughnuts. "Breakfast, anyone?"

Matt ran over to him and took the outstretched box. "Thanks."

"No problem. Just save me a chocolate glazed."

"No problem." He placed the box on the counter and rifled through them, taking out a marble-frosted one.

Steve strolled into the kitchen and lifted a mug toward Fiona. "Coffee?"

"I need the whole pot." She felt as though she hadn't slept in days, which she hadn't. Instead of taking the night to get rest and a clear head, she'd intertwined her emotions and every other part of her with Jason. The result was a tangle of emotions and hair combined with seriously bloodshot eyes. She hadn't bothered to go into the bathroom to fix herself up, so she took the pause in the activity to slink back into the bedroom and into the bathroom. The face in the mirror looked like she'd had one hell of a good night. Her hair was partially matted on one side and had straightened out on the other. Her face had no makeup but bite marks were on her neck and her lips appeared a bit too swollen. Damn it.

She rinsed her face with very cold water, brushed out her hair and braided the top back, securing it with a rubber elastic she found in a drawer. It would hurt like hell to pull out later, but she functioned better when she was satisfied with her appearance. She didn't have the heart to put on her outfit from the day before, so she remained in Jason's oversize sweatpants and his shirt.

Jason and Fiona glanced at each other as she walked in the room. His hair was as tousled as hers had been, although he didn't seem to care that he was advertising the extent of their reunion the night before. For Matt's sake, she wanted him to go shower and change, or at least straighten himself out. This whole experience could mess Matt up, although dying would mess him up more than his parents having sex. She shook off her insecurities about the night before. They had much bigger things to think about.

Jason leaned against the counter, sipping his coffee black as he always had. A thousand unsaid things bounced between them. He'd watched over her for years, but not enough. Had she known her husband had been in that type of danger, she'd have had a security detail with him at all times. From the look of it, it seemed his team had about five people involved. How did he make an income if he had his resources all on her?

Matt came over to her, a small white frosting mustache under his nose. "How long are we going to stay here? I was hoping to go over to Ethan's house tonight."

"Count out the weekend. I need more information before I can make plans for you going into public or even to school. I guess I can call your teacher and claim you have mono. That will give you a few weeks of Zoom class."

The frown on his face broke her heart. "That's not fair."

"It isn't, but it's the reality." She ruffled his hair and pulled him into a hug.

"Do you know who is after us?"

"I know enough to know they're lethal and relentless." And they could be after Matt. An eye for an eye. The thought churned in her gut, but she couldn't allow it to linger inside her. She had to push back on the emotions so she could do her job. Her job skills had a significant amount of cobwebs over them as was evident from the way she couldn't neutralize the intruder in the house or the men trying to pull her into the car.

Steve turned to her. "Noah can remain here with you and Matt. We'll handle things at the office."

Fiona felt torn. The weight of responsibility bore down on her—she should be protecting Matt, but the office held answers she craved. She had to find out if someone from her own past had caught up to her, or if Porras had hired the men to attack them. Whoever they were, they couldn't care less about her or Matt. "I need more information. Information I can only get if I meet my attacker."

Jason shook his head, chiming in, "We think it's best you stay here, Fi."

"We? Who is we?" she asked, her patience fading.

"The team," he replied.

She carefully controlled the tone of her voice to not sound too aggressive, well, at least not extremely aggressive. "I never hired your team, so as far as I'm concerned, I make my own decisions. If you want to assist me, that would be fantastic, but do not limit my access to information. You lost the right to love and protect when you didn't trust me."

Steve and Noah both stepped back toward the doughnut box, within listening distance, but not in the direct line of fire.

She could and should remain with Matt, but something inside Fiona was restless, a gut feeling that wouldn't be silenced. She looked at Matt, his young face etched with confusion, then back at Jason. "I'm going with you," she said firmly.

The men exchanged looks, their expressions a mix of surprise and concern.

Jason began, "Fi, we thought—"

"I know what you thought," Fiona interrupted. Her mind was a whirlwind, juggling the roles of mother, former operative and wife. "But every fiber of my being tells me I should be at that office with you. I can't explain it, but I have to be there."

Steve raised an eyebrow, the weight of Fiona's insistence evident. "But Matt…"

Fiona's heart ached, torn between maternal instincts and the pull of her intuition. "He'll be safe with Noah, right? I am unable to sit here and wait for whatever the enemy is planning. If I have some sense of what we're up against, I'll feel more in control. After leaving me out of control for so long, you do not have a say."

Matt had always been a smart and competent kid. As much as her gut told her she had to go out and interview their attacker, she also felt certain Matt was safer here. She watched as Matt peered at Noah, his unease at their unfamiliarity palpable. The pang of guilt hit her hard. She would be leaving her son with a near stranger.

"Look, if anything happens, I need to know we did everything we could," Fiona continued, her voice heavy with emotion. "And that means me being at that office."

Jason gave a resigned nod. "All right. But we stay together."

Steve and Noah agreed.

Matt walked back to his mother, so young compared to the men in the room, yet he had a calm and perceptiveness that gave her hope that everything would be okay. "Go ahead," he said. "I know it will drive you crazy to just sit around watching over me. Noah was pretty cool to talk to in the car on the ride over yesterday. Now that I have more information about what is going on around us, I can probably ask better questions."

"Okay." Fiona hugged him tight. "If any harm comes to you, it will be coming to him as well."

Noah frowned but acknowledged Fiona's maternal need to protect her child.

As the group prepared to make their move, her heart struggled, the love for her son overwhelming her. Every choice had its price, and she prayed she was making the right one.

# *Chapter 9*

Jason and Fiona drove toward headquarters in the Expedition, following Steve in his Tesla. Jason was glad for the private moment with his wife. The night before felt as though he'd been in a nightmare that somehow twisted into a dream and he needed some grounding to convince himself that he had indeed been able to hold his wife in his arms one more time. Holding Fiona close had been a bittersweet reminder of what he had lost. Not that she was acting as though their night together meant anything. The scare of the morning sent her right back into fight or flight mode, not that Fiona was ever in flight mode. She was too focused on Matt's safety to back down. That strong personality had been one of the reasons Jason fell in love with her.

"Are you sure you don't want to stay with Matt?" he asked, hoping she'd stay inside the bunker with their son.

She turned toward him. "I want to make sure that we're not forced underground for the rest of our lives. I didn't spend the past five years raising a strong, intelligent and personable kid to now tell him that he has to dim his light so that no one notices him ever again."

"It won't be that bad. I'll find a way to stop the threat."

"You aren't even positive what threat you're protecting us from. You had five years just sitting in limbo, waiting for someone with a deadly vengeance to find us. If the man in the house had been a sniper, Matt and I would be dead right now. I wasn't anticipating something so sinister arriving at my front door."

Jason had no words to counter hers as she spoke the truth. "I blew it. Somehow, I trusted that they would never find out I was alive. If you could imagine it though, others could too. It was all my fault."

"It was all your fault that you didn't tell me and prepare us, but it wasn't your fault that the assignment you were on had such a tragic ending." She placed a hand on his and sighed. "My anger at you is also fear for Matt. We lost so much when you disappeared. Now he's at risk too. I couldn't bear to lose you again and with him in danger, I'm overwhelmed."

"I'd say let's let the past be the past, but that's a steep order. I promise I'll make it up to you. I'll do whatever it takes to protect Matt and you."

"How about we act as a team. We protect each other."

Jason knew Fiona's past didn't only involve economic treaties, but she never spoke about her job with him except to casually mention far-off places that she'd visited as though she were a travel influencer. Perhaps some of her expertise did relate to criminal organizations and dealing with them. If that were the case, then he would be the biggest idiot of them all by not trusting her with his secret. Somehow it had all seemed so simple five years ago. Disappear and allow her and Matt to carry on without ever having to look over their shoulders at the boogeyman coming after them.

"Agreed," he said as he twisted her hand inside his and squeezed.

"No more secrets?"

"None." He wanted her to trust him as she had in the past. At least while they could still be together. If he couldn't think up a way to take down the entire Porras cartel, his only choice would be to sacrifice himself to save his family.

They pulled up to his office, which on the outside looked like a large storage-unit facility with faded blue paint and rows of white-and-pink impatiens—enough of an effort made for the building to appear cared for but not enough to seem like something special was inside. The building was a master class in deception. He'd always taken pride in creating things that concealed more than they revealed. Fiona scanned the area as they drove through an automatic gate and into an underground garage.

"This setup keeps people less curious," he said.

"I'm not sure. Aren't storage units robbed often?" she asked, always focused on exactly the right questions.

"I'm sure they would be if they didn't have the security system we have around it."

Her brows lifted. "Like the security system you put in my house?"

He bit back his reply. She was right. He'd half-assed the security. Instead of a twenty-four-hour presence watching her house, he'd split up observing her comings and goings with Meaghan. And the alarms that were triggered when the intruder broke inside did nothing but warn them of any current danger without an adequate means to neutralize the intruder until someone arrived.

He parked the car next to Steve's. Fiona followed them to the entrance. Jason watched her face closely as she stepped into the office. The headquarters of Fresh Pond Security included ultramodern offices, an open conference room with an impressive screen covering almost half the wall and a lobby area that held a living wall filled with golden pothos and peace lilies. The lighting and design inside the facility had to make up for the lack of windows. Plants offered a calming atmosphere for a job that called for long hours and strenuous work conditions.

"It's not what you were expecting, is it?" he mused aloud, addressing Fiona but not revealing everything just yet. He wanted to drip-feed the details, to keep her intrigued, to watch her piece the puzzle together.

She turned to him, her eyes reflecting a mix of surprise and admiration. "I was not expecting this at all. I imagined more a Dick Tracy-type office in a brick building with a coat stand where you'd keep your trench coat and fedora."

Steve laughed. "If he had his way, that's where we'd be. This place is better. It's much more space than we could afford in an ordinary office building, and it keeps people from finding us too easily. We tend to meet up with clients at their houses or places of employment in order to get a better perspective on what they are expecting of us and if we want to handle the matter."

"Hidden in plain sight," Fiona said on a sigh. "It makes a lot of sense." She waved her finger across the conference room, the furniture of the lobby and the long hallway of offices. "Must have cost a pretty penny."

"It took us three years to afford this place. Before

that, we worked out of Steve's basement until his wife kicked us out." Jason led her down the long hallway, remembering those first few years where he'd been a mess. He missed his family and had no desire to create anything, much less a successful company. If it hadn't been for Steve taking Jason's idea and creating a business out of it, Jason might still be in a rented hotel room with a bottle of Jack and a death wish.

Fiona followed Jason through what seemed like a technologically advanced office space, although she'd been out of the workforce for a while, so perhaps this was more common than it had been when she'd relied on the government for her perspective.

Steve came up next to them. "You can have the small conference room. We have some information about Federated Security and a list of possible clients who might have hired them."

"A list?" she asked. She had no reason to think her own past had caught up with her, but perhaps she was being naive. She'd done a lot of questionable things in a lot of places to a lot of people, and although she'd never been caught, there might be a file somewhere that would incriminate her. The day she retired from the service, she'd been handed a small pension and a list of federal laws she'd break if she ever spoke a word of her past. Her position with the Department of State had been embellished and her shadow work disappeared. Jason's work in the military, however, had not been scrubbed. She'd easily accessed with her internal contacts why he'd been in Colombia and how the whole assignment had gone up in flames. Perhaps he had other assignments that had also created enemies. There were too many possibilities.

"What about the Porras cartel?" she asked.

Jason frowned, as though the name alone pissed him off. "We can't count them out. Porras has a great business mind, but his ego gets in the way. He'll hunt me down if he thinks I'm alive. But we have no direct proof that they're the ones involved."

"The break-in and kidnapping attempt were not random. Someone is focused on our family."

"I agree. Once we learn who, we can direct all our energy to shutting them down."

Fiona hated waiting for information. She preferred a more direct means of obtaining the intelligence she needed. Perhaps she could find someone to hack into Federated Security's records. It would be safe and would give a decent snapshot of who was paying their bills. Her mind spun with all the different avenues to go down, but felt somewhat assured that Jason had people around him who might be able to obtain the information needed.

A few steps further down the hall, she froze at the sight in one of the offices—Meaghan, the last person she expected to see sitting at a desk here. Meaghan, her hair twisted in a messy bun, looked up and nearly fell back in her chair as she spotted Fiona. *Why the hell was Meaghan in Jason's workplace?*

"What are you doing here?" Fiona asked as her world shattered more and more with each heartbeat. This was her best friend, the one person she trusted to spill her heartache, loneliness and fears for the future. A hundred reasons rushed through her head. She was there being interviewed or perhaps Jason had offered her protection too.

Before Meaghan could answer, Jason stepped forward. "Fi, I was meaning to tell you."

Her gaze jumped between them, a mix of anger and hurt. "Any time before me running into my best friend and neighbor at your workplace would have been a great time to tell me."

Meaghan's deference to Jason told her Meaghan had some sort of connection to him and that nearly knocked Fiona on her ass. There was a knowing between them, as though they'd been through many things together and they understood things about the other a mere acquaintance wouldn't. "Tell me you two aren't together?"

"I work for Jason," Meaghan said. Her unwavering stare directed at Jason, filled with hostility, only added to Fiona's questions.

This was a nightmare. Meaghan knew all of Fiona's flaws and her mistakes and her mishaps and her incompetencies. That she could have been writing those things up in reports and handing them over to Jason for the past five years shattered Fiona's remaining hold on reality. She couldn't breathe. She sat down on a chair in front of Meaghan's desk but missed and crashed to the floor. She struck the back of her shoulder into the corner of the chair. The pain, both new and old, hammered through her.

Meaghan and Jason rushed to assist her.

She lifted her hand, unsure whether she was stopping them or wanting to strike them both down. "Back up."

"Fiona, I was assigned to watch over you, but the friendship was real." Meaghan squatted next to her and remained at her side despite the command.

"Friends don't lie or set up friends with men like George." She swallowed hard and pushed her hair back from her face. "Unless they were instructed to do so by their boss."

It was one thing for her husband to lie to her, but to have her best friend lie too made everything exponentially worse. Fiona pulled herself to her feet. She could use a shot of whiskey to cut through the heartache and the lingering pain from her injuries from the night before. Meaghan whispered something to Jason. Her hostile demeanor directed at Jason only added to Fiona's confusion.

"I feel so bad about everything that happened to you," Meaghan said to her, returning to the other side of her desk as though she'd been placed in time-out.

"I'm sure you do, but I honestly don't care."

"Don't take your anger at me out on Meaghan. She's a workhorse. She's a talented bodyguard and has been looking out for you and Matt this whole time." Jason nodded toward her like a proud parent.

"Stupid me. I thought she worked nine to seven every weekday at an insurance company." Fiona stared at Meaghan. "No offense, but if you're such an amazing bodyguard, then why did I have to fight off some ape of a man in my house and then almost get kidnapped at the book signing?"

Meaghan crossed her arms. "I never left Matt's side at the bookstore. He was safe. I also knew there were three other people watching over you inside and outside the bookstore. As for the break-in, I agree I blew it. I'd been getting lax after years of nothing happening. You had no activity whatsoever. I promise you though, I'll never let my guard down again."

Fiona could see the self-reproach in Meaghan's expression. It was one she'd worn when she let something get by her in the past. "Okay, that wasn't fair. You had a job to do, but I have the right to be angry that I was not included in any of the plans on how to protect me. I'm not that clueless when it comes to security. Right now I have to get my head around a new reality, one where my dead husband is alive and my next door neighbor, the one who nurtured me during my most difficult days, works for him. I'd cried in your arms so many times, and you knew the truth."

"No. I thought your husband was really dead. I only found out that Jason was your husband last night. He went by DJ and never used his actual name. I swear."

Fiona's gut told her Meaghan was telling the truth and the majority of her anger bounced back to him. "So you took me on as a work assignment?"

She nodded. "He hired me to protect your family almost five years ago, but after a few months, I wasn't doing it just for the paycheck from Fresh Pond Security, I was protecting my best friend."

Fiona reached out her hand to Meaghan. They had a solid history and like it or not, she was Fiona's closest friend in the world. In that moment of reconciliation, the significance of her friend's words dawned on her with surprising clarity.

"Fresh Pond Security is the name of your company?" She stared at Jason, overwhelmed by the ping-pong emotions of the past twelve hours. Jason had proposed to her on the edge of Fresh Pond in Cambridge.

Jason shrugged. Although he'd always had difficulty

expressing his deepest emotions, she could see the corners of his mouth fall. "I named it after one of the happiest days of my life."

Her breath deepened. For five years, the love of her life lived a few miles down the road and worked at a place named for their love story. For five years, he watched his wife and son carry on with life without him. For five years, she suffered a depth of heartache she never wished to go through again. "That doesn't make it any better. In fact, it hurts even more. You've screwed with every part of my life. I don't even want to think about the press from the disaster at yesterday's bookstore signing. Janet must be completely overwhelmed with people trying to figure out if I've been kidnapped or if that was a publicity stunt. And don't forget about Matt. Not only have you harmed him psychologically, you also placed his life in danger."

Jason nodded.

Fiona wanted to go back to sleep and wake in a world where she could trust those she loved. And yes, it was hypocritical of her to think such things as she'd never been able to be entirely honest about her occupation with Jason. Her body ached and her concern for Matt grew with each minute away from him, but she had to find out who was after them. From the sound of Steve and Jason's investigations, they still couldn't be certain it was Porras.

She inhaled the sweet smell of the cut gardenias on Meaghan's desk. They had come from her garden, a place where Fiona and Meaghan had spent hours sipping tea and sharing their trials and tribulations. Meaghan's office contained a lot of her personality, the personality

she'd allowed Fiona to see. A large laptop that Fiona recognized from her visits to Meaghan's house sat open on
her desk next to a bloodred stoneware coffee cup. The
paintings on the walls displayed rustic landscapes, one
of a farm by a lake and another of a cabin resting next
to a wooded stream. Across from her desk, a variety of
screens showed an array of information. On one, the
news played in mute, another contained a digital cal-
endar and to-do list and a few had surveillance camera
feeds. One of Fiona's house, the back and the front. Another house was displayed next to hers. Finally, a man sat
on a chair in what appeared to be an interrogation room.

The man in the video seemed very familiar. He had the
buff arms and thinned waist of her intruder. Handcuffed
to a metal chair that appeared bolted to the floor, he wore
medical scrubs, a spot of blood on one of his thighs where
she'd stabbed him. His face had been obscured by the
darkness and a black mask. Yet here he was.

"Who is that?" she demanded.

"No one you need to be concerned about," Jason said.

Fiona was so sick of being pacified as if she were
brainless and defenseless. She'd have protected her iden-
tity forever because she had always respected the rules.
But not now. Not when her child was being hunted.
"Who is that? And don't lie. Is that Robert Harper?
Locked up here?"

"Yes," Meaghan replied, not looking over to Jason
for permission to hand out information. "He works for
Federated Security."

Federated Security out of Houston employed men and
women who had no morals. They'd lie, steal and kill if
the price was right. Although Fiona had never fully jus-

tified her own actions, at least she'd believed at the time she was doing it for some greater cause. One that would make the world safer for the vast majority of people. "I want to see him," Fiona declared, her determination cutting through the thick tension. She needed answers.

"Not a chance. It's not safe, even with him under lock and key." Jason shifted to block her path to the door.

"I need to know why he was there." The weight of her husband's and best friend's combined disapproval might have stopped her before. But not now. Now, she needed clarity, more than ever. "Can I just have a minute?" She sat in the chair in front of Meaghan's desk and put her head in her hands.

Jason and Meaghan stepped out for a minute. She could hear them speaking about Fiona's stability. That was fine. If they thought she was falling apart, they wouldn't anticipate her next move. She slipped behind Meaghan's desk and yanked out the cord to her portable power bank. She slipped the three-foot long cord into the pocket of the sweatpants she'd borrowed from Jason. Her outfit didn't make her appear that intimidating, but perhaps it would make her look a little unstable. That could be used to her advantage.

"I'm done asking for anything," she murmured to herself. No more lies. No more secrets. She was taking control.

She exited the office with a soft, pretty expression. Steve had joined Meaghan and Jason in the hall. They all stared at her as she walked over to them. She focused her request on Jason as he had an abundance of guilt she could manipulate. "After all you put me through, you owe me. I want to talk to Harper."

"What are you going to say to him? He's trained to keep his mouth shut. He won't leak a word without someone waterboarding him and I'm against that practice, personally." Jason stood with his hands in his pockets, trying to appear in control.

Then Steve made a very stupid mistake. "Come on, Fiona. This is not the place to act out your storylines. We've trained for years to handle these situations."

"You're right." She stepped toward him, nodding with all the regret and sadness she held in her heart over the state of her current life. Steve placed an arm over her shoulder, offering comfort. By the time she spun away from him, she had his gun in her hand.

Steve's eyes widened in surprise and Jason yelled out, "Fiona!"

"I need to see Harper. Where is he? And don't think I won't use this. You're already dead, Jason, but your son is very much alive and I intend to keep him that way."

Other employees of Fresh Pond Security had already gathered, drawn by the commotion. No one dared to approach her. She had the upper hand.

Jason granted reluctant approval. "Fine, but I go in with you."

"I want to be alone with him." Her voice strong and unflinching. The gun in her hand brought her back to a time where everything she did risked her own life and took the lives of others, but not once had she been caught. She had a million regrets from that time in her life, but none right now.

Jason protested, "Fi—"

But she cut him off. "Do it."

As the door to the interrogation room opened, Robert Harper looked up. At the sight of her, his lips curled into a sneer. The wound from where she'd stabbed him with the pen kept his leg stretched out in front of him. She stared at it, causing him to remember and feel the pain she'd inflicted upon him.

She turned back to Jason. "Close it. Give me five minutes. I promise, that's all I need."

He didn't have a choice. Not with her waving Steve's gun around in what appeared to be an unstable mindset. Knowing him, he probably didn't believe he could take it from her without someone being hurt. "I'm watching the monitor. If you appear in danger at any point, I'm coming in."

"Fine."

Between the handcuffs, the bolted chair and her skill set, she wouldn't have any trouble.

Once the door closed, Harper started in on her. "Just wait until I get out of here. I will slit your throat and gut your son."

She stormed over to him and stomped the heel of her boot into his knee, dislocating it. His screams lasted a few seconds longer than his ego wanted. When he shut up, she pointed the gun at his head. "Who hired you?"

He stayed silent. She slammed the butt of the gun into his already swollen nose. "Who hired you?"

Blood dripped from his nose, over his lips and down his chin. She pulled out the cord and slipped it around his neck as he fought to get loose.

Her interrogation techniques were ones she had learned in the darkest corners of the world, reserved for the worst of the worst. "You don't get it. I would sacrifice myself for my son without a second thought. Going to jail for murder is nothing." She pulled back on the cord and could feel his breathing slow. "I want a name."

He tried to lift his hand to get her to stop. She loosened the cord and waited. If he didn't say anything relevant, she would tighten it again.

"Andres Porras wants you dead," he muttered, his hostility growing despite his acquiescence. "And your son. And nothing you do will stop him. And if he doesn't kill you, I will."

"You have bigger worries than little old me. Porras is going to want you dead for betraying him. I'm sure it will be slow and painful." She pulled her phone out of her pocket and replayed him giving up Andres Porras.

"You bitch."

"And you're nothing but a stooge. Good luck in hell." She turned and saw Jason.

He must have entered while she was focused on Harper. He stopped at the sight of Harper's face and the blood sprayed over Fiona's clothes.

"I might need a change of clothes and he might need a doctor." She stepped past him into the hall.

Jason approached cautiously. "Fi, what did you—"

"You're right. Porras is after me," she said, her voice low with a mix of fear and rage. "And our son."

As he reached out to her, Fiona stepped back. "Now isn't the time to reconcile." Despite the fact that they had been quite reconciled the night before. "Now that we know who is attacking us, we can make a better plan. There's no hiding from a man like Andres Porras. Matt's in danger," she said, a chilling look in her eyes. "We have to get back to him."

# *Chapter 10*

Jason stared at the bloodstains on his sweatpants and the T-shirt he'd loaned to Fiona. A few drops had sprayed on her face, probably when she broke the man's nose in the same place Jason had broken it only a week before. After the rage she'd carried into the room, brandishing Steve's weapon and ranting about protecting Matt, she had transformed into a calmer state. A very similar state to when she returned from her work trips so many years ago.

When they were married, she'd never exploded in a rage or even shown a higher level of anger. Of course they had had arguments, but neither one of them would ever raise their voice over the loud shout one might make at a crowded bar. The way she'd slipped Steve's gun from his holster, which was located behind his hip, not directly on it, was something a person had to have practiced many, many times in order to pull that trick off with someone trained in law enforcement.

Meaghan, a woman who had spent years with Fiona, also appeared stunned at Fiona's change in temperament and her new skill set. She'd observed Fiona wave the gun around, never once going up to stop her or challenge her. In all of their heads, it seemed there was an intuitive understanding that Fiona knew how the Sig Sauer worked and would use it if she needed to.

As they watched her beat the hell out of Harper, not one of them rushed in to help him. Perhaps the image in front of them seemed too much like a trick of the mind. Fiona was a diplomat and a writer, but here she was breaking a man's nose. When she wrapped the cord around his neck, Steve told Jason to stop her. He agreed and rushed inside the interrogation room as she stepped back from Harper with her phone in her hand playing a recording of Harper ratting out Porras.

Jason, lost in a maelstrom of emotion, felt a strange detachment from the scene before him. He looked at Fiona, her familiar features seeming alien, every contour and line hiding a story he couldn't read. The woman he had vowed his life to, laughed with, cried with, had become an enigma to him. He felt a piercing nostalgia for the days of blissful ignorance, for the moments when he believed he knew every corner of Fiona's soul.

"What the hell?" The words, so small yet laden with anguish, escaped his lips, more a sigh than a question. He struggled to find his footing as though he'd just been caught in the blast radius of an explosion.

Fiona's voice, usually so direct and warm, held a shadow of guardedness as she responded. "I don't want to talk about it. We need to get back to Matt and make a more permanent plan."

Steve's voice broke through the thoughts rushing around Jason's head. "Seems you aren't the sole custodian of secrets, Jason." With an outstretched hand, he accepted his gun back from Fiona. "Don't do that again."

She shrugged. "Don't let it happen again." She turned to Meaghan. "I need to change."

"I have some backup clothes in my office. They may be a bit long on you, but otherwise will fit."

Jason stayed silent while Fiona followed Meaghan back to her office for a change of clothes. She strode away from him with not a flicker of regret slowing her steps. Meaghan matched her pace as though she found Fiona 2.0 even more appealing than the original version. Jason had no idea what he felt except bulldozed.

Sam had tried to get information out of Harper all night. The guy wouldn't say a word to him, not even a nod of the head. Then a few hours later, Harper openly taunted Fiona and when pushed by her, he gave up a client guaranteed to seek revenge.

"To be fair, when Sam had interrogated him earlier in the week, he merely talked to him, while Fiona beat the crap out of him." The violence was extreme. Her entire past as a diplomat now seemed questionable. She flew around the world to negotiate trade deals? Something didn't add up, but she was right. Now wasn't the time to focus on it.

Steve shrugged. "You're not seeing the bigger picture. Sam was doing a job, Fiona was saving her family. Although I will never relax in her presence again. She's got a very specific skill set. Her capabilities seemed even more brilliant when she pulled out her phone with Harper telling her it was Porras who had hired Federated Security. I bet we're only scratching the surface of what she's capable of."

Jason agreed. He called Noah while he waited.

"How is Matt?" he asked, hoping there was some stability in his world.

"He's great. Just kicked my ass in *Grand Theft Auto*."

Jason exhaled some of his stress. "Okay. Look, we now know for sure that the Porras cartel is involved. Be extravigilant and do not open the door for anyone except me, Steve or Meaghan."

"Do you think this site has been compromised?"

"Anything can happen and with their unlimited resources, it's very likely." Which made Fiona all the more correct in saying that they had to get back to Matt.

Meaghan came out of her office.

"Is she doing okay?" Jason asked.

"She's preoccupied with Matt's welfare. She has blinders on for anything else."

Jason nodded. "Steve, can you stay here and get any information on Andres Porras's whereabouts?"

"No problem."

"And Meaghan, why don't you follow us to the bunker. You can give Noah a break and Fiona might talk more freely with you there."

"Or she'll still be furious I kept my relationship to her a secret. It's not like this job allows me unlimited opportunities to get to know people. If I don't hang on to Fiona as a friend, I don't know if I'll get another one in the next decade or so."

"She'll come around."

"She has melted a bit. She complimented my office decor."

Jason saw the worry in Meaghan's expression. He'd always appreciated Fiona having such a decent person as Meaghan around her. The thought that he might have messed that up didn't sit great with him. "There you go. You're back at being best friends."

"I wouldn't go that far, but I have no problem going out there. Want me to leave now?"

"Sure, if you feel comfortable explaining your presence to Matt."

"Absolutely. I'm throwing you under the bus," Meaghan said.

"Go ahead. I seem destined to be run over a hundred times today."

Meaghan strode away as Steve slapped Jason on the back and headed to his own office, leaving Jason alone, waiting for his wife. He checked his watch. They'd been gone for three hours. It was time to go back to the safe house. Perhaps he could call Meaghan to pick up some subs on the way. The kitchen had food, but it was more necessities than luxuries. Cans of soup, pasta, beans and rice. There were some half gallons of ice cream in the freezer, but generally, the pickings were slim.

When the door finally opened, Fiona walked out with a clean face and a short blond ponytail, dressed in Meaghan's workout clothes—bright blue leggings, a concert T-shirt and New Balance sneakers. Her expression had softened more, which eased a bit more of Jason's stress.

"Ready?" he asked.

She nodded.

They walked to the Expedition in silence. She looked quite fit and competent. Had she always been that way and he'd only seen the sexy side of her? Her figure did make a perfect cover. No one would expect the sexy blonde woman to be able to take them down with a kick to the knee in sneakers. She could probably take out an aorta wearing high heels.

They remained in their own thoughts until he hit the turnpike, then she turned to him, her lips tight. "I'm sorry for taking things so far. If anyone comes after you for Harper's injuries, I'll take the blame."

"His employer doesn't want to be caught in a breaking and entering case and if Porras ever hears about his confession, he'll disappear."

"I don't want that to happen. I'm not vindictive."

"Right." He paused and thought about how to phrase his next question. She had certainly hidden something from him. "When did you learn how to torture prisoners?" A bit too direct, but under the circumstances, necessary.

"I took a few self-defense classes as part of my employment." She stared straight ahead at the cars in front of them.

He didn't believe her at all. The inability to trust the person he loved was a bludgeon to his chest. Something Fiona had felt for a day now. "Ever had to use those skills in real life?"

"Occasionally," she admitted. "How long have you had someone interrogating Harper with no answers?"

His employees had worked on Harper for days, but he didn't want to admit his tactics had failed. Sam should have been able to break him without getting them arrested. Fiona crossed over into felony assault. She did, however, get the information in five minutes. As promised. And looking back at what she'd done with more scrutiny, he understood she'd been angry, but never out of control. It was far too easy to label a woman who had strong feelings as someone unable to think through consequences, and she took advantage of such presumptions, gaining access to the interrogation room and Harper.

"It doesn't matter. My people don't beat the hell out of people in our custody," Jason said defensively.

"Don't act so superior. As a private citizen, you can't hold that man against his will. And I didn't initially break his nose, I only compounded an existing injury. Someone between my house and that room must have had a slip of the fist—but go ahead and be upset with my tactics." She glanced at the cut on the middle knuckle of his right hand. She didn't miss a detail.

They didn't speak again for a few miles. They both had their secrets, but most of his were now out in the open. Hers seemed to stretch down an endless hole of lies and misinformation.

He had been happy in the knowledge that he could rush into dangerous jobs that he'd never speak to her about while she worked in the more mild-mannered field of diplomacy. But she'd been in far deeper than he'd ever realized. "I guess we never really knew each other at all."

Fiona hesitated before looking at him. "I wouldn't say that. I know for certain I love the person who sat with me that day in the library. I know you would never do anything to harm our family on purpose, although you did have a massive fail declaring yourself dead five years ago."

Jason sighed, rubbing the bridge of his nose and thinking of his words carefully. "I love the woman I met in school. The woman who had ambition and intelligence and the ability to see straight through me. I love my bride and the mother of our child. It's the person who sat with me for coffee on Sunday mornings who I don't recognize."

Her expression remained soft, almost wistful. "Remember all those times you took off to parts unknown and I kissed you goodbye without knowing if I'd ever see you again?"

"They were the hardest days of my life until now."

She nodded. "Me too. Why did you never tell me what you did when you had to fly overseas on assignments?"

He looked down, his hands tightening and loosening on the wheel. "The information was classified. It would be breaking the law."

She tilted her head, challenging him. "So why would you expect me to break the law for you?"

Jason's mouth opened, but for a moment, no words came.

"You're a hypocrite. And all the assumptions you had of me over the years were the ones you put in your own head. I never told you what I did or did not do when I traveled for work. You created a beautiful fiction for yourself and that worked fine for you and your fragile ego, but don't get all angry at me for being who I am." Her calmness wrapped over him, moderating the tension.

He thought back to conversations where she'd avoided any mention of the country she'd visited or the people she traveled with. Had he opened up his mind, he'd have seen the signs all around them. The congenial phrases in Farsi and Korean she used whenever she met someone who spoke those languages seemed a useful way to connect to people in her field. Did she know those languages more fluently than she let on? She'd once whispered a threat to a man at a bar who had been harassing a young college woman. Whatever she said to him had him rushing out of the bar without a backward glance. Jason laughed about it at the time, although the ability to scare someone double her size had been impressive to him. She'd also shot a perfect set at a carnival with an old BB gun that no one else could aim correctly. The crowd teased her about being lucky, but maybe it was pure skill. Her appearance tended to cause malfunctioning in the brains of most men who met her. Steve could now be included in that group. If Jason had to hire someone who would be completely overlooked as a potential risk, no doubt it would be her. Now that he'd taken off his rose-colored glasses, he could see her as someone with far more abilities than he'd allowed himself to imagine.

"I'm sorry for underestimating you," he said as they arrived at the farmhouse.

"It's preferable to be underestimated at times." She reached a hand toward him. "When we have some downtime, I'll give you an abbreviated version of my CV. For now, let's focus on Andres Porras."

He nodded and scanned the area. Everything appeared as it should. There were some open fields behind the house covered in goldenrod with a small vegetable garden that was tended by the caretaker. Meaghan had already parked her black Corvette next to Noah's car.

When they went inside, Noah and Meaghan were talking in the kitchen and Matt was still on the couch. When he saw Fiona, he stood up and trotted over to her, giving her a hug. "I'm glad you're back."

"Me too."

Before Jason could say anything to his son, the force of an explosion outside the house knocked him off his feet. Fiona pulled Matt to the ground and tucked into the edge of the kitchen as Jason looked at the damage and tried to ground himself.

He yelled into his phone for Steve to send help, as Meaghan and Noah rushed outside, guns raised.

The fortified hideout had been built to hide their clients, not protect them from a bombing. Jason focused on getting Fiona and Matt to safety.

"Stay low." Jason pointed to the corner of the kitchen.

Fiona nodded, as she and Matt remained hunched between the island and the refrigerator. Matt crouched by the island, observing everything. Not once did he lose control in the chaos. His intensity reminded Jason of Fiona.

The sound of multiple shots from outside pushed him to get up and back up his team. He directed Fiona and Matt toward the back of the house. After seeing her performance at headquarters, he wasn't as nervous to send them out alone. He opened a door to a basement. "Turn left at the bottom of the stairs and keep going until you reach the barn. Wait in the back of the Range Rover."

Matt rushed down the stairs.

Before Fiona could follow, a second explosion blew out the wall where the television had been. She hit the floor as debris showered over her. Concrete, brick and electronic parts blocked the door to the basement and Matt.

Jason rushed to the door he'd sent his son through and pushed, kicked and tossed away the wreckage to get through. Fiona was at his side assisting him, and based on her intensity in trying to reach their son, he didn't stop to assess her health.

Once through the door, he rushed downstairs, Fiona

right behind him. The three cars in the barn were all there. A Range Rover, a beat up Ford F-150 and a BMW, but the barn doors hung open and Matt was nowhere in sight.

"Matt?" Fiona yelled out, her panic echoing off the concrete walls.

Jason opened every door of every car, calling out his son's name. "Stay here," he called back to Fiona before rushing outside. The house was in flames as well as the side of the barn. Meaghan's Corvette had bullet holes through the side. The Expedition's tires had been slashed.

"Have you seen Matt?" Jason called out to Meaghan as she hunkered behind a rusted tractor.

"No."

He'd thought Fiona would always be safe with him out of the picture. Instead, he'd left her wide open to attack. If someone had wanted her dead, she would be. The thought tortured him.

Fiona arrived at his side from the house. "He's not inside."

They both whipped around as a helicopter dropped into the field near them. The sound thundered through him and the wind swirled dirt around, making visual observations limited. Two men dressed in black dragged Matt, fighting like a cornered tomcat, toward the bird. Jason ran toward them, but was too late. It lifted off. Once in the air, he couldn't shoot it down. Not with his son inside.

Fiona cried out, "Matt!" Her aching cry stabbed through his heart. This was everything he'd tried to protect them from. He'd been a fool to think he could control such a huge source of evil.

# *Chapter 11*

A whirling haze of emotions consumed Fiona as she watched the last traces of the helicopter vanish into a cloudy sky. Beside her, Jason stood, every line of his face etched with agony.

He lifted the phone to his ear, but before he spoke to the person he called, he glanced over at her and whispered, "I'm sorry."

She didn't respond. No words could fill the gaping hole blown into her by Matt's disappearance. Especially knowing that Andres Porras wanted him for one specific reason...revenge for his own son's death.

Flames roared behind them, consuming the secluded safe house that was supposed to be their sanctuary. Thick plumes of smoke billowed into the sky, yet neither Fiona nor Jason spared it a glance. Material things could be replaced, but Matt's disappearance—that shifted the axis of the world to Fiona. Nothing would ever be the same after seeing her son taken away from her in such a violent way. The fading whir of helicopter blades overhead was an all-consuming focus, its receding noise carrying away their son.

Jason finally turned away from the sky. His gaze met

hers, and for a fleeting moment, the ferocity of their emotions threatened to spill over. His anguish and rage inflamed her own. Under any other circumstance, he would reach for her. She knew that as surely as she knew he would blame himself for this. With one step forward, he could bridge that gaping distance that had grown between them. But not now. This wasn't the time or the place. Their son was out there and that eclipsed everything.

Seeing the love Jason had for his son healed a small part of their brokenness. Not perfectly, but in a way where she could see trying to be with him again. If they could ever get back to what they had. But that time had ended and they had no future until Matt came home.

"They found us," he said, his voice a gravelly monotone. "That's on me."

Fiona didn't want to hear excuses. She wanted her son back by her side. She hardened her shell of a heart and squared her shoulders. "We don't have time for guilt or finger-pointing. We need to pivot, adapt, hit back." Her eyes remained dry as tears were generally foreign to her, but if they weren't, they'd be tears of fury.

He nodded, pushing a torrent of emotions into that well he'd always used to keep life at home more balanced. "You're right. We have to be tactical. They won't see us coming."

Before either could step away from the apocalyptic scene, Jason's phone vibrated. Steve's name flashed across the screen.

"What the hell happened out there? Is everyone okay?" Steve's voice sounded tense.

"No. Matt's gone, airborne. I can't see Noah or

Meaghan." Jason strode back and forth, his eyes scanning the sky, the house and Fiona.

"Check in with them and then get back to the office. We can go over the camera footage of the area and try to pull as much information from the video as possible. Does Kennedy know?"

"I'm calling her now," Jason said.

Fiona had no idea who Kennedy was, but she'd better be someone with a connection to the air traffic control system.

Jason hung up the phone and punched in a new number. "Kennedy, I need you to track a helicopter in the air right now."

Fiona let out a deep breath. His connections were deeper than she'd imagined. She was so grateful. She stepped closer to hear the conversation.

"Where?" Kennedy said, adding no pleasantries. The soft tapping of computer keys could be heard in the background.

He gave her the address and the direction of the flight.

Fiona stared back toward the spot in the sky where she'd seen the helicopter fade from view. From what she saw at the end, Matt had struggled some, but he didn't fight too hard, which was for the best. Fighting trained professionals would result in something broken and maybe a tranquilizer.

Jason put his phone back in his pocket. "Kennedy can find anything in the air or on the water."

"Let's hope they stay in the area. Where are Meaghan and Noah?" She was prepared to run back into the house, but her gut told her they wouldn't be there.

"Noah!" Jason yelled out, voice raw.

She hadn't seen Noah or Meaghan since the first explosion, although gunshots had echoed in the distance until the helicopter disappeared. A dread crept through her. Maybe something had happened to them. She couldn't bear more violence, even from her. She harbored not one regret that she'd retired so early from her government employment. The life she'd created with Matt, being a mom and writing thrillers was more than enough excitement. If she could bring her husband home to live with them, it would be perfect.

Emerging from the smoke and haze around the house, Meaghan, appearing like she'd just climbed Everest, supported Noah, who had a definite limp on his right side. Blood seeped through his clothes from a wound near his hip. The sight gave Fiona flashbacks to a time when blood meant a job well done. The nightmares from that time never left her.

"What happened?" Fiona rushed to him. The bullet had pierced the area above his hip. There was a chance it missed the most important organs, but his chances for a full recovery would be exponentially better in a fully equipped trauma center.

"They ambushed us," Meaghan said, the words growled through clenched teeth. "They shot Noah and got to Matt before I could react."

Noah's legs started to go out, but Jason rushed over to him to hold him up.

Fiona lifted his shirt and saw the raw edges of the wound. She instinctively pressed down to stop the flow of the blood. Warm, sticky and thick, the wound had to be treated immediately.

"Hold on," she murmured, trying to convey strength she wasn't sure she felt. She'd never been great with medical issues, but neither Meaghan nor Jason stepped in. "Can we move him to a car? He needs to be transported yesterday." She could see the shock in his eyes, and she tightened her pressure on the wound as Jason and Meaghan walked him to his car.

"We should be chasing that bird." Noah spoke through his pain.

"You need some hard-core first aid."

"Bullets are just a minor inconvenience," he replied. "As soon as I'm clear, I'm taking down an entire cartel if I have to to get Matt back." His feelings for their son were evident despite only knowing him personally a few hours while competing in a video game.

Jason leaned close to him. "You'll be needed. For now, hang in there. I can't use you until you're fully cleared."

"I'll be fine then. Go. Neither of you will be safe here. They may have someone coming back to finish the job." Noah pointed to the Range Rover in the barn and then said a whole statement to Jason with one nod of his head.

Meaghan paused at the side of her car, a river of oil flowing down the incline from under the hood. Both the engine and the door panels were riddled with bullet holes. "So much for that."

"Take my car. No one touched it. That's why it's better to get a less flashy car." Noah pointed at Jason's Expedition with the flat tires. "You guys have too fine a taste for your own good."

He headed toward his almost ten-year-old Acura, but

lost a step. Jason held him in his arms and helped him into the back seat. Fiona slipped in next to him.

"What are you doing?" Jason said through the open door.

"I'm holding him together while Meaghan drives. Get the Range Rover and meet us at the hospital."

After Meaghan was buckled in, Jason shut the back door.

Fiona scanned everything around her. A calm Noah buckled in with an injury that must be overpowering him with pain, the burning house and barn—the remnants of Jason's plan to protect them. So much for her current life. That chapter had ended and she had no idea what was to come.

Jason ran toward the half-burning barn, his phone to his ear, as they drove away at top speed. A few minutes later, the Range Rover pulled in behind them on the road.

Meaghan spoke without turning around. "We saw two vehicles—looked like a pickup truck and a smaller black sedan—drive away after we ran outside. I'm wondering if they set the blasts as a diversion so the helicopter crew could shuttle Matt away. I'm not positive Matt was the target. They may have been going after either of you."

"I'm not so sure. If Andres Porras lost his son, he could be targeting Jason's son." Fiona could only hope that Matt kept his cool and stayed safe until they could retrieve him.

A medical team waited with a stretcher as they pulled up to the hospital emergency bay. Fiona lifted her hand from Noah's hip and stepped back to let the professionals do their job. She stood in silence as they rushed him inside the automatic doors that slid closed after them.

"You should wash up," Meaghan said.

"I'm a walking biohazard today." Noah's blood had leeched onto Meaghan's borrowed leggings. "I know what I'm getting you for your birthday this year."

Meaghan waved her off. "It's a risk of the job."

They both entered the hospital and a nice woman at the reception desk handed them each a mask and directed Fiona to the bathroom. Meaghan followed. While Fiona scrubbed her hands, Meaghan rinsed off her face.

"So, you're not in insurance?" she asked the friend she knew nothing about.

"Former law enforcement."

Fiona nodded. With hindsight, she could see Meaghan in a uniform. "What made you leave?"

"The town I worked in had a good old boys' club. It was hard to get them to see me as more than a traffic cop. Jason saw my frustration and offered me a job. A very lucrative job. So I took it and have never been happier." She stopped her before they left the restroom. "What about you?" Her expression told Fiona she wasn't accepting her State Department story.

"I can't say, but let's just assume we had similar training." Sort of.

Jason stood by a vending machine, waiting for them. He held two packs of M&M's and a Snickers bar. He tossed one bag of the M&M's at Meaghan and the Snickers at Fiona. "Noah is in good hands. Meaghan, can you wait here for an hour to get an update and meet us at headquarters?"

"You gave me chocolate. I'm at your disposal."

"Thanks. Fiona, we need to go."

She agreed and followed him out to his car. As soon

as she got in, his SUV sped off. "Can we swing back to the bunker? I just want to see if someone left us a way to track them."

"It's swarming with firefighters and police right now and that would slow our investigation. There are more resources available at the office. Steve has been lining up video and Kennedy might have more on the flight path of the helicopter. As for you, you're not leaving my sight. This past day has been a nightmare. Everything I've done to protect you is unraveling." He sped down the road so fast, she had to brace herself on the curves.

If he thought she was going to be tethered to him because he wanted to be in charge, he had another thing coming. She bit back her harshest replies, but her self-control teetered at the very edge. "You're in a nightmare? How dare you come back and destroy my whole life and then ask for pity?"

The road curved through farmlands and past small New England town commons. He zipped around several cars, causing the drivers to send obscene gestures out their windows. The flash of some headlights in his rearview mirror pulled his attention from the past to the present. The isolated location had actually made it a perfect place for an ambush.

A car, some low-to-the-ground sports car, perhaps a McLaren, followed at a distance. There would be no outrunning something with six hundred horsepower, but they had to try.

"Lose them," Fiona told him, needing to have every precaution adhered to so they could focus on Matt and not saving their own hides. He swerved into a field and headed straight across what seemed like soybeans. The car followed, bouncing across the uneven terrain. As they approached the halfway point, a fairly deep brook crossed their path. Jason sped up and after a short liftoff, the front slammed and thumped as though the struts took too much impact. To Fiona's surprise, the SUV straightened out and continued forward until they made it to the road. The car following them stopped before the brook, then backed up and turned around. They'd be long gone by the time it circled the entire farm. Fiona leaned back in her seat and took a deep breath. This was going to be a marathon and she had to treat it as such. The time for panic and hyperventilating had come and gone before she could even contemplate wallowing under all the turmoil.

When they arrived at Jason's office, the place was buzzing with activity. Steve met them at the door. He had an intensity he hadn't worn when Fiona had met him, not even when she was assaulted at the bookstore.

"Kennedy has a fix on the bird," he said without preamble, leading them to a dimly lit room.

"Where?" Jason asked.

"Nantucket Sound."

That wasn't so bad. It was close enough to get there quickly. "That's good, isn't it?"

"Yes and no. We can get to Woods Hole in an hour and a half, but if they're on a boat or get to an airplane, they can go anywhere. We don't have the resources to follow easily."

Steve broke the silence, "We're tracking every vessel around Martha's Vineyard. If Porras is there, we'll find him."

Fiona's eyes sharpened. "And when we do?"

Steve squared his shoulders. "We end this nightmare for your family."

Calvin, their computer wizard, rushed in the conference room. "They've made contact." He placed a printed email in the middle of the table.

Jason reached for it, fingers trembling ever so slightly. Fiona stood by his side, her stance defiant. Jason cleared his throat and began to read aloud.

Jason or should I call you DJ?
Welcome back from the dead. Don't ever think you will outlast or outsmart me. If you want to see your son again, come find me. Alone. I don't like uninvited guests.
—AP

The initials meant the worst thing that could happen had happened. That Andres knew Jason's new identity also meant he could come to their office and hurt all the people on his team. Fiona had to get a better profile on Porras. The only thing she knew about him related to his need for revenge and his quest for domination and power.

Jason looked up, rubbing his temples, the weight of years evident in his eyes. "Andres Porras... I never thought I'd cross paths with him again. When I encountered him in Colombia years ago, it was like looking into the eyes of a serpent. Cold, calculating. He would burn entire villages if he believed someone had betrayed him."

Steve, ever the analyst, added, "It's not just his ruthlessness—it's his reach. I've tracked his finances. The man's got connections in every underworld market you can think of—arms, drugs, human trafficking. His web stretches globally, and the center of it all is him, always making a profit, always staying a step ahead."

"The people I've spoken to about the Porras family say the same thing. You cross Porras, and not only do you pay, but your entire lineage does," Sam added.

Fiona's eyes hardened. "So, we're dealing with a megalomaniac. What's our next move?"

"First, we find out his actual game," Steve answered. "He may want Jason in order to make him suffer the way Andres suffered the day his son died."

She glanced at the bottom of the email and read out the coordinates.

19T 0379904E 459460N

"Matt will be at this location." She typed into her phone. "He's got to be on a boat."

"Why?" Steve asked.

"Because this location is in the center of Nantucket Sound." Fiona fought the urge to rush to the bathroom and expel the limited food she'd eaten in the past few hours. Never had the stakes been so high when doing such a dangerous job. She could lose both Matt and Jason. The thought tormented her and hurt her ability to think clearly.

Jason paced back and forth as he spoke. "He needs me to show up or he can't make his next move. Maybe that's our play. If I go, he'll be focused on me. That could buy us the time we need to locate Matt."

"But it's a dangerous game," Sam interrupted. "Porras will be prepared for whatever we plan. His family hasn't been in this business for decades without intelligent risk management."

"I know," Jason responded. His pace picked up as he rubbed his fingers into his temples. "It's a risk we might need to take."

Fiona could hear the strain in Jason's reasoning. He had always been unflappable in the most extreme situations, but this was his son. She understood. The stakes had never been higher for either of them.

Steve directed everyone to look at the large screen in the conference room as he pulled up satellite images of the coordinates between Woods Hole on Cape Cod and Martha's Vineyard. "There are several large vessels out there. Some container ships, a few mega-yachts lingering before their migration to Florida or wherever they wintered. Wherever he's sending you, we need eyes on the inside before making a move."

Jason focused on the images. Fiona could see the tension in his expression. There were too many choices—and what if Matt was on a small fishing boat?

"I might have the tech we need," Sam piped up. "I made some tweaks on my microdrone. It's discreet, emits minimal buzzing that will be hidden under most engine noise, has some heft to keep it moving through the wind out in the sound and has great visual and audio. Too much rain, however, can knock its capabilities out."

Jason nodded, "Then check the weather. While you handle reconnaissance, Steve, dive deeper into Porras's network. There's always a weak link."

Fiona added, "We need diversions too. Distractions. Porras might be expecting Jason, but he won't anticipate our other moves."

Steve smirked, "Like Trojan horses? We do have some contacts in the area that owe us a favor."

Jason pulled everyone's attention. "All right, here's the plan. I go in as the bait. Sam, you handle tech, make sure we have a constant feed. Steve, contact our allies. We need eyes on the ground and diversions at the ready. Fiona, I need you coordinating from here. It's essential Porras believes I'm alone."

Fiona's eyes met Jason's, his silent plea passing between them. She wanted to disagree, but he had to focus on his assignment—literally being the bait.

She nodded at the plan but had her doubts. Criminal organizations couldn't be killed without a massive defection or an army of law enforcement and even then, they replicated like a Hydra cut down over and over again by the skill of one opponent, thus making the next rounds more and more difficult to win. With Jason and his team working with her, she stood a better chance of helping Matt. They had the resources. She had to understand the game and the rules, and then she'd play to win.

The room was a flurry of activity. Maps, devices and a clear strategy in place. Andres Porras may be a formidable adversary, but he'd now instigated a war. From the look on the faces of the people in the room, this team was willing to go to the ends of the earth to protect their own.

Every action, every step was for Matt, and they would move mountains to ensure his safe return. Fiona would be there with them. Following directions and trusting their orders. And if it all fell apart, she would have her own Plan B to implement.

# *Chapter 12*

Jason remained quiet, trying to release the mountain of stress pressing on him. He had always thought of himself as the one who could remain cool and collected under the worst conditions imaginable, but this was about his only child. If he failed, Matt wouldn't survive. No. Failure was not an option. He had to use all his resources and get in and out with his son. Porras was smart, but Jason considered himself smarter. He also had the best of the best backing him up. They couldn't be found within thirty miles of the pickup point, but they would have the ability to track him and help out if his plan stalled.

"I'd be better in the field," Fiona insisted. An intensity in her eyes said she'd be willing to blow up half the world to get her son back.

But her need for action didn't change his plan at all. He wasn't going to risk Fiona's life on this. He had to handle it alone. He glanced over at the team. They would react in case he was hurt or killed and couldn't get Matt to safety, but Fiona was not going. "You stay here and wait for updates."

She frowned. "I'm more capable than I look."

"I understand, but I'm not ready to do my job and worry about you. Please stay here."

"You don't understand. I would wager I'm more capable than you. I would be an asset. If you had told me what happened in Colombia, I might have been able to help keep us together."

Maybe she was right, but he couldn't count on her understanding of the ins and outs of their team. "Please stay here. I love you too much to lose you."

"That's a lame excuse to exclude me. Love can do amazing things sometimes. It's not a cage. If anything, love should create an environment that expands, not limits. You say you trust me but you want me locked away? You've already forced me into widowhood for the past five years. That decision wiped me out, and now when the stakes are even higher, you want to take away my ability to rescue Matt? I don't think so. So you better start thinking of a plan that involves a cooperative effort. I love you too. We can weather even your prior deception, but only if we start acting like a team again." Fiona reached out, her hand gripping his.

Jason felt her familiar warmth, a reminder that, despite the secrets, the essence of the woman he loved never changed. A woman he couldn't bear to see hurt.

His fingers brushed over her soft skin, grounding him. The feel reminded him of the night before and the trust they'd put in each other, in just existing in each other's company. "We'll get Matt back."

She nodded. "Let me help."

While her intentions came from the right place, he was not going to bring her into a situation where she could be caught in the same hungry lion's den he was headed into while trying to save their son. He couldn't wonder about her safety and remain focused on rescuing Matt too. He didn't care if he survived this ordeal as long as he could make certain his family would pull through and thrive into the future.

He wanted Fiona involved, but at a distance, and yes, he was being a hypocrite, because if the situation were reversed, there would be no way she could keep him from rescuing their son. Yet, his own insecurities blocked him from trusting what his heart and head both told him about Fiona. "Porras will see through any effort we take to minimize the risks. Even the small drone might cause them to just kill Matt and flee. I refuse to let that happen. We have to follow their requirements. The team can work in the background. If I get close to Matt and find an opening in their defenses, I can cause a disruption that will allow backup to board the boat."

"So you go it alone to an isolated place where you have no assistance? And we wait it out until you find a window of opportunity, *if* you find a window of opportunity?" Steve asked, his frown not supporting Jason at all.

"I don't want anything to risk Matt's life." His mind had already started racing, and his thoughts turned darker and darker. The whole mission seemed more and more impossible as he allowed doubt to consume him.

Fiona watched him, her eyes not filled with fear, but with a piercing intensity. "Jason, we need to think this through logically. Going directly to them could be a trap."

He turned sharply, his eyes blazing. "They have our son, Fiona. What choice do I have?"

"You always have choices," Fiona responded. "You need to take a step back. Your reluctance to disconnect from your emotions is limiting your ability to see the big picture. We have to break every aspect of this operation down in order to understand what the risks are and formulate ways to reduce those risks."

"We don't have a week to do a whole project analysis on what will work and what won't. I have to be there in—" he looked at his watch "—three hours. It'll take me two hours to drive to Woods Hole."

"Figuring out a plan won't take longer than thirty minutes if the people you've been bragging about to me are as capable as you say they are. Besides, you can work in your car to finalize smaller details." She leaned back in her chair and raised her brows in that way a middle-school teacher did when handling headstrong preteens.

Steve, Meaghan and Sam nodded in agreement with her. Fiona had transformed from someone the team protected to a valued member of the team with zero deliberation from Jason. In reality, he'd never hire someone like her. Her background had layers and layers of walls protecting her from discovery. She'd never disclosed any of her past work, nor had she ever explained the details of her actual skill set either during their marriage or in the past few hours since beating the hell out of Harper. Too much risk for a fledgling security team to take on. Yet, here she was, making plans and collaborating with the team he'd put together. Somehow, their allegiance had crossed over from him to her.

"Although I don't know your past, as you won't disclose it, I doubt you've ever experienced this scenario," Jason said to her.

"You'd be surprised, although I admit my emotions for the safety of Matt have altered my usual distance from this sort of thing. What I do know is Porras blames you for the death of his son," she said. "What makes you think he won't enact the same revenge and kill Matt right in front of you? Once you're there, that's the first thing he might do. Get it out of the way and then head back toward South America."

Jason felt as though she'd hit him with an axe. The possibility of Matt being killed so soon after he arrived on the boat had been on his mind, but hearing Fiona articulate it made it all the more chilling.

She continued, "You charging in there is exactly what they're expecting. I'd bet they also have some pretty decent firepower that would take out a rescue boat or even a helicopter. Why give them what they want?"

Jason hesitated. The immediate rush to save Matt dissipated. "Then what do you propose we do?"

Fiona picked up a pen at the table, tapping it gently over a pad of paper as she laid out her thoughts. "First, we should inform law enforcement. I know we're afraid they'll hurt Matt if we involve the police, but there are ways they can help covertly."

He shook his head. There was no way he was going against their directives without solid assurances that the authorities wouldn't rush in for an arrest without regard for Matt's safety. "It's too risky."

"Riskier than you going in there alone and unarmed?" she challenged.

"What's your second idea?"

"Use a minidrone equipped with a camera as Sam suggested. We'll send it to scout the area first, take stock of what we're dealing with. We need information, Jason." The tapping continued, a nervous tic he'd noticed about her when they were in college.

"And third?"

"Third," she paused, taking a breath, "we negotiate, and while doing so, we use the time to gather as much information as we can to form a tactical advantage. This can be through the police, through surveillance or even through a third party. We cannot just walk—sail—into what could be an elaborate revenge scheme."

He sighed, his eyes meeting hers. "They will not negotiate. They have all the cards. You know this too. If we had something they wanted, besides me, I'd agree with you, but if Porras doesn't get his way, there would be nothing stopping him from leaving tonight."

Fiona moved closer to him. "I concede that point, but if we all put minds together, we may realize we have something they want and would be willing to bargain for. We'll get him back, Jason. And we'll do it by being smarter, not just braver."

With newfound resolve, they turned their attention to enacting Fiona's plan. When the sun disappeared behind the bank across the street, Jason appreciated Fiona's approach. He of all people understood that bravery wasn't about charging into danger—it often involved having the courage to change course, especially when guided by a voice of reason.

When the plan was nailed down into a reasonable operation, Jason drove alone to Woods Hole.

The traffic wasn't too bad and he made decent time onto Cape Cod and into the small community at the southern point. Seagulls soared overhead, their silhouettes contrasting against the moonlight. The docks were mostly empty, save for some fishermen returning with their catch of the day, a line of cars waiting for the next ferry and a few tourists taking an evening stroll.

Jason parked his car in a dimly lit corner, away from prying eyes. His heart raced with a mix of excitement and anxiety. The operation they had planned had to be precise, with no margin for error. He got out of the car, stretched his legs and walked to the dock where a subsequent email from Porras said the zodiac boat would be located.

Hidden between two large fishing vessels was the gray inflatable boat with an outboard motor. A GoPro camera had been rigged onto the motor, to watch the happenings on the water. No doubt he'd locate a tracking device if he took the time to look, but that wouldn't matter. Everyone knew where he was headed.

As he pushed off in the small boat, he set the entire plan into motion. It was a gamble, but so was sailing straight into enemy hands. At least this way, they held a few cards and were active participants in this very deadly game.

The lights from the waterfront shops faded as he traveled farther from shore. The slapping of the water on the bow provided a rhythm to his journey, something to calm his mind as he prayed for everything to fall perfectly into place.

# *Chapter 13*

Fiona didn't want Jason to drive away alone, but knew he'd be monitored as he arrived near the boat. He'd been so focused on rescuing Matt at all costs that he'd let caution and planning fall away. It had been a risk to challenge him in front of his team, but she remembered the days after learning of Jason's death. Her intense grief prevented her from handling her job. The only reason she'd been able to get out of bed had been knowing Matt had lost his father and needed her more than she needed to hide under her covers. The pain of knowing Matt was now in such a dangerous situation made breathing difficult and she too was losing her ability to objectively work out a rescue plan, but like before, Matt would not be saved by her falling apart. She needed to keep it together for both Matt and Jason.

Jason had left a half hour before. That was a decade if he ended up needing backup, but they had to make sure no one saw their involvement. She walked into the conference room, now the control center for the entire operation. The soft glow of computer monitors lit Sam's and Steve's faces. A concentrated energy filled the space as they worked against the clock, finalizing coordinates, updating maps and checking intel.

Meanwhile, in a government building somewhere outside Washington, DC, Kennedy stayed glued to her monitors, tracking every movement on air and on the water. She and Sam stayed in constant communication.

Calvin had remained hidden from Fiona, in his own space, since the technology wasn't so easily transported into the conference room. She located him in a room where screens around him displayed data streams, video feeds and encrypted messages.

"Come on, Porras," he muttered under his breath, "Give me something." With every keystroke, he delved deeper into the web, trying to uncover any hidden trails Andres might have left behind.

"Do you need anything before I leave?" she asked.

"Just for you to get that family of yours back together in one piece. Jason has been a bear for the past year and even with everything going on around him now, he's got a different attitude. A better one."

The news made her focus even more on her task.

She waved and met up with Meaghan. "Ready?"

"Yes." She'd changed into black pants and a black rain jacket.

Fiona was still in Meaghan's yoga pants and T-shirt, although she borrowed a blue hoodie from Noah's office. The word from the hospital was that he would be fine after some exploratory surgery and time off. That he'd risked his life for Matt made her forever indebted to him.

They drove south in Sam's car, a small silver Prius. It had some zip and blended in with the cars around them, as Noah's had done.

"How are you holding up?" Meaghan asked her.

"I'm scared, angry, exhausted and my muscles ache. Otherwise, I'm perfectly fine."

Meaghan laughed. "Sounds like you're ready for our objective."

"The idea of floating out to sea at night isn't my idea of fun, but I can't leave Jason out there alone."

Meaghan parked the car near a private marina, and Sam and Steve pulled up next to them. Sam unloaded the drone, while Steve carried a mini mobile command post with tracking and satellite gear. Fiona stared out at the waves crashing to shore and hoped Jason and Matt were safe. His plan had been to fall upon their mercy or to infiltrate them, grab Matt and somehow leave the boat and return to shore with both of them alive. It wasn't much of a plan, and from what she'd read about that group they would have enough resources to keep a former military operative from taking down a boatload of trained mercenaries. This plan was better, she hoped. There were no guarantees in this business, but risks could be reduced with planning. There was no way Jason had headed into this without a bit of bravado, and that might help him or hurt him. Between their two different approaches, Matt's chances of getting off the boat increased.

Jason had told the rest of the team he had to go to the boat alone. If they were as competent as he claimed, they'd be there as backup without Porras knowing. The only team member she knew, or thought she did, was Meaghan, who was currently focused on loading their small boat with supplies—two extra life preservers, a first aid kit and a few weapons. For just short of five years, Meaghan had lived next door to Fiona and pretended to sell insurance policies. And here she was about to embark on a sea rescue against members of a drug cartel. Fiona was more than a bit impressed. She also felt as though she could confide in Meaghan more. They had similar backgrounds and although Fiona could never disclose what she had done in her past life, she could remain vague and still find connection. She wouldn't be critical of Meaghan for spying on her, as Fiona had hidden her own secrets and would continue to do so. According to Jason, Meaghan had not known her boss was related to her and Matt. She handled the assign- ment like a true professional and had been as betrayed as Fiona by Jason's lies. It would be interesting working with her as a team.

They exchanged a few brief words, double-checking every last detail of the plan. Meaghan's determination to get Matt back safely gave Fiona the confidence needed to jump back into this world with two feet. Matt's life, and Jason's, depended on her.

Steve approached them with a tablet in his hand. "I've got a live feed from Kennedy's satellite connection. It'll give you both a bird's-eye view of the yacht. I've marked the potential entry points on it. Hold back until Sam can confirm it's the right one with the drone."

"Can Calvin track my phone? I have no GPS," Fiona said.

"A GPS is part of the life preserver. Don't take it off," Meaghan replied.

"What about Jason? Are you tracking Jason?" If Fiona could have microchipped Matt, she would have. Per- sonal liberty meant squat when the person was dead. She shook that thought from her mind and held on as a large wave lifted the dock a few feet higher, then dropped it back down.

"We're tracking Jason. We'd never let him go without something to locate him quickly."

Fiona knew that, but with under an hour to organize this and years on the outside doing nothing to remain in shape or up-to-date, she wasn't quite as capable as she'd been telling herself. That thought scared her the most— that Jason had been right about her. She'd not only be in the way, but her lack of preparation would hinder the rescue and possibly place her husband and son further in harm's way.

"Thanks, Steve," Meaghan said, glancing over his shoulder to look at the screen before taking the tablet from his hands. "This will be helpful. How's the chatter? Anything on the Coast Guard's channels?"

"So far, it's quiet. Calvin is listening to them and will contact us with updates. Be quick. We don't have a big window."

Fiona focused on what they were saying. She had a good idea of the entire team and their jobs within the organization. "We'll stay connected as much as we can. Sam, you've done similar operations on boats of this size. Any last-minute tips?"

"Stay low, keep quiet. These yachts often have more guards than they show. Matt is our priority and Jason. Revenge, justice and any other bullshit you're bringing with you is secondary. Steve and I are going to head out first to give the drone a chance to find openings and learn the situation." He had a calm confidence to him. It reassured Fiona that she was dealing with a highly professional team, although the proof would be in how well they implemented the plan. As she'd seen at the bunker, the element of surprise and unlimited resources could destroy even the most prepared team.

"Once you're ready, signal us. We'll be able to slip in closer and get a better viewpoint." Meaghan slipped on a black life preserver and handed the other to Fiona. "How did you end up with the speedboat?"

In the shadows, a sleek, black speedboat bobbed gently, its powerful engines making the smaller boat seem more like a rowboat than anything tactically useful. Although Fiona would have preferred to be on something a bit larger, a bigger boat would also be a bigger target.

"Seniority. Let's go." Steve, wearing all black like Sam and Meaghan, boarded the larger vessel and Sam followed behind with two silver cases.

After Meaghan hopped on board the smaller boat, Fiona stared at the open water between Woods Hole and Martha's Vineyard. Then she turned east toward Nantucket, an island that wasn't visible from Cape Cod. If she overshot or undershot her direction, they could end up floating out to the Atlantic Ocean and miles and miles of isolation.

# Chapter 14

The inky black of Nantucket Sound stretched forever before Jason. Without lights on the zodiac, his main means of navigation were his phone and the lights on the large boat waiting for him. The waves rose and fell, making his stomach reel from the bag of chips and soda he'd grabbed on his way out of the office. As each minute passed, he came closer to his son, but he had no idea whether he'd be able to rescue him. Fiona was right. Without backup, both he and Matt would never make it out of this alive.

Moonlight broke through the cloud cover, offering fleeting, celestial beams over the water, each one a beacon guiding him to the yacht anchored in the distance.

As the yacht emerged from the shadows, two figures signaled him to approach. After another forty yards, the two men came into focus. From their silhouettes, they each carried an AR-15 but wore jeans and surf shirts. Despite blending into the preppy environment, there was no mistaking their purpose on the boat.

"Hold up." The command cut through the lapping waves as Jason cut the engine, allowing the zodiac to drift toward the yacht. The two men moved with military precision, and one climbed down and boarded the zodiac, his hands rough as he searched Jason.

"You won't need this onboard." The second man grabbed Jason's phone from his hand, pulled the battery out and tossed all the pieces into the salty water. He then frisked him for anything else he was carrying. He found nothing.

The welcoming committee then pushed him toward the ladder and told him to start climbing by jabbing the rifle into his back. He scrambled up from his tiny boat, climbing until he reached the rich teakwood deck of the yacht. There was no easy escape from here. He would need backup or a boat. He looked around for Matt, but couldn't see him. Instead, he saw a woman lounging by a hot tub and several more men with weapons lingering about.

Sitting like a king on a lounge chair in the moonlight, Andres Porras nursed a glass of crimson wine. Although Jason had never met the man, he'd done his research in the years since the botched operation. Porras was the reason he had to hide himself away to protect his family. Despite all those years of planning, his nightmare had come to life on a multimillion-dollar ship. Strands of gray threaded through his enemy's otherwise dark hair. When the man's eyes locked onto Jason's, determination masked all other emotions. Determination to bring about his version of justice by causing Jason to suffer as much as he had. His logic was flawed, however, as he'd been the person who sent his son to his death, and Jason had merely been the last person standing at his botched raid.

"Welcome, Jason Stirling." Andres's voice dripped with icy calm. "I've waited so long for this."

Jason remained as composed as he could. "That's a

lot of energy you put into someone who has never done anything to harm you or your family."

Andres tilted his head as though Jason's words made no sense. "You don't believe that. Why else would you fake your own death?"

"To avoid this very confrontation. You want to make up for your own bad ideas. Instead of looking inward, you've decided to lash out at the only survivor of the raid that you set in motion. I never hurt your son. I can honestly say I never even saw him. I'd been knocked out in the IED blast that you set on my unit before any of your men arrived at the scene. My handgun was still in its holster when I woke up in the back room of someone's shop. I didn't hurt anyone that day, but I sure as hell lost all of my colleagues." The memories of the slaughter swarmed through him, crashing loss and pain over his body as icy as the sea below him. If Andres thought he'd get an apology from Jason for merely being at the wrong place, he was wrong. Jason would never forgive that bastard for the senseless murder of so many. That Andres lost his own son in the raid should rest on his shoulders alone, although now was not the time to antagonize him. Not until he knew Matt was safe.

He looked around the deck and found him. Matt, on the floor by the bar, was tied at the hands by duct tape. Otherwise, he seemed unharmed so far. Jason's emotions welled. "Matt!" he shouted and stepped toward him but was immediately blocked.

Andres rose, his pale tan pants and loose white shirt giving off Caribbean vibes. With an easy wave of his hand, he called off his men. "First, we talk." His every word hung heavy in the salty air.

A mental battle waged in Jason's head. The trained soldier in him needed to focus on the enemy, but the father in him could only see the stoic face of his thirteen-year-old son and want to reassure him that everything would be okay, not that he knew what the future held for either of them.

Andres chuckled, the sound hollow. "He's a strong boy. Got in a few good swings at Alex before taking a long nap. Perhaps I shouldn't kill him at all, just take him and raise him as my own. He'd fall into line quickly with the right motivation." He gestured to where Matt was bound.

Matt's eyes burned through Andres. It would take a lot to break that spirit and Matt would either die or lose a significant part of himself in the process.

Jason's voice broke, "Let him go, Andres. This is between us."

Andres leaned forward, eyes sharp. "My family and yours are bound together. My son David's death tied our fates. You could have put an end to this a long, long time ago, but you chose to hide. Luckily, Montana was a fan of your wife's books. Intriguing plots, but nothing that affected me, until her last book. She gave me something I haven't had in a long time. Hope. And here you are. I must thank your wife in person someday."

The considerable implications of Andres's words lingered, a cloud of what-ifs and philosophical meanderings. But the sudden drone of another engine broke their standoff.

Jason walked to the edge, unsure if it was too late to wave them off. Even if it wasn't anyone on his team, anyone innocent caught up in this nightmare would be at risk. Two men shoved him to the ground and secured his hands behind him around a post with mooring line. Matt was seated across the deck, against the edge of a bar.

An urgent shout from the front of the yacht confirmed Jason's worst fear. "Boss! Boat approaching!"

Through the darkness, the faint hum of an engine grew closer. His heart raced, a single thought consuming him: Fiona.

Andres smirked. "Expecting company? I told you to come alone."

Jason met Andres's gaze and tried as hard as he could to contain his alarm. "I don't know who that is." Every fiber in him tensed, thoughts of Fiona dominating his mind. Her safety, her tenacity. Would she attempt to board? He knew damn well she would, and she'd have the whole team supporting her decision. Hell, if they continued like this, she'd be running his whole company before the end of this fiasco.

Andres, with an uncanny ability to read him, raised an eyebrow. "Your backup, perhaps? Or something... more?"

Summoning every ounce of control, Jason met Andres's stare, voice steady. "I told you, I came alone."

Andres smirked, an unsettling blend of amusement and malice. "Then you don't care if I eliminate them." He gestured, and three armed men walked over to the side of the yacht and pointed their rifles in the direction of the sound of the engine.

Fiona's grip tightened on the edge of the boat, her fingers damp with salt water and anxiety. Beside her, Meaghan's face was taut. Fiona could see the police training that had honed her abilities and felt foolish to think Meaghan had ever worked a desk job.

The radio buzzed to life, casting a pale light over Meaghan's face. "Communications to Boat Two. Target located and we have visuals on both Jason and Matt. They're on the main deck by a hot tub. So far, we have confirmed six men, one woman, and Andres are with them." Sam's voice crackled through the speaker.

A pang of fear punched into Fiona. The mere name of Andres Porras and all the violence he'd committed in the name of profit was enough to send shivers down her spine. She tried to picture Jason and Matt held by such predators. The urge to swim toward the yacht and board it rushed through her, but there was no easy way up the sides of such a large vessel and she didn't want to risk Meaghan's life. They were supposed to be following at a distance in an observation role, allowing Steve and Sam to stay far enough away to avoid any aggression or any panicked moves by the crew to get rid of their victims quickly.

Her grip on the sides of the boat loosened as she went through some of the gear they carried. She slipped a small knife into the pocket of her life vest. The roar of the larger craft's engine sounded as though it would drown out their small engine's noise, but if they moved too close, the occupants of the yacht would hear them. "Are they okay?" she asked.

"There's no sign of physical harm, but be ca—" Before Sam could finish, the unmistakable sound of gunfire interrupted the transmission. The bullets struck the water around the boat, sending plumes of water into the air.

"Meaghan, get out!" Fiona yelled.

Without hesitation, Meaghan swung herself over the side, clinging to the boat's edge, the side facing away from the yacht. Fiona needed to pull the gunfire away from Meaghan, so she took a deep breath and dove into the chilling water. She could feel adrenaline pumping through her veins, numbing the cold bite of the ocean. Her life vest fought her body from descending too deep into the water. Her lungs screamed for air as she swam. When she finally broke the surface, the yacht was within arm's reach. From the rifle barrels pointed in her direction, she knew she'd successfully drawn the attention away from the small boat and Meaghan. She glanced back at it. The boat seemed powered by a ghost, motoring away from her in a large curve. Meaghan needed to stay hidden until she was out of sight and everyone on the boat focused more on her. Fiona assured herself that Meaghan would be fine. She had the right mindset to survive anything. There was nothing else Fiona could do for her.

Reaching the yacht, Fiona hoisted herself up the ladder, her movements driven more by urgency than strength. Her body ached from the cold, but she focused on seeing her husband and son and making sure she was able to do something to help them. Standing back in the basement of a storage facility would never have been an acceptable role for her to play in this. Not when so much could go wrong and so much already had. She was still annoyed that Jason had thought he was helping anyone by going at this alone. He had to see that being part of a team was always preferable to being the lone wolf. Even when she'd been sent out on her own to finish her assignments, she'd always had someone looking out for her interests, at least from afar. Without ten other people on the ground around her, she'd never have been able to accomplish all she had.

Two guards greeted her as she arrived on the main deck, their rifles aimed at her, expressions unreadable.

One of the men, attired like a fraternity brother in shorts and a blue linen shirt who had overstayed his welcome on campus by ten years, pointed the cold metal of an AK-15 in her face. "Stop there." He was a bit overcautious. She wasn't going anywhere with so many weapons trained on her.

Another casually dressed man stood next to him. He frisked her and located the knife she'd slipped into the pocket of her life vest. The presence of a weapon, even one only a few inches long, seemed to make them all the more paranoid. They stripped her of the life vest and let her remain standing in dripping wet clothes.

Above them stood a woman dressed in a pale yellow maxi dress with a straw hat over loosely braided hair. She watched silently, her slim figure wrapped in a shawl. Standing to the side, she had a storm brewing behind her eyes. Fiona could tell she was unhappy with the direction things had taken, but there was a resigned set to her shoulders that suggested she wouldn't dare challenge Andres. Without knowing her role in all of this, Fiona couldn't decide how to leverage that emotion. The man behind her, cruelty etched onto his face, caught Fiona's attention. Andres. He was the only man who could stop this. He held up his hand, signaling the others to hold their fire. His piercing eyes assessed Fiona, scanning over her wet hair and drenched clothes.

The yacht's engine roared to life. Meaghan would be safe in the water. Fiona wasn't sure if she'd just signed her own death certificate, but she never second-guessed decisions she'd already made as that wouldn't change them. It was time to understand the situation and bend it toward her will.

"Fiona Stirling," Andres said with the confidence of someone who had stalked her whole family.

She ignored him for a moment while she turned around in a circle, looking for Jason and Matt. She squared her shoulders when she found Matt across the deck. His hands were secured by tape, but otherwise, he had no restraints on him. If she needed him to run across the deck to hide, he'd be able to. He looked scared but determined. She gave him a small wink, a silent promise that she would do everything in her power to make things right.

Jason, on the other hand, wasn't going anywhere. His hands were tied together behind his back, attached to a column for the upper deck. Two burly guards stood on each side of him. They certainly weren't underestimating him, but maybe they'd underestimate her. Jason wasn't too welcoming toward her presence. His whole body was coiled tight, ready to explode at any moment. More anger radiated toward her from him than toward the actual enemy.

She faced her husband's incensed gaze.

"Damn it, Fiona." Jason hissed, a mixture of relief and anger on his face. He'd expected her to remain a safe distance away, but he should know she'd never leave him and Matt at risk. "Why would you put yourself at risk?"

She met his eyes with a fierce determination. "I lost you once already. I won't lose you again."

Andres, leaning against the ship's railing, eyed them both. "Such passion," he mused. "I've watched couples sacrifice each other for nothing but a few thousand dollars. But you two… There's a fire there. It's…touching."

"Honestly, your admiration means zero to me. Just let Jason and Matt go. If you need someone to kill for your little revenge, kill me." If she died saving Matt and Jason, she'd die, not a happy person, but satisfied she did the best she could.

Matt, however, wasn't feeling grateful for her sacrifice. He looked between his parents, torn between his loyalty to them and fear of Andres. She could see his slow, even attempts at pulling apart the duct tape holding his hands together.

Jason's face reddened at her words. "What the hell, Fiona?"

Andres chuckled. "This has become much more interesting. What will Captain Jason Stirling do to save his wife and son? What would happen if he had to choose between them? That would be a very interesting question. And how much love would you two have for each other if your son dies while you both watched? The bond you two share… It's your greatest strength and your most profound weakness." He paused, looking thoughtfully at Jason. "It's like Christmas in September."

"Let them go, Andres. They have nothing to do with this," the woman said. An Instagram perfect beauty, the kind men killed for, she watched Fiona as though she could read the future and it was bloody and bleak.

"And yet, here they are, Montana," Andres retorted with a smirk. He considered Fiona for a long moment, his eyes narrowing. The silence was almost unbearable. Finally, he shook his head. "Sorry, Mrs. Stirling. No deal."

Fiona squared her shoulders. "Jason abandoned us for five years. I doubt losing us now will have an effect on his life. Perhaps you can take one of his colleagues. He was much more attached to them." And not one of them were there to be harmed.

Andres tilted his head with an air of malicious amusement. "Oh, I think you will be more than sufficient for what I have in store for him. Because, as you said, you'd do anything for family and I'm sure he would too." He let the words hang in the air.

The weight of her decision to board pressed down on her, but she wouldn't let Andres see her falter. She met his gaze, unyielding. "Good luck with that."

From the side, Montana spoke up again. "Let her family go, Andres. We've made our point. We have so many bigger issues to deal with back in Bogotá."

Andres frowned, clearly irritated by the interruption. "This is not your business, Montana."

She shook her head and turned away, walking down the stairs to the interior of the boat. Fiona hated seeing her go. She seemed to have a conscience and might have been able to prevent harm from coming to them. It seemed that Andres's obsession with revenge for his son made him blind to everything else around him. He was taking a lot of chances lingering so close to shore. This was not international waters. Regretfully, he didn't seem to have a decent set of advisors with him. He was commanding the crew with his ego and leading himself along with his heartbreak.

One of the Abercrombie henchmen pushed Fiona next

to Matt and wrapped her hands with duct tape in front of her, as they'd done with Matt. Matt had been moving the tape back and forth until the ends twisted over and stuck together, a nightmare to get apart. She'd need a knife to help him.

"Leave it alone," she whispered to him. "You're making it harder to break."

His fidgeting hands froze and from the look on his face, his thought that he would be free vanished and panic rolled in.

She received a sharp smack on the right ear by the idiot closest to her for talking. "Shut up."

She tried to appear apologetic so they'd let her remain there, but another guy walked over and dragged her about fifteen feet from Matt. Now they were all separated. She tried to stay in the moment, but Jason seemed about to blow his top, and Matt was fading under the stress of it all.

# *Chapter 15*

Jason had never been hypnotized by wealth. Once he'd lost his wife and son, nothing seemed to matter except keeping them safe. Now he was trapped in this floating prison, waiting for some super wealthy villain to destroy them all. The dimly lit deck cast long, undulating shadows that melded with the steady rocking of the boat. The silence outside of the clanging of pans from the kitchen and the heavy footsteps of their guards added to the chilling tension aboard the ship.

Jason couldn't pull his hands free. They were tied together behind a thick pole, its cold, unyielding surface pressing against his back. The rough rope dug into his skin with every futile movement he made.

Fiona seemed downright content to sit there and wait for the worst to happen. His anger at her simmered under the dread of what could happen to her. Matt's breathing had become more shallow since his mother appeared. Jason would do anything to prevent them both from being harmed. If the team had followed the plan, they might have backup soon enough.

"Andres," he said, his voice hoarse, "there has to be something, anything, you need. Is it money? Assets? Influence? Just name it."

But Andres, a silhouette against the dim light, smiled at Jason's offer. "You think this is about material wealth, Jason? What did you make last year? Two hundred thousand? How adorable. How much can you offer to me? A used Range Rover or that burned-out house you called home?" He laughed, a hollow, mocking sound that echoed over the waves. "I have riches beyond what you can comprehend. I just need closure on this part of my life so my son will have a sense of closure in the afterlife."

"Hurting my family will never bring closure to this. You sent your son to his death. I had nothing to do with it. Perhaps you need counseling. I can't pay for a private jet, but I'll buy you some therapy sessions. Imagine learning to understand how your own actions affect the world."

Andres stepped over to him. Jason expected an argument—instead, he received a kick in the face. The toe of the leather boat shoe hit the side of his mouth, crushing his teeth into his cheek. He spit out blood onto the shiny deck. He took the injury, thankful it had been focused on him and not on Matt. Time and distance, however, were their enemy. If they went too far out to sea, their chances of rescue would decrease.

A few feet away, Matt stared at Jason's face. No doubt the violence brought the danger they were in to the forefront of his thoughts. His muscles tensed and he tried to slip his hands out of his bindings. Matt's subtle efforts to escape caught the eye of one of the guards, a man no more than in his mid-twenties. With a swift, almost casual move, he kicked Matt sharply in the shin, no doubt spurred on by the violence of his boss. The force of the blow and the sharp pain made Matt cry out. Jason, a person who had held to a very tight code of behavior in the military, wanted to kill that man. After the shock of the attack settled, Matt's eyes narrowed, the intensity almost asking the guard for another blow.

Fiona's eyes, usually so soft and full of warmth, ignited with a fierce protectiveness. Her chest heaved with suppressed emotion, her hands clenched despite being wrapped together in duct tape. Yet, she treaded carefully—any sign of an escape attempt or insubordination would get her beaten up as well.

Jason regretted so many things. Had he gone after Andres years ago, he'd never have had to fake his own death. Instead, he hid like a coward and did nothing but wait. Watching his son get hurt while he was rendered immobile was a torture worse than any physical pain. Andres knew this. Yet, Jason couldn't help trying to help him. "Leave him alone," he yelled out, pulling all eyes toward him.

Andres, a new drink in his hand, had sat down on a lounge chair without the slightest hesitation in his plan. "Every ounce of your pain," he said, savoring each word, "is a gift for my son."

Seeing her son in pain sparked something inside Fiona. She held an arsenal of skills capable of reducing the beast who harmed him into nothing more than a quivering mess, but with her wrists bound, she remained as helpless as Matt. His anguish echoed in her ears, amplifying the rage boiling within her veins. The tape around her wrists was the only barrier holding back the storm of retribution that lurked beneath her restrained exterior. The grimace on Matt's pale face gave her pause. Whatever she did, it would have to be intelligent, deadly and fast enough to not gain the attention of the men surrounding her.

She made a quick assessment of what they were up against. On a boat, in the middle of Nantucket Sound, a mile or so off the coast of Martha's Vineyard. An occasional recreational boat could be seen on the horizon, but not close enough for their occupants to see what was going on. The ferry lane was located farther south, so that wouldn't help them. There were several guards who lingered around Andres. The woman, Montana, and maybe a chef and other staff were belowdecks. There had to be a captain driving the boat, which meant they had too many people to fight off, considering neither she nor Jason had their hands free.

She struggled with the tape, loosening it, but not enough. It was too sticky and any jerky movements would bring too much attention to her, and she'd be no help to anyone dead. Besides, she didn't want to fold over the edges of the tape as Matt had done in his attempts to get free. It would make breaking out of it all the more difficult.

Jason had pulled at his bindings so much when the guard kicked Matt that blood dripped from his wrists. He'd done everything in his power to protect Matt and her from this exact situation and she'd unwittingly written a map for Andres to follow to find Jason. The thought made her sick. Tied to the post with enough guards to prevent him from pulling free, he was completely sidelined. He'd told her several times that this had been the reason he'd hidden himself from the world. He'd done it for Matt and her. She should have respected that. Instead, she'd thrown his concern for them back in his face. Everything he'd warned her of had come true. Yet, she had to be fair to herself too. She'd never have imagined this scenario when he disappeared. She was doing the best she could under the circumstances.

Matt remained passive. No fight, but he didn't have the look of someone who had given up either. He was thinking. Exactly as his father was doing. Going over details, trying to assess the situation. He held himself together not like a thirteen-year-old, but more like a seasoned marine.

"You're an asshole," Jason called out to Andres.

Andres stood up and walked over to Jason. "Your pathetic attempt at saving your son makes this all the more satisfying." He kneed him in the face as he spoke the last word. Jason's head snapped back at the force, leaving him with a bloody nose in addition to a swollen lip. "Can you now imagine waiting to hear from your son, and learning some bastard had gunned him down. He was only seventeen years old."

He stepped toward Matt, presumably to kick him as well. Fiona couldn't yell out to stop him, because that would stir him on. Despite that, her heart raced inside her. Watching Matt suffer was something she'd never be able to tolerate.

Montana returned and Fiona then noticed the large diamond on her ring finger. Fiona had no idea if Andres was married, but Montana's ability to say what she wanted did mean her relationship with him was built on something stronger than sex. "That's enough. I can't deal with blood all over the floor and furniture. Have someone clean this mess up." She waved her hand across

the deck. "Come inside, cariño. I'm starving for you."
She looked away from the Stirling family and sashayed
down the stairs.

"Want me to stand guard over them?" one of his flun-
kies said.

Porras hesitated. He stared at Jason and then at Montana's retreating figure. It wasn't clear whether he'd been
persuaded to follow her or whether he preferred sticking
around to shoot his perceived enemies. If Montana was
his wife, was she also the mother of the lost son? If so,
she carried as much grief as he did, maybe even more
because she could do nothing to stop her husband from
sending her son into battle with the US and Colombian
governments. If Montana could persuade her husband
that murdering an innocent family wouldn't honor their
son's memory, they might survive this ordeal, but grief
was a funny animal, cycling back and forth between
anger and sorrow.

Just as Fiona felt a huge relief at Andres following
his wife, he turned back. Something had changed his
mind, but Fiona had no time to think through what that
might be, because he headed straight to Matt and lifted
him to his feet. "You are nothing compared to my son,
David. He was a man—you are but a boy."

Matt tried to twist away from him, but with his hands
tied and Andres's strong hands on him, he didn't stand
a chance. Matt scanned everything around him and relaxed for a moment, which was the right thing to do.
Fighting Andres would get him killed.

Jason, still tied to the pole, pulled at his bindings, but
they were too tight and thick to break free. The wounds
from his prior attempts looked painful, but Jason was fo-

cused only on Matt. His anger and fear surfaced, as clear as the moon. Her heart broke for him. After missing the past five years of Matt's life, he couldn't lose him now.

Fiona shut her eyes to reduce the tension and clear her mind. Acting out in fear and chaos wasn't the answer. A splash in the water and Jason's screams of pain opened her eyes. She watched the dark sea in horror as Matt broke the surface, struggling to keep afloat. There was no way he'd survive without being able to tread water for a long, long time.

Jason fought, making his wrists bloodier, even though he wasn't able to save him. But Fiona was. She waited for a moment, her heart punching into her chest, gearing her up for the biggest fight of her life. The boat had slowed but was still moving away from Matt and he'd soon be lost to them.

"A life for a life. I feel better, but not one hundred percent." Andres gave Jason the finger and walked downstairs.

"You bastard," Jason shouted, but Andres continued walking away.

When the other men turned away from the railing where they had tossed Matt overboard and toward Jason, Fiona made her move, hopping up on to her feet, racing across the deck and diving over the railing of the boat. Holy crap, it was a long way down. The last thing she heard was Jason screaming for her to stop. Too late. She tumbled around in a most inelegant manner and struck the water butt-first. The cold water woke up all her senses as she submerged and descended lower and lower under the water. Before her momentum slowed, she kicked to the surface, the moon guiding her up. Salt water filled her throat and nose. Her head popped up and she coughed out the seawater and sucked in huge gulps of fresh air. It only lasted a moment until a wave struck her and knocked her back. She didn't have the assistance of the life vest to keep her afloat as she did before, and her tied hands made staying afloat nearly impossible.

First things first, she had to get her arms free. The salt water made the loose duct tape into a far more malleable force. She didn't have time to slowly maneuver her hands through the tape. Yes, the tape was failing in the salt water, but she had to swim back to find Matt. Pulling a leg between her hands and her chest, she yanked her hands away from each other at the same time she jammed her knee between them. The tape split. Her hands were free. She shook her shoulders and glanced over toward the boat. It was much smaller now. They didn't want to see Jason's family die? Cowards. Not that she was complaining. She had enough to handle without someone sitting above her taking potshots.

She did a one-eighty and saw Matt's yellow T-shirt far-off. He was still afloat, but struggling. An athlete like his father, he should be able to kick for a few minutes. Maybe a few minutes had already taken place. She couldn't be sure, as time was rushing through her head at alternative paces—too fast, too slow—and for a moment when she'd first heard the splash, time stood completely still. She swam toward him using the shirt as a homing beacon. One goal. Get to her son.

Although never the best swimmer, she'd done a triathlon once and had a swim instructor teach her how to keep a steady pace without expending all her energy. It was the only way she got through the swim portion.

Stroke, stroke, glide. She stayed underwater until her breath was gone and then spotted her son again. Stroke, stroke, glide. He was so much farther than she'd thought. She should have jumped as soon as Andres threw him overboard, but the chance of his men grabbing her was so much higher and then she wouldn't have had a chance in hell of saving him. Stroke, stroke, glide. She lifted her head and could no longer see him. Her entire body began to fight the cold water, the stress of the waves and the panic of not making it in time to save her son. She still had about twenty strokes to go when she saw him fade under the water. Panic rose, obliterating her rational side. She couldn't let him die, and she was more than willing to risk her own life to save him. She took the biggest breath of her life and dove underwater, hoping she could pull him up in time.

# *Chapter 16*

Jason looked out at the fading image of Fiona with disbelief and anguish. His eyes were transfixed on possibly the last place in the world he would see his wife and son alive. The last thing Jason had seen of them was Fiona's blond hair fanning out over the violent waves as she disappeared beneath the surface of the ocean.

She'd jumped overboard in a desperate bid to save their son. If he'd been able to, he would have done the same thing. Staying onboard would only allow Andres to torture them. Their chances of survival were slim, but they had a chance—at least that's what Jason told himself.

After all this time of protecting them, only to see Matt thrown overboard and Fiona, his heart and his soul, follow him into the icy depths, destroyed him. Time stopped and the world as he knew it became stained with the blood of his family.

A perverse laughter echoed across the deck, turning Jake's blood to ice. Andres, a picture of sadistic satisfaction, stood at the railing edge. "It's quite poetic, isn't it, Jason? Your wife killing herself like that. To be honest, I would have been happy for the men onboard to have had some fun with her. Pity. Well, enjoy the evening. My own beautiful wife is waiting for me."

His amusement was made even more grotesque by the scenario—a chilling testament to his warped sense of justice. However, not everyone aboard the yacht shared Andres's sentiment. Montana, half-hidden in the shadows, listened to his speech with a face white as porcelain. She bore the look of someone witnessing a gruesome accident, unable to look away despite the horror.

She crossed the deck, her steps hesitant, to stand beside her husband. She reached out, touching Andres's arm lightly. "Andres," she said, her voice barely above a whisper. "This...this isn't justice. It's murder."

Her words halted the mirth on Andres's face, yet he quickly resumed his sinister smirk. "This is justice, Montana. David can rest in peace now. Tomorrow, Mr. Stirling can join his family at the bottom of the ocean. And they'll be together for always. I find that somewhat romantic."

"Romantic? It's barbaric." Her voice cracked, her gaze flickering to Jason.

Andres clasped her hand and pulled her away. She followed him without argument, but the temperature in their bedroom would be frigid.

A chilling silence remained on the deck after they left. The waves of the sea rose and fell nonstop, refusing to provide a chance for Fiona and Matt to float peacefully and wait for rescue. Bound to the post, Jason could do nothing but obsess over the fate of his family.

Fiona's heart pounded in her chest as she tried to locate Matt. The frigid water felt like a thousand icy needles against her skin, robbing her of breath. But she fought against the shock, forcing her body to continue on her search. She would not stop until she found him.

Matt was somewhere in this chaotic expanse of water, swallowed under waves. Her focus fought through her panic and all of her maternal instincts toward sacrifice and suffering. A levelheaded mind was so much easier when the task didn't involve one's child.

Salt water stung her eyes as she forced them open, struggling to make out anything in the shadowy depths.

She swam farther down, the weight of the water increasing, pressing on her chest and crushing her resolve. The cold crept into her bones, numbing her. Her body grew weary, her lungs burned for air, her eyes stung. She rose up and took a large gulp of air, fighting off the despair and forcing hope to push her farther than her body wanted to go. Diving down again, she kicked in a circle around the spot where she'd submerged, knowing that the currents were pushing and pulling her in a direction of which she had no control.

But then, she saw it. A spot of color in an otherwise gray and hazy environment. His yellow T-shirt, its vibrant hue contrasting against the darkness of the water. With a renewed surge of energy, she propelled herself toward him, her arms aching with the effort. When she reached him, she saw his eyes wide with terror and confusion, faint bubbles of precious air escaped from his lips as he struggled.

She maneuvered him into a lifeguard's hold, pulling his back against her chest, linking her arms under his. His hands were still tied together with the duct tape. Kicking with all her might, she swam toward the surface, feeling her own breath leaving her. Her lungs screamed, her muscles burned, but she kicked, focused on that shimmer of moonlight to lead them to air.

They broke the surface. She gasped for breath, but held tight to Matt. He coughed, his body trembling. Fiona secured her grip on him, doing her best to calm him despite the wild beating of her own heart.

When they had a moment to release the strain of that first obstacle of drowning, a wave lifted them higher but didn't crest over them. Fiona took that as something positive. The wind had died down and the sea was growing calmer. Yet, looking around her, she had to fight with everything she had to ignite even the smallest flicker of hope. The vast, empty horizon offered little positive to dwell on. Not one distant light, a ship…anything. All she saw was the yacht disappearing toward the open ocean with Jason aboard. Where the hell was the drone and the rest of the team?

Fear chilled her to the bone, but she shifted her mindset back to survival. They were together and she had been able to rescue her son from drowning. Holding on to him, she reassured herself that getting captured had been the best thing. She'd been there when Matt was thrown overboard.

"Hold on, Matt," she murmured, her voice a shaky promise against the storm of emotions inside of her, "We're going to make it. I won't let go."

As the sea rose and fell around them, Fiona and Matt clung to each other. The endless expanse of water offered no reprieve, no floating debris to cling to. The bitter cold was slowly sapping their energy.

She tried to stay calm, tried to keep them afloat, occasionally filling his shirt with air to give them a small reprieve, but his hands had to be free for that technique to be really effective. Her fingers pulled at the duct tape, using the water to help her until she could unravel it. The gray tape was about four feet long, far more than they had used on her—he'd been their only prisoner at the time and they had taken their time to secure his hands. They probably assumed he had more strength than Fiona. No matter. All hands were now free. She shoved the tape into the pocket of her yoga pants. Just in case.

Mathew squeezed his hands together and pulled apart from her for a second. The current moved them farther apart and he struggled to swim back to her.

"That's not going to work." She pulled off her sneaker and between rest periods, untied it.

"What are you doing?" he asked.

"Tethering us together. It's too much effort to try to swim and remain next to each other."

"But what if I start to go down? You'll get pulled down too."

"I won't let that happen." She sounded more confident than she was. If they could no longer stay afloat, she was going down with him. But that would only happen after she did everything under her power to keep them afloat.

In the moments between waves, they took turns resting, supporting the other's weight while they fought to catch their breath, their bodies numb from the cold. Fiona remained positive and as strong as she could for Matt. Their situation was dire—survival growing more and more unlikely as time stretched on—but Matt remained calm.

"Do you think Dad is okay?" he asked.

"He's still onboard, at least he was when I followed you over the railing." She hoped he would survive this. Her gut told her Andres had more in store for him. Jason was a survivor. Hopefully, the team would find the yacht soon.

"I can't believe they threw you overboard too."

"They didn't exactly. I figured the two of us together would have a better chance of survival than only one of us."

He turned toward her. "You jumped?"

"We're a team. That's what teammates do." Fiona looked into Matt's eyes that bore an uncanny resemblance to his father's. "Your dad will be okay without us. For now, let's think about staying above the water and then we can plan his rescue."

"It's hard to believe we finally have him back and all this happens. I wish he'd told us."

"I agree. But your father…he didn't know they'd ever learn he was still alive. He couldn't have known this would happen."

Matt spit out some seawater. "I know, Mom… I don't blame him. I'm scared for him too."

"Have some faith. I've been in worse situations and have come out fine."

"Worse than this?"

"My job was complicated," she replied.

"Mom, I… I knew you did something different when you worked. Remember the Little League coach who wouldn't let me play and you asked him nicely, then he freaked out on you? You literally stood still and stared at him until he got nervous."

"I don't think he was nervous."

"Yeah, he was. He always put me in after that and

never said another word about benching me. I even caught him looking at you whenever I was pulled from the field," Matt said, his voice barely audible against the wind. "You gave up your job just to be with me."

Fiona blinked against the stinging salt water, a shaky smile gracing her lips. "You've made being your mother easy."

She would do anything for her son. Literally anything. If she had a chance to meet up with Andres and his band of thugs, she would make them regret tossing a teenage boy to his death.

Her plans hung in the air. She had to believe they'd get out of there. Otherwise, they might as well just let go and descend to their graves. Cold, tired and scared, they held on to each other in the turbulent sea and reminisced to keep each other awake and alert and able to hold on for a little bit longer. Their plans for the future and shared fear and concern for Jason fueled their will to survive. And as long as they had something to fight for, they could last a little bit longer.

# Chapter 17

The more Jason thought about it, the more thankful he was that Fiona had followed him. She was in a position to possibly help Matt. Not that either of them were champion swimmers, but they both had grit and determination and he had to believe that she'd find a way to keep Matt alive. The team should have followed them at a distance and hopefully would come across them, although the darkness made any rescue attempt difficult.

Two of the guards sat at a nearby table, nursing beers and laughing in Spanish about the tough guy who watched his son and wife die from the boat. He didn't bother replying to them in Spanish. The less they knew about his skill set, the greater the chance they'd spill something he could use to escape.

He shut his eyes and tried to rest and think his way out of this nightmare. He definitely didn't want to be like Porras, spending his life on revenge for something he had done. Instead, he plotted various means of escape under a bunch of different scenarios, including being thrown overboard, getting loose and stealing a gun and sending up rescue flares. The mind games helped ease his stress and the fear of losing Fiona and Matt once and for all.

Soft footsteps came up behind him. Montana. She was in a light bathrobe tied at the waist. Her long hair over one shoulder. This was not a meeting he wanted. Her husband seemed like the jealous type, as well as the sadistic type and the asshole type. He didn't want to risk a slit throat for even seeing her.

The two guards glanced over but resumed their conversation. Apparently she didn't warrant any intervention. Which meant she might have more power than Jason had given her credit for.

"Have you eaten?" she asked.

"I'm fine." Jason tried to be as blunt as possible to not push a conversation.

She wasn't taking the hint. She put a drink in front of him with a straw. "It's nutritious. You need the nutrients. I fear you might be here a long time."

He shook his head, not wanting to accept anything from anyone.

"I'm sorry," she whispered. He could hear the distress inside her. Perhaps the memory of her son tormented her even more with the cruelty of her husband.

He could taste the blood from the cut in his mouth and thought of Fiona and Matt freezing to death and maybe worse. "Sorry doesn't bring my family back to safety."

"I know you never hurt David. It was Andres. He insisted he was old enough to be a soldier. He was just a boy. Only seventeen," she admitted, her voice too low for the guards to hear. "Please drink this."

"And if you want to poison me?" Jason said, his voice laced with suspicion.

There was a hesitation in Montana's demeanor. "If I wanted you dead, I would not go through all this trouble. I'd have one of these men shoot you and toss you overboard."

He couldn't disagree and nodded when she offered the drink again. He took a sip through the straw. Some sort of smoothie with mango and banana. The taste hid the taste of his own blood.

Montana wiped away a tear. "I just want my family safe. Like you do."

Understanding bridged the distance between them. They both understood each other on a level no one else on that ship would. Not even Andres with his hyperfocus on all the wrong things.

Jason fought the glimmer of hope that sparkled in the back of his mind. "I don't trust you."

"I'm offering to help," she replied.

Before he could garner any details, Porras came rushing toward them, rage in his eyes. "Montana? What the hell are you doing here?"

"I'm giving humanitarian aid to a prisoner."

"Don't be foolish. He'd just as soon slit your throat than let you help him. Go back to bed."

She backed away from Jason as Porras approached them and fled back downstairs, leaving the smoothie. The two guards were now standing, acting as though they'd been there the whole time.

Porras stood over Jason. "Don't get any funny ideas. She'd help a dog that bit her in the arm." As he walked away, he kicked the smoothie into Jason's leg. The cup turned over and soaked his pants with the golden liquid.

The guards laughed, but left the contents of the cup to seep further into his clothes. They returned to their beers at the table nearby.

Jason tried to move the cup with his leg, and then saw something that most definitely didn't belong.

A nail clipper.

Fiona's body was beginning to shut down. Matt was shivering uncontrollably.

She'd never felt so helpless in her life. The sea tormented them endlessly and the cold was sucking away her energy and her sense. Even her heart was beginning to break down, the potential loss of her son and husband slowing the beating down to a low, sorrowful drumbeat.

Although she'd taught Matt how to tuck in his shirt, blow air into the wet garment, and seal the neck opening with his hands, she knew that this crude floatation device wouldn't help if their minds became muddled with the confusion that accompanies hypothermia. They only had minutes left before the cold took them both.

Her eyes scanned the water, trying to find anything that could help them.

Something swam by her. Something large. She swallowed down her fear to keep Matt calm. "Matt," she said to him in a voice as steady as possible, "stay still."

But it was too late. The sleek form of a shark, illuminated briefly by the soft light of the moon, circled closer.

Matt looked down. She wanted to get between him and the shark, but he was in front of her. As the shark approached, Matt pulled away from Fiona's arms and moved toward the shark, punching it in the snout.

The shark reacted like a chastised puppy, arching back and then circling away from them.

She was speechless, her son having just defied every

bit of advice she'd ever given to him. "That...was incredibly reckless," she choked out, "and incredibly brave."

Matt, breathing hard, looked at his mother. "I saw it on *Shark Week*. I couldn't just let the monster eat us."

Fiona refused to think about becoming a meal for a shark. That was one more threat she wasn't able to control. Instead, she grinned, the release of some of her pent-up tension. Pulling him close, Fiona said, "You handled it better than I would have." She didn't know what she would have done if it had approached her first, but was doubtful she'd thrust a fist toward its face.

They switched positions for a moment, giving her a short rest.

The far-off sound of a motor rose up in the distance. It was dark and impossible to see Fiona, dressed in darker colors. Not the easiest outfit to spot at night. Perhaps the yellow of Matt's T-shirt could catch someone's eye. She wished she still had the knife from her life vest. It would shine if hit by a light.

"Do you have anything in your pockets?"

"I don't know. I had my keys and a few coins. They took my phone."

"Let me see the keys."

He struggled to search for them as he stayed afloat. "They might be at the bottom of the ocean."

"That's okay. I'll get new ones made."

"I have a quarter." He lifted up his hand, clenching something in his fist.

"Perfect." She took it from him. "Can you tread for a few minutes alone?"

"I'll try."

She aimed the flat of the coin toward the boat. It was headed a few hundred feet away from them.

"Wave your arms and try to get their attention."

She screamed toward the boat and Matt waved his arms. The boat didn't turn off course.

Then a spotlight scanned out toward them. Matt, with renewed energy, waved his arms and Fiona aimed the coin toward the light. She had to believe they would see the weak shine off the dull old quarter. This was their last hope. Her arm hurt as she held it up, keeping as much faith in her plan as she could. She could feel Matt losing energy as he went back to treading water.

"This isn't going to work," he said, his voice defeated.

"Don't stop believing. This is our way out of here. I know it."

"Like you knew Dad was dead?"

"I didn't know he was dead. I was told that and acted accordingly. I'm now taking all the information I have and using it to get us out of here. If you think that's absurd, then go ahead and let go of me. You can pull me under and it will all be over."

His legs kicked harder, keeping his weight from dragging her down. "I couldn't. I don't want to die."

"Then don't." She continued aiming the coin toward the boat. It had to work. She was running out of options.

The boat motored away, the lights fading into the distance, but then the spotlight swung back in their direction.

# *Chapter 18*

Jason waited until the two men supposed to keep an eye on him closed their eyes. He then leaned forward and shifted his legs until the nail clipper was by his hip and he could grab for it with his fingers. He took his time and nicked at the rope tying his hands together. When one of the men stirred, Jason slowed his movements to remain undetected. Eventually, the guard returned to sleep and Jason finished the job, pulling the rope apart where it had been frayed.

He had several options. He could hold the sides together and pretend it wasn't broken, but he'd be subject to another beating or a gunshot to his head if Porras became bored of his presence. Those options didn't appeal to him. So he had to escape, but they were too far out to sea for him to dive over the side of the boat and swim to Fiona and Matt. Instead, he had to hide somewhere on this yacht, where no one would find him. He scanned the area. The life raft would be the first place they'd look. The upper deck was all open spaces, except for the pilot-house, and he'd need to move carefully to avoid coming into view of the captain. Although he'd love to take over the boat and send out a distress signal to someone, the men inside the main control room would be armed and not willing to give up control so easily. The main deck where he was located now was also too open for him to hide. He had to sneak downstairs.

The cool breeze in the air gave him the energy to move. He took the rope and tossed it overboard and tip-toed belowdecks. The first landing had a long hallway with what was probably the main bedrooms and the dining area. Jason wouldn't be safe there, so he went below one more floor and passed by the galley, where someone was already banging pots and pans, preparing for breakfast. Beyond that, a "caution, no entry" sign on a door invited him inside. The door opened to the engine room, a gleaming white and chrome space, heaven for engineers. He could hear footsteps above him in what seemed like a control booth, complete with large computer screens high on the walls. That was his destination if he could wait it out until the man inside left. He stayed low and glanced around for a safe place to be close but not seen. There were a few hot-water tanks wrapped in white insulation, double engines and a large generator. He couldn't find any place to hide, except in an access panel in the engine.

The space looked far too small for him, but he had little choice. He opened the hatch. The motor rumbled in a high-priced-sports-car kind of way. The floor seemed clean without any oil or dust and the insulation wrapping the pipes kept the heat contained, mostly. So he ducked inside, his arms and legs pulled tight.

Had Porras held Fiona or Matt as a captive, Jason might have folded to whatever demands Porras made of him, but he had nothing over Jason now. And if Jason had the chance, he'd bring that asshole to justice. For now, he practiced deep, slow breathing and hoped for a miracle.

The confined space became suffocating as the minutes dragged on. His body, pressed against the insulated pipes that weren't burning, but very hot, vibrated under the constant hum of the engines.

Footsteps passed nearby. There seemed to be some urgency in their tempo. His absence might have become known. That would keep him inside this hellish engine for a bit longer. The oily scent of machinery clogged his nose, and his focus was off. But he stayed as still as possible.

He reviewed what he knew of the yacht's layout in his mind. Getting into the ship's communications system was his objective, but not with so many people walking around.

The engines' hum escalated into a deafening roar; the yacht was picking up speed. He had to get out of this space. The cuts and bleeding at his wrists tormented him. But every sharp sting reminded him of watching Matt being thrown away as though he were trash. His stomach roiled with the anguish of what had happened to him and Fiona.

More footsteps, some muffled shouting between men and then footsteps rushing away. He was safe for now.

A rush of energy shot through Fiona as the boat came closer to them. When she caught sight of the silhouette she squeezed Matt's arms. "It's the team. They found us."

His entire demeanor swung from bleakness to elation. The energy shift resonated through his expression

and movements. "What were the chances of them finding us?"

"One hundred percent. What is happening now is
what-is—let's ignore all the what-ifs. There's no time
for that. Look. Steve's waving a towel toward us. And
Meaghan made it back on board. We're going to be just
fine."

The boat pulled up close to them and Steve reached
down, pulling Matt out of the water first. He received
a large hug and was immediately wrapped in a towel.
Fiona treaded water for another minute until Steve
reached for her. The speedboat was higher from the
water than the one she and Meaghan had taken out only
a few hours earlier, but it also had enclosed areas where
they could warm up and get dry.

Once on board, Meaghan ran to her, flung a towel
around her and gave her a bear hug. "Damn. Your life
vest is on the yacht. We would have flown past you if we
hadn't seen something shining from the water."

"They took my life jacket the minute I got on board.
Porras thought he'd drown Matt to make Jason suffer,
but I was able to dive over the edge after him." She took
a sip of water and spit it out over the railing.

"I punched a shark," Matt said through chattering
teeth.

"A very brave move, but as a mother, I don't think I
could live through a reenactment." Fiona shook her head
at the memory. There were too many times she could
have lost him. Now that he had a team backing him up,
she turned her thoughts back to Jason. "Are you tracking the boat still?"

"We lost the drone when they fired at your boat. One

of them noticed it and took it down. We're following the yacht through Kennedy's systems. We have the specs for the boat and a map of every floor. Now we need to figure out a way to get aboard."

"Did you contact the Coast Guard?"

"Yes, but they're a half an hour out. Kennedy has been monitoring three Coast Guard vessels in the area. Their closest asset is assisting a sailboat that flipped over. Another is still in port in Hyannis, and the last one has to maneuver around the elbow to reach us."

Fiona bit back her frustration. "They're our best chance at slowing their escape."

Her body shivered as she stood with the team. They moved below to the small area inside, while Sam and Steve switched places—Steve now piloting the boat above, Sam sitting at a table helping them think of their next steps. Meaghan went to a microwave and heated up two cups of tea for Matt and Fiona. When Fiona held the warm cup between her hands, she sighed. The heat was wonderful.

"Can we catch them?" Fiona asked.

"Yes, but they'll see and hear us coming and Jason could be killed before we board." Sam tapped his fingers on the nautical map in front of him.

"Can we sneak in, disarm the guards and allow the speedboat to come alongside it?"

"Like you did before? Because that was a clusterfuck," Sam said with too much truth.

"I admit I drove the boat too close," Fiona said. "But they didn't sink her and you came to my rescue in time."

Meaghan stood next to her. "There's got to be a way to slow them down. Ram them?"

Sam shook his head. "They'll detect us before we arrive."

"Right." Meaghan, her fingers tented together, sighed. "Too bad we couldn't stop the engines."

Sam appeared struck by lightning. He picked up his phone and called someone over the satellite link. "Can we jam their engine and scramble their radar for a few minutes, enough to stall their engine and enable us to slip behind the ship and get aboard?... Doubtful." He looked at Meaghan, then spoke into the radio again. "Okay. I'll ask them and get back to you."

"What did Calvin say?" Meaghan asked.

Sam stood and pointed up to the bridge. "Let's include Steve in this."

They left Matt below, wrapped in a blanket and drinking the tea Meaghan made.

When they reached the bridge, Steve looked over his shoulder. "I have them at a distance, mostly tracking them with Kennedy's guidance and the radar. Any ideas on how to stop them?"

Sam nodded. "We should be able to stall out the boat for about five minutes, but it won't stop, merely glide without engine assistance. Once their computer system runs an override, the engine will click back on and we'll be out of luck. We have literally minutes to get close enough to the boat to board without them seeing us. I doubt they'd let anyone climb up the ladder again, so it looks like the rear portholes are our best bet. The specs I found say that they're just under two feet wide. The rest of the portholes are only one foot and we'd never be able to fit anyone through them. They're located at the stern.

It's risky, but once I get on board, I can cause enough chaos to allow Steve to pull up on the side."

Meaghan shook her head. "You couldn't fit through such a small space, especially in a wet suit. Steve couldn't either. I guess it's me."

"And me," Fiona added.

"No," both Meaghan and Steve said at the same time.

"You can't go in alone," Fiona insisted. "There's too many of them, and you'd never be able to climb up to the porthole without help."

"It's too dangerous. You've already been exposed to the cold water, your body may not tolerate another long, cold plunge during the same night," Steve said, his eyes focused on the radar.

"I'm more than capable of making it back to save my husband. Especially if you have an extra wet suit." She hoped. Part of her wanted a nap and a sleeping bag, but she needed to save Jason.

Steve continued staring ahead at the water in silence. Sam made a face, but Meaghan nodded. It was a slow nod, nothing too enthusiastic, but definitely accepting.

"There are only three people on this boat who can fit through those windows. Me, and I'm already going, Fiona, who has proven she can fight enough to stay alive for at least a few minutes once she's on board, and Matt."

"Matt is not an option," Fiona declared. There was no way he was going near danger again.

"Then we have our team." Meaghan pointed between Sam and Steve. "You guys better carry out the plan to perfection, because we'll be counting on you. Jason will too."

Sam's shoulders dropped enough to let Fiona know he wouldn't be arguing over this anymore.

Steve shrugged. "Fine. It's settled. Be ready in twenty minutes. And you two better not die."

Meaghan gave him a thumbs-up. "We're huge fans of being alive."

Fiona returned belowdecks to check on Matt. He was bundled up and fast asleep on the cot. She kissed his cheek and pulled the blanket under his chin, then leaned back on a large bench at the stern of the boat and stared through the opening to the moon, praying Jason could see the moon too and was safe.

# *Chapter 19*

Sam dropped the dinghy to the side of the rescue boat. The boats smacked each other as they floated along, side by side. As the dinghy tapped against the larger vessel, water splashed onto the wooden bench. Fiona looked over the railing and saw how far down she'd have to climb to get aboard. Having been in the water only thirty or forty minutes ago, she wasn't super keen about slipping back into the cold waves and swimming to a place where they not only wanted her husband dead, but they already thought they'd killed Matt and her.

Sam helped Meaghan down into the smaller boat, their hands linked together. Her entire weight was held by him as he lowered her over the side, not that it appeared to be a problem for him—he had the build of a football player. She remained focused on not falling into the water as she dropped into the middle of the dinghy without making it rock too much to either side. When she was safe, they all turned to Fiona.

"Are you sure you want to go through with this? I can try to fit through the window," Sam said.

She looked him over. There was no way he'd fit through the porthole. It was her or Matt, and there was no way in hell she'd send her son into combat. "I appreciate the offer, but you wouldn't fit. Imagine climbing up the side of the boat, only to end up wedged with your feet waving to the fish and head inside the boat unable to stop someone from using your face as target practice."

He made a face. "Good description, but when you rescue DJ, tell him I offered but you refused."

"Absolutely. We'll disrupt things enough to put everyone else off their guard so you guys can come and save the day." She wouldn't let anything stop her from making sure her non-dead husband was still alive at the end of all of this.

He nodded. "You make a lot of sense. If you have trouble, just contact me through the earpiece. It should work submerged in water."

"Should?"

He shrugged. "We've never had a sea rescue before."

"Good to know." If she and Meaghan were Jason's only hope, she'd better get it in her head that this was her most important mission ever.

"Turn back if you get nervous. It's better to be safe than sorry."

Meaghan called up to them. "Sam, we're grown-ass adults doing our jobs. At least I am. Fiona will be fine with me by her side and if she isn't, you'll have Jason to deal with. Or not. Who the hell knows anymore."

Fiona saw a new side of Meaghan—focused, confident—and yet for this split second, she could sense Meaghan's fear as well. A little fear never hurt anyone during an operation. In fact, she found just the opposite in her years undercover. A reasonable amount of fear made people double-check plans and ensure that safe-

guards were in place and functional. Overconfidence
created gaps in the plan, areas that should run smoothly
but without double-checking might result in chaos. The
team had enough professionalism to understand the risks
involved, try to alleviate them as much as possible and
strike out even if things seemed stacked up against them.
Although she hadn't met all of the team, those she'd met
had impressed her. The love and loyalty they carried for
each other showed.

She wished she could give them information that
would give them more confidence in her, but she didn't
have authorization to release that information. If she
ended up in jail because of a security breach, Matt could
end up alone. That was not an acceptable outcome. She
shook her head and ignored the fact that she might not
make it back from this task. Now she had to make sure
she didn't let any of them down. They had no idea what
she was capable of and yet they trusted that she would
at least not get in the way. From her understanding of
revenge, Jason needed to suffer a bit longer. No way was
Porras going to kill Jason to relieve him of the pain of
watching his family die.

That Jason would think she and Matt had been lost
after all he'd been through broke her heart. She should
have forgiven him when she had the ability to do so. Holding grudges never made life better. Forgiveness was not
necessarily an easier path, but it led to better outcomes.
A moment of love, of connection, of understanding.

"Ready?" Sam asked her.

She nodded. She was more than ready.

He gripped her hand the way he'd gripped Meaghan's
a moment earlier. "Godspeed."

She gave him a nod and a smile in return and then tightened her hold as he lowered her over the side. Meaghan reached up and grabbed her by the waist, helping her down.

"Fiona, this is Steve." He spoke through her earpiece. "Can you read me?"

"Yes." His voice was loud enough to hear, but not biting.

"Meaghan?"

"Loud and clear," Meaghan replied.

They motored away from the bigger craft toward the signal coming from Jason's earring.

"Is there any way of getting a message to him? Like is the earring a communication device as well?"

"We kept it simple. Every one of us has some simple or cheap piece of jewelry that wouldn't attract attention. Mine is a belly-button ring," Meaghan said, lifting her shirt to show off ripped abs and a small diamond hoop in her belly button. "It allows us to track the person, but they can also take it off if they aren't on the job. Most of us leave it on all the time. I prefer having it with me in case a blind date goes wrong."

"Like the one you sent me on?" Fiona asked.

"For the record, George appeared quite upstanding when I met him."

"And the first thing you thought was that he was the perfect person for me?"

Meaghan shrugged. "Hindsight is twenty-twenty, isn't it?"

"I hate to interrupt you both on this interesting conversation, but I have the boat in my sight," Steve called in. "It's probably best for you to swim from here so they don't notice. It's about a quarter of a mile. Are you okay with that? The sound is fairly choppy."

"I'll be okay," Meaghan said. They would be abandoning the boat.

Fiona nodded. She'd rested enough to get some of her strength back and had been wrapped in a large blanket before putting on the neoprene bodysuit. This outfit would have made her time floating at sea with Matt much more comfortable. "Ready."

Meaghan went first, easing into the water over the edge of the boat so as not to tip it too much to one side. "Oh my God, it's freezing."

Not the words Fiona wanted to hear as she psyched herself up. She followed Meaghan into the water, tensing at the cold biting her limbs.

Meaghan swam in such a way as to minimize her time on the surface. Slipping under the water and kicking, then twisting on her back to grab a breath and continuing on. Fiona tried that technique but took in a mouthful of water. In order to make it, she'd have to glide just under the surface like an underwater breaststroke and turn her head at every fourth kick. Not as clandestine as Meaghan, but it shouldn't draw too much attention.

As they drew closer to the boat, Fiona, out of breath and barely keeping up with Meaghan, who seemed part seal, began to panic. Would the window be open still and could she lift herself up into it?

She needn't have worried. They both arrived to find the window still open, although it seemed much farther up than she remembered.

"I'm not sure if I can climb up that high."

"You're going to spring me up there and I'll reach down and pull you up," Meaghan replied.

She explained exactly what Fiona had to do. Float, head down, and maintain stability. "One, two and three."

In one huge movement, Meaghan lifted herself onto Fiona's back, stood up and leaped up to the window. Fiona missed the end of the acrobatic feat as her entire body was shoved underwater. She came to the surface and watched as Meaghan gracefully pulled herself the rest of the way without making a sound.

She twisted around and reached her arm down for Fiona. Fiona needed a second to get her bearings after being pressed underwater and then stretched out her arm. Meaghan had to do all the work because Fiona had nothing to hold on to.

Within seconds, they were both sitting drenched on the floor of a bathroom.

"Towel?" Meaghan handed her a fluffy white towel and took one for herself. "We need to be as dry as possible and a change of clothes will help if we need to fight."

"Montana's bedroom is somewhere on this floor."

"That will be great if Montana isn't inside."

They crept through the hall, hearing voices in the dining area, and slipped into an elegant bedroom that was made for days on the ocean, white-and-blue shells decorating the walls and bed. An entire wardrobe was available to them.

Meaghan, being all legs and small chested, fit into a pair of shorts and a T-shirt while Fiona could wear Montana's sweatpants, but required a sports bra and a tank top to keep herself as comfortable as possible while trying to save her husband. Knowing Matt was safe gave her the confidence to take more chances than she had when his life was in the balance.

A noise down the hall had them both slipping into the small closet together. Meaghan rested her chin on Fiona's head, while Fiona pressed as much of her curves as possible into the wall space behind her. When the footsteps passed the bedroom, they both relaxed for a moment. The footsteps returned and this time the bedroom door opened. From the deep sound of them, they were the larger boots of a man, not Montana's. She'd been in sandals when Fiona last saw her, before Matt was thrown overboard and she followed.

Fiona could feel Meaghan on the verge of a sneeze. There was nothing she could do to prevent it, so she prepared to fight her way out. The door opened and closed again and the footsteps traveled back toward the bow of the boat. Meaghan let her sneeze out in as muffled a manner as possible.

"*Gesundheit*," Fiona whispered.

"*Danke.*"

They slipped back into the room. Fiona hadn't truly gone into a fight situation since Matt had been in elementary school. She took a deep breath and visualized herself as strong and competent with all that muscle memory coming back in the nick of time.

"Ready?" Meaghan asked.

Fiona nodded.

"You can stay here, you know. It's going to be brutal and we're the underdogs."

"Thanks. I'm okay."

Meaghan and Fiona slipped down the hall and past the dining room. Montana sat at one end of a long wood

table. Porras sat at the other. They had dishes and flow-
ers and fundamental differences in morals between
them. Not that Fiona had time to analyze their relationship; she had to rescue Jason. Meaghan waved Fiona
downstairs now that they saw that the route was clear.
Meaghan would search for Jason on the main deck. It
was better that way, because Fiona would be too invested
in saving Jason to focus on her assignment. The longer
she stayed apart from him, the better.

As Meaghan crept up the stairs to the main deck,
Fiona listened at the engine room door to make sure it
was clear.

# Chapter 20

Jason's jaw throbbed from the beating, but the pain eased the strain of picturing his wife and son drowning, unable to be saved. He could taste blood in his mouth, whether from a loose tooth or a broken nose, he didn't know. He didn't care. The weight of his despair threatened to destroy him. Nothing on Earth mattered to him more than Fiona and Matt.

Sharing that intimate moment with her only a day before showed him exactly what he'd lost. The love of his life. The only person he wanted by his side. It was impossible to think about how many ways a heart could be broken, but in the past few days, it had been crushed, shattered and destroyed in every way possible. There would be no coming back from this. How did one survive when all hope drained away? The despair edged him closer to a dive into the deep, cold water where he could rest his weary soul near his wife and son. It would be so easy to do.

The engine slowed and then stopped. In fact, the entire room went silent as though something had shut an off switch on the entire vessel. One of the men ran inside and rushed past the engine to the control area. The silence gave Jason hope. His team, with their connections to some of the best technology blocking devices, might have done something to sabotage the ship's controls.

The thought of Steve and the rest of the team carrying on this assignment, more dangerous than anything they'd ever handled together in the past, provided Jason with a reason to hold on in the dusty cramped space. A group of people was out there. They wouldn't let him down, and he sure as hell wasn't going to fail them. While he couldn't wipe away the despair on losing Fiona and Matt, he could function enough to survive. Steve had all the brains, Sam had ingenuity, Meaghan had guts and Calvin had the tech skills. Noah, a man who took a bullet to save Matt, was in the hospital right now aching to get back into the storm with them. These guys deserved Jason's best. He couldn't quit on them or the important work they did. Life wasn't easy. It was tough and challenging and punishing. Yet, as long as he could help make this place better for even one person, he had to go on. His family would expect nothing less.

His back cramped up in the small space, but he remained silent. There was a slight rustle of sound outside the engine room door. When the door opened, a single figure came inside. Barely audible footsteps but the slim figure blocked what was left of the light coming through a porthole.

For a split second, the shape of the shadow appeared as if Fiona had floated right back into his life. The tiny silhouette pushed past his slight view into the engine room, a sliver of an opening from under one of the engines. He tilted his head for a better view. The silent sprite's light hair was wet and pushed behind her ears.

But that couldn't be Fiona. He'd seen her go over the edge, diving into the ocean in an attempt to save Matt.

A shuffle of a man came downstairs from the control room, the actions both sudden and scared. The ghost of his wife pulled something out of her pocket and flung it toward the man. He went down with a thud. Jason couldn't be sure if she killed him, but from the gasping and then silence, she probably had. She then went over to the engine controls and speaking in a whispered voice, responded to someone somewhere.

"Yes… The red one?… Okay, I've got it." The voice was all Fiona.

A moment later, an alarm blared.

With the alarms blaring, Fiona could barely concentrate. She preferred having the ability to hear people come up behind her, but this was an exceptional situation. She scanned the area. The guard who had been at the control panel had blood from the knife in his neck soaking into his blue linen shirt. Fiona hadn't wanted to kill the man, but he'd pulled a gun on her and dodging bullets would have seriously stalled her rescue of Jason, and the gunshots would have alerted the others that someone had infiltrated the ship. She refused to place Meaghan at risk.

The engine remained stalled out with whatever Sam and Calvin had concocted to destabilize the technology aboard the boat, but they'd insisted that she set the fire alarm off to override the generator from starting up automatically. Although she expected someone to arrive soon, she never expected the grate under the engine to open. She pulled out another knife, ready to defend herself, but recognized the rough skin and long fingers of her husband. The area he was attempting to extricate himself from seemed impossibly small for his long body.

She hustled to his side. Touched his arm as if to see if he were real. "Jason?"

"Fi. Are you okay?" He smiled up at her, then twisted his leg from under the quiet engine.

"I was going to ask that of you. How did you get there?" She pointed to the impossibly small space.

"I didn't think anyone would look for me there."

"I definitely wouldn't have." She wrapped her arms around him, knowing it could only last seconds, but gaining strength from the contact with the man who she would risk anything for. "I'm good and so is Matt. Steve found us floating in the water. It was a miracle." She didn't have time to go into specifics. They'd have to reconnect over the details when they were safe and away from Porras and his men.

He lifted her chin and kissed her with an intensity that welcomed her back from the dead and apologized for all the pain he'd put her through. She kissed him back with her own apology for her lost faith in him and a promise to never give up on him. They pulled apart reluctantly.

"Tell Jason we have his back," Steve spoke into her earpiece.

His presence in her ear calmed her. Help was on the way. "Steve and Sam are intending to board the boat in a few minutes," she told Jason. "Meaghan is on deck looking for you."

He shifted toward the side of her face. "You can't get here fast enough, partner." He spoke directly into her earpiece before nipping her earlobe. "Okay, let's go find her."

She nodded and they slipped out of the engine room, making sure they didn't run into anyone in the hall. The loud scatter of men rushing here and there made for a slow, jerky trip from the engine room to the main deck. They slid up the stairs after several close calls but eventually hid behind the bar and waited. What they found made Fiona's blood boil. While she was having a reunion with her husband, Meaghan had been captured and handcuffed to a chair. A very heavy chair that could take her to the bottom of the ocean if someone decided to toss her overboard the way they'd sent Matt.

They must have assumed she was the only one on board, because their urgency was more in getting the boat going than searching for someone. Until the dead man by the control panel was discovered. Several cries for assistance came from underneath. One of the two men standing guard over Meaghan rushed off to see what had happened belowdecks. The other looked out toward the sea, watching over their position, looking for anyone following them.

Fiona and Jason had only a moment to create enough chaos to rescue Meaghan and allow the team to board.

Jason pulled a fire extinguisher off the wall, while Fiona lifted a tray of empty glasses not yet carted away to the kitchen.

"On three," Jason whispered.

Fiona nodded.

Footsteps climbed the stairs. Heavy ones that were probably attached to someone who was heavily armed. Fiona held her breath for a moment and said a quick prayer that luck would fall on her side in this situation.

She looked back at Jason, who mouthed the word

"three." There would be no going back from this. She'd fight to save the people she loved or die trying. There was no in-between in this game. She hustled to the other side of the boat and tossed all the glasses at once onto the floor, then backtracked. She could hear the men scurry over to the area away from her position.

Now she'd have to trust that Jason could fight them back while she released Meaghan. She rushed over to her. Meaghan looked at her, the relief evident. Fiona placed a finger over her lips to keep her silent.

She took out a pin from the knife holster and pulled Meaghan's hands toward her. The sounds of gunshots rang out behind her. She only had seconds. She wedged the pin into the slot, shifted it back and forth and then twisted until she heard a slight click. One cuff opened. That was enough for now. She dropped the pin into Meaghan's free hand, before turning to face whoever was running into the area.

The crew member who had rushed belowdecks had come back, gun in hand. He pointed it in Meaghan's face, then pivoted to Fiona. Fiona held her breath. Meaghan remained calm and kept her hands behind her as though they were still secured behind her back. Fiona lifted her arms up in a surrender. She stepped toward the man, allowed his gun to press into her skin. The proximity would only help her. Remembering how Porras had treated his men when she'd been a prisoner, she worked under the assumption that this guy didn't have the authorization to kill her, and he'd be punished for doing so without a direct order. That second of indecision that passed through him provided her with an opportunity to clasp her hand on the barrel of the gun and twist it in a way that yanked it from his grip.

She turned away from him, the gun now in her hand. With a low drop to the floor followed by a swipe of her leg under him, she dropped him. He landed with a thud on his back, still reeling from her first attack. She stood over him, the gun pointed at his chest.

"Don't move." She stared at the man with such intensity, she left no doubt in his mind that she was more than willing and able to pull the trigger. Meaghan stood by her side, the cuffs now dangling from her finger.

"Cuff him," Fiona said.

Without a word, Meaghan turned the man over on his stomach and yanked back his arms in a move that an experienced police officer would be able to handle in their sleep. She put one on and then secured him to the same pole they'd tied Jason to.

"Where's Jason?" Meaghan asked, a question in her expression.

"He's holding off two other men. I hope." She sped away to where she'd broken the glasses. There was one man on the ground, his head bleeding from what had probably been the fire extinguisher. Jason and the other man were at a standoff. Jason still holding the fire extinguisher and the man holding on to a military grade rifle.

Without a word, Fiona pointed the gun at him, baiting him away from her husband. He took the carrot and turned his weapon toward her. As though in slow motion, she saw Jason call out to her, and could hear Meaghan yelling to her to get down, but there was no moment to contemplate every possible choice, every possible outcome. Instinct, muscle memory, a keen survival instinct.

They all churned together to make the decision for her. She shot him dead before he got to her.

As his body tumbled to the ground, Jason reached her side. He stepped in front of her and took the gun that had only a moment before been pointed in her direction. Meaghan knelt down beside the man and checked his pulse, but the shot had been almost point-blank into his chest. The blood loss enormous. The damage inside not survivable.

Jason pulled her into his arms. "Are you hurt?"

She shook her head. Nothing physical, and she wouldn't allow herself to think of the psychological damage until she had her family intact once again. "I'll be fine. We need to get off this thing."

"Meaghan?"

"I'm fine too," Meaghan said from behind them.

The tension in Jason's face diminished. He rubbed Fiona's back, probably as soothing to him as it was for her. "This whole situation has been more stressful than anything I've been through in my life."

"How adorable. A family reunion." Porras stepped forward and pointed his gun at Fiona.

A sharp, searing pain ripped through her right leg, causing her to gasp and stumble backward. He'd shot her. She clutched her wounded calf, feeling warm blood soaking through her fingers. Panic over Jason's and Meaghan's safety flooded her as she looked up to see Porras, his eyes cold and calculating, continuing to point his gun at her.

"You should have stayed out of this," Porras said, his finger tightening on the trigger.

Fiona refused to let fear paralyze her. With a burst

of adrenaline, she pushed through the pain and lunged behind the bar, praying it would shield her from the hail of bullets.

Jason rushed to her side. Before he could reach her, Porras caught sight of him. Porras sneered as he raised his gun again. This time, it was aimed at Jason. "You can't escape your fate, Jason. You will watch your wife die."

She couldn't see Andres, only Jason's expression. So much hatred and a flickering of fear. Without a weapon, he could do little to protect her.

Yet, in the moment she prayed for his safety, he chose to push away from Fiona and launch himself at Porras, knocking the gun out of his hand. The two men struggled for dominance, fists flying fiercely in a desperate struggle for survival.

Fiona could only watch from the sidelines, the gunshot wound stripping the strength from her. She shredded a dish cloth she located on a shelf to tie above the wound and stem the flow of blood already puddling through her sweatpants onto the floor.

As Jason fought to overpower Porras to her right, Fiona caught a glimpse of Meaghan's struggle. Her friend fought with every ounce of strength and skill she possessed against two men on the deck. The more she fought, the more they came back at her. Blow after blow landed on Meaghan. Her eyes teared up from the pain. Fear for both of them surged through Fiona. Her energy crashed and she watched, helpless to protect them. Jason landed a sharp uppercut to Porras's chin, sending him stumbling backward, momentarily dazed.

At the same time, Meaghan found an opening and

delivered a swift and devastating strike that left one of the men unconscious on the deck.

But before they could fully savor their victories, a second gunshot rang out. Jason stumbled back into a chair. His face paled and his eyes fluttered closed. The momentum sent him careening out of her view. As Meaghan dove on the man who had shot him, Fiona screamed out.

Her heart wouldn't bear losing him again. Summoning every ounce of determination, Fiona stood and faced Porras, fury blocking out the pain burning through her leg. They circled each other, both battered and bleeding, but neither willing to back down. She didn't care if he killed her as long as she could take him out with her and end this senseless attack on her family.

Beside her, Meaghan sent one of the men overboard with a roundhouse kick, then was pushed back into a wall, a fist to her face. Blood dripped from her nose, but she continued to fight, even overpowered.

As Fiona stepped toward Porras, something hit her from behind. She struggled to remain standing, but her strength was draining as fast as the blood flowing out of her leg. The ship blurred around her though she fought to stay conscious, her vision narrowing to only the dark sky overhead.

Before the outcome of their struggle could be determined, darkness claimed her, and she succumbed to the void, praying that Jason and Meaghan would somehow find a way to survive. In the depths of her unconsciousness, time stood still, and her mind drifted through a haze of memories and dreams. She saw glimpses of her old life with Jason—their laughter, their love, their hopes for the future and sweet moments with Matt. A sharp pain shot through her and her mind twisted, conjuring the vivid faces of people she'd been tasked to eliminate when she'd worked for the government. Her sins coming to take her to hell.

# *Chapter 21*

Jason had tumbled backwards into a chair, a bullet skimming his shoulder. He glanced back at Fiona. Her skin had turned a ghastly pale, her leg soaked in blood from the gunshot wound. At the same time, Meaghan fought against overwhelming odds, her luck shifting downward. The pressing need to rescue both of them and get revenge for Porras destroying his family's peaceful existence crashed over him, but he was too outnumbered, at least for now.

His thoughts were interrupted by the roar of engines. Looking out over the stern of the yacht, he caught sight of a speedboat advancing at breakneck speed toward the yacht. Steve was at the helm, with Sam holding a rifle in his hands. For a moment, Jason felt the weight lift off his shoulders, but a gunshot from behind him toward the boat had him terrified he'd lose everyone he cared about today. And each loss would be tied directly to his lie.

The last of the men protecting Porras had turned their attention toward the incoming boat, their own vessel still crippled by the cyberattack. Jason took that chance to throw one of the men overboard and punch another so hard with an uppercut, the man fell flat to the floor, losing his rifle to Jason in the process. Steve never swerved off his destination, despite the gunfire. As the large boat skidded to a stop beside the yacht, Sam leaped onto the lower deck, taking out one of Porras's men in the process. Their timing couldn't have been better.

Jason sprinted towards Meaghan, her face swollen from the beating and slammed aside the asshole using her as a punching bag.

"Thanks," Meaghan breathed, stumbling back and shaking out the impacts. Before Jason could respond, she lunged at the same man. He never saw the punch coming, and with a satisfying thud, he dropped to the deck, knocked out cold by one very pissed-off woman.

Porras and the two remaining guards had fled to another section of the boat, no doubt to reorganize and get more ammunition.

Fiona remained motionless on the ground. Jason squatted beside her. Her pulse carried on as a faint rhythm, assuring him she still had a chance of surviving this, but not for long.

"We need to get Fiona out of here," Jason called out to Sam, who was circling the deck, making sure the area was clear.

After disabling another guard who had wandered into the area, Sam rushed over to help. Together, they carefully lifted Fiona and made their way to the speedboat.

When she was placed behind Steve, his eyes narrowed on her injuries and her weakened condition. As he secured her in a blanket on the floor of the boat, he pointed a handgun and shot over Jason's shoulder. Jason spun around and saw one of Porras's thugs drop.

"Anyone else need medical care?" Steve called out to him.

Jason's shoulder was bleeding, but not too much. He didn't have the luxury to step back, not while Porras was still hell-bent in chasing down his family. He glanced at Meaghan, her face now swollen. She shook her head. He'd never get her off the yacht until she either took out the cartel or died trying.

"Not yet, but we have this. Go. Fiona's losing too much blood to survive much longer."

"I'll get her to the mainland for medical assistance."

Jason paused, afraid to let her go without him, but he had to finish this here and now. "Okay. Take care of her."

"Always." Steve pushed the throttle and turned away from the yacht, reaching top speed toward the mainland.

As the speedboat roared away, Jason turned his attention to the cause of this hellscape. "Porras!" he shouted, his temper seconds from detonating.

Sam waved down from the bridge. He'd taken it over and somehow restarted the engines. Jason could feel the lean of the boat as it turned toward the mainland, following Steve's course. He ran back to the bow and found Meaghan, blood dripping from her nose and a black-and-blue mark on her cheek and under her eyes, pointing a rifle at five men with their hands up and their weapons kicked out in front of them. There were two casualties on the ground in front, and she seemed primed to take out anyone else who stepped toward her. Jason backed her up, using the men's own duct tape to secure them, then scanned the area for anyone else free. Porras was nowhere to be found.

When Meaghan tied up the last thug, Jason descended

into the belly of the ship with Meaghan right behind him, adding to his arsenal as he searched for Porras.

They moved systematically through the ship's quarters. They entered each bedroom, knocking open the closets and bathrooms, checking under every bed. When they reached the galley, Jason caught sight of a man, cornered and looking like a caged animal. Montana was beside him, her expression a mix of fear and defiance. As Jason approached, the man in front of him came into focus. This was a fourteen- or fifteen-year-old boy. Same hair and build as Porras, but slighter. His eyes wore the same tension as Montana's.

Jason's hand clenched around the grip of his pistol. Another son? The thought drained his rage. This would never end. It would cycle over and over again for generations if he didn't find a way to stop it. Another Porras, someone who could hunt down Matt for years. Every fiber of his being screamed at him to pull the trigger, to end the cycle of revenge and pain. But he remembered Fiona's plea from days past. "An eye for an eye will only make the whole world blind," she'd whispered.

He agreed with her. He'd never kill an innocent boy. He couldn't.

Letting out a deep breath, he lowered the gun and Meaghan came around next to him. "I have nothing against you or your son," he said to Montana, his voice cold. "Porras, however, shot my wife and wants to kill my child. Where is he?"

The boy made a sharp move, pulling a gun from behind him. Before he could even point the gun, Meaghan lunged, expertly disarming him. A swift kick to his knees brought him crashing to the ground. Jason moved in, tying his hands behind his back and those of Montana.

Montana didn't fight him. Instead, she dropped her head, a tear sliding down her cheek. "You could have killed him," she whispered.

Jason met her gaze. "I could have. But your husband's cycle of violence ends here."

As they made their way back to the deck, the yacht was eerily quiet. Sam remained on the bridge, on the radio with the Coast Guard. Meaghan led Montana and her son to a seat close to where Porras's men were tied up.

Jason searched for Porras but couldn't see him. Meaghan pointed off the starboard side at the tender with a small outboard motor, almost to the horizon. "He abandoned ship leaving his family and team behind. So much for loyalty," she said loud enough for everyone to hear how their wonderful leader didn't care enough to save them.

"You've got to be kidding me." Jason stared at the boat carrying the man who wanted his family dead now getting away. "Tell Sam to go after him."

But before they could get into a chase, the piercing beam of a spotlight from a helicopter sliced through the darkness, followed by the deep growl of an approaching Coast Guard vessel. Jason wasn't going anywhere until he passed through a whole mountain of bureaucratic BS.

"US Coast Guard. Lay down your weapons and raise your hands!" came an authoritative voice through a megaphone.

Meaghan exchanged a glance with Jason. They knew they were on the side of the law, but the scene—the two of them, heavily armed, with a whole boatload of people tied up—could easily be misinterpreted.

Jason placed his weapon on the deck, raising his hands in surrender. Meaghan followed suit, placing her rifle next to Jason's. The Coast Guard personnel swarmed the yacht, several headed to the men tied up and several others to Jason and Meaghan. No one resisted arrest. Jason tried to explain how they came to be on the boat, but they ignored him and focused on securing the area. They were not interested in explanations. A few moments later, Sam came down from the bridge with an officer, his hands behind his back in handcuffs.

Jason stared at the aftermath of his failure to confront this problem years ago. He should have done something besides hiding out and not protecting all the people who mattered in his life. Matt had almost lost his life and Jason had no idea how much psychological damage this would do to him. Fiona was bleeding so profusely that she might not make it to the hospital in time. Meaghan and Sam both were in handcuffs. And Meaghan had undisclosed injuries she wouldn't complain about because she was that type of person. It was all on him. One hundred percent.

"These guys kidnapped my son," Jason explained to a Coast Guard officer, a stern-faced man with a silver streak in his hair.

"Where is your son?"

"He's with the state police in Bourne," Sam replied.

"He is?" Jason said. He thought they'd transport him somewhere else.

"It was the safest location for him while we came back out to get you."

"You can call them, Officer," Meaghan added, although she received a pretty angry expression in reply.

"And you only contacted us after you took control of the boat?"

Jason was the one who put them in this, so he answered for the team. "We have a lawyer, Barbara Singer." Jason had found Barbara's expertise in criminal law helpful in the early years of the business. She told them what lines they could cross and what lines they absolutely couldn't go near. She would not be happy about this situation. Not at all.

Montana shouted over everyone else, "They kidnapped us. This is all a setup. They killed those men." She pointed to the area where there were several dead men on the deck.

The officer raised an eyebrow, then turned to Jason. "Your lawyer better be damn good." He turned to Montana. "You're all coming with us for questioning."

As the Coast Guard crew began the process of transferring everyone from the yacht to the lower deck of the Coast Guard cutter, Meaghan whispered to Jason, "We have the kidnap demand letter. It'll work out."

Jason nodded, watching the members of the cartel as well as Montana and her son being led away. "As long as Fiona and Matt are safe," he murmured, the roar of the helicopter blades echoing overhead.

As the Coast Guard vessel motored away from the yacht, now commandeered by Coast Guard personnel, Jason, Meaghan and Sam sat next to each other on a long bench, under armed guard. Montana stared out the window while Porras's son wore a stony look of contempt. It wasn't an emotion that would simmer away quickly, but Jason had to believe that he'd soften over time. Not that he was worried about their feelings when Fiona's life could be draining away.

"That was a tough call back there," Meaghan said, nodding towards the kid who almost shot them. Jason had had a shot but Meaghan handled him without having to kill him, even after she'd been beat up by the other men.

"It was an easy call," Jason admitted. "I never want to hurt anyone. Even these assholes. But if they're going for me or someone I love, I'll do what I need to keep everyone safe. Your method was risky, because he could have taken you or me out. Total badass move. I owe you."

She smiled. "I could use a raise."

Sam leaned his head back to rest on the wall. "Combat pay."

Jason nodded. "Fair enough."

But Jason wasn't so quick to claim victory as they were ferried back to the mainland. Porras may have lost his protection, but both Matt and Fiona remained at risk as long as Porras himself was free in the world. His family couldn't survive living under the constant shadow of revenge.

Jason sat with his hands cuffed at a steel table in a gray conference room overlooking the ocean. Last night had seemed like a never-ending nightmare and yet here he was, caught in a state of limbo with Commander Grogan, a man who wanted hard answers from Jason, but refused to offer any news about Fiona or Matt. Jason remained as silent and calm as possible as the officer grilled him over and over about why he'd trespassed on

Porras's yacht. After two hours, Jason's patience wore thin at the Coast Guard officer's continued interrogation.

"My son was being held captive and the ransom note said I had to go out there alone to get him back. So I did." He spoke in a monotone voice as he had repeated this same line about fifty times.

"Alone? Some of your staff at your little security service also headed out there."

"I followed the demand on the note," he replied, not giving Grogan the answer he wanted. "They chose to follow me."

"They went out on their own without orders from you?"

"I did not give an order to follow me." Steve made that call with Fiona's urging.

Meaghan and Sam had been sent to other rooms. Jason warned them on the boat ride back to shore to remain silent no matter what they were accused of. They had enough experience to handle themselves like the professionals they were. Steve would most likely be back at headquarters with Calvin, Noah was still in the hospital and Kennedy had disappeared back into the cubicle where she lived in the Pentagon. The more he thought about it, the more they looked guilty of something. Hopefully, the blown-up house couldn't be pinned on them. They had quite a few murder charges looking straight at them. Sure, it was self-defense, although self-defense while trespassing was a difficult mountain to climb.

His thoughts remained consumed by concerns about the safety and whereabouts of his family. He had to know if Matt was safe, whether Fiona's gunshot wound had been treated in time and if Porras posed any lingering threat to their lives. The unknown gnawed at him. Yet, Commander Grogan wasn't sharing anything. The officer annoyed him. For the moment, Jason was in the dark.

The officer leaned forward, his eyes fixed on Jason, and said, "Mr. Stirling, you and your team took matters into your own hands, and there are definite consequences for your actions."

Jason clenched his jaw and refused to respond. The door to the interrogation room swung open. Barbara, sporting her usual navy suit and annoyed expression, entered the room, plopped a briefcase onto the table and stared down Grogan. "I'm Barbara Singer, Jason's attorney. And you are?"

"Commander Grogan, CGIS."

"CGI what?" she asked, with not even the smallest look of confusion.

"Coast Guard Investigative Service."

"Right." She took a seat next to Jason and said, "How are they treating you?"

"I'm good, but I don't know what's happening with Fiona and Matt."

She turned to Grogan. "Can we have a minute alone?"

He nodded and left the room.

As soon as the door closed, Jason spoke. "Matt is supposed to be with the state police. And I have no idea what happened to Fiona. I last saw her on a boat with Steve, bleeding profusely."

"I understand. Steve contacted me. He's with Matt at Falmouth Hospital waiting for Fiona to come out of the operating room."

"How is she?"

"So far, stable."

"Does she have security?"

"Steve's there, and local police have been notified that Porras is still at large."

It wasn't a perfect scenario, but Matt was safe with Steve and Fiona was stable, so far. But he had to get out of this interrogation room. He had to get to Fiona's side.

About fifteen minutes into their conversation, Commander Grogan returned. He immediately started in on his questioning again.

Barbara turned her shotgun gaze toward the officer. "My client is a concerned father who acted out of desperation to save his son from a dangerous criminal. We intend to cooperate fully, but we also expect his rights to be protected."

The officer hesitated, his composure slipping. "I understand, Ms. Singer, but you have to realize the seriousness of the situation here. Mr. Stirling and his team took the law into their own hands. Two of the guns found on board the ship were licensed to his business. Can you explain that?"

Barbara frowned. "Can you explain why the father of a kidnapping victim is being subjected to a harsh interrogation while the actual villain in all of this is running through the streets of Massachusetts without nearly half as much animosity thrown in his direction?"

Grogan glanced between Jason and Barbara, realizing that the power dynamic had shifted away from him. Barbara goaded him on for a few minutes, then commented on how the press were going to react when they learned that he'd kept a man from seeing his injured son and dying wife while the El Chapo of Colombia was on the loose. Jason knew she was bluffing, because of all the things he'd demanded of her when he'd sent her a retainer was the utmost privacy in all their dealings. His business did very well without any involvement from the press. Commander Grogan, however, did not know she was bluffing.

Barbara pressed on, her voice resolute. "Our priority should be to focus on capturing Andres Porras. My client may have obtained valuable information that can lead to the arrest of Porras and dismantle his criminal network. Jason is more than willing to cooperate fully if he is accorded some decency in this matter."

"Let me speak to my commanding officer," Grogan said before rushing from the room. He'd underestimated her, and it was becoming increasingly evident that he didn't fully grasp the intricacies of the situation.

"That went well. Thanks." Jason appreciated her on his side and hoped she didn't have to help him out of too many more jams, especially ones that involved Homeland Security.

"Give it five minutes. He'll send an underling to release you so he can save face."

Five minutes later, an ensign appeared, who apologized that Commander Grogan had been called to another matter. She handed Barbara and Jason a business card.

They left the harshly lit interrogation room, the weight of the world slightly lifted from their shoulders. Meaghan and Sam were waiting for them. The air outside seemed fresher, the corridors less confining, but Jason couldn't shake the nagging worry that gnawed at him like a persistent itch. Was his family safe?

Barbara must have sensed his unease because she placed a reassuring hand on his shoulder. "I'll drive you all to the hospital. If Fiona's half as stubborn as you are, she'll be fine," she said, her voice steady and calming.

Meaghan laughed. "They're pretty equally matched in that department."

As they stepped outside into the bright, sun-soaked day, Jason couldn't help but feel a renewed sense of determination. The hunt for Porras had begun in earnest, but his heart was torn between locating him and rushing to Fiona's side.

# *Chapter 22*

Fiona's eyes fluttered open, and the sterile white of the hospital room flooded her vision. Her head throbbed, and the pain in her leg was a constant reminder of the gunshot wound she'd sustained while trying to save Jason. She groaned, memories of the terrifying events flooding back.

"Mom?"

Fiona turned her head to see Matt sitting in a chair by her bedside. He looked different now, dressed in gray Massachusetts State Police sweatpants and sweatshirt. Her heart filled with relief at the sight of him, but her thoughts were consumed by the well-being of Jason, Meaghan and Sam.

"Are you okay?" Her voice was raspy as she reached out to touch her son's face.

"I'm okay, Mom," he said, taking her hand as he had when he was much smaller. "Steve took me to the police, and they were pretty cool." He turned his head toward the door and there was Steve, leaning against the doorframe, holding a large coffee cup. He looked as weary as she felt.

"Steve," she said, her voice low. "What's going on? Where's Jason? Meaghan? Sam?"

Steve walked into the room and set the coffee cup on the bedside table. "There's a lot to tell you," he began, taking a seat next to her. "On a good note, Jason, Sam and Meaghan are all alive."

Fiona exhaled as though she'd been holding her breath for a year. "I'm so relieved."

"Don't party too soon. They were caught up in a Coast Guard mission to intercept the yacht. They arrested everyone on board. Everyone, except for Andres Porras. He escaped before anyone could stop him."

"How could he escape in the middle of the ocean?"

"A dinghy. An expensive one with an onboard motor and enough gas to get him anywhere on Cape Cod, Nantucket or Martha's Vineyard. He's on the loose. There's reason to believe he's coming after you and Matt."

Fiona's heart sank at the mention of Porras. He'd done so much damage to her family. And he was still out there looking for them.

"Where's Jason now?" Fiona pressed, her fear escalating.

Steve hesitated for a moment before continuing. "Jason, Meaghan and Sam are all in custody. They were swept up in the investigation of Porras and his operation. It didn't help that our guns were scattered across the ship."

Fiona's mind reeled with the news. Her husband, her friend and Sam, all in custody?

"Don't worry. Barbara is taking care of everything," he added.

"Barbara?"

Steve cleared his throat and nodded, understanding her confusion. "Barbara Singer is an attorney Jason hired years ago for this exact situation," he explained. "Not this exact situation, but something close. She's the best of the best. Intimidating as hell. I sort of feel bad for the Coast Guard officers put in charge of speaking to her."

As Fiona held Matt's hand, she couldn't help but wonder where Porras was headed. It didn't take a whole lot of brain cells to realize he was coming after Matt and her.

A nurse came inside and told Steve that visiting hours were ending. Fiona demanded that Matt get to stay, and the nurse caved for him, only him.

Steve smiled in that way that told her he had everything on his end under control or as in control as he could get it. "I'm going to find doughnuts. I'll bring you back some." He waved and disappeared down the hall.

Fiona had only just met Steve, but in that short time, she understood why Jason had decided to go into business with him. Cool under pressure and he seemed to have an understanding of all the chess pieces in this game. She was grateful for his help.

"Are you really okay?" Fiona asked Matt when they were alone.

He nodded. "I was worried about you and Dad, but otherwise, I'm okay."

She loved that Matt was holding himself together, but he'd need to break down all his feelings eventually as she had after too many situations where blood stained her memories. Her first priority after everything calmed down was to find a decent therapist for him. Perhaps she could enlist her own therapist to give her a good recommendation. She'd need her own double sessions for the next few weeks to get over the immense rage bubbling up inside her.

The hospital room door swung open, and Jason rushed inside. He looked like an impossibly beautiful mess of a man. Rugged, with a steely determination etched into his features, his dark hair hanging disheveled onto his shoulders. Bruises and scrapes marred his gorgeous face.

His clothes were torn and stained with blood, evidence of the gunshot wound to his shoulder that he had miraculously survived. She'd so wanted to believe the bullet hadn't hit anything vital, but she had no idea. That lack of knowledge shook her to her core.

Despite the physical toll, an unwavering determination had him rushing to her side.

"Fi." His voice filled with emotion as he closed the distance between them. He enveloped her in his arms, and she clung to him as if her life depended on it.

She pulled back at the slight wince from him as she touched the wound on his shoulder. "Have you seen someone?"

"I couldn't do anything until I saw you and Matt." His embrace tightened, and he kissed the top of her head, his lips warm against her hair.

She looked up toward him and he kissed her lips. A kiss that reaffirmed their love and their unbreakable bond, a kiss that promised they would stay with each other and never let each other go.

As they pulled away, he turned to Matt, who had buried his head into the phone he was using, most likely to avoid the awkwardness of his parents making out next to him.

"Hey, champ." Jason's voice emitted as much warmth as a man who had been fighting for everyone's life for hours and hours could. He reached out and pulled Matt into a tight embrace. "I'm so glad to see you."

Matt embraced his father back, and Fiona could see the love and relief in his eyes. "I'm glad to see you too, Dad."

Jason straightened up, his expression turning serious. It was a look he had rarely used in their marriage. He'd always been the carefree, lighthearted guy at home and from what she'd heard from his former colleagues, seemed the same at work, until something threatened them, and then his attention became laser-focused. He addressed both of them. "Listen, we can't let our guard down. Andres Porras is headed in our direction. We need to be prepared for anything. How long are you planning on being in bed?"

Fiona didn't have the physical strength to fight off an attacker in her hospital room. "Say the word, and if someone else drives, I'll go anywhere to keep Matt safe."

It wasn't a difficult choice when he was standing over her with so much fire in his eyes and a willingness to do anything for Fiona and Matt. Jason's presence made her feel more secure, but she wouldn't be able to rest easy until Porras was no longer a threat.

Jason's fingers traced the edge of Fiona's hand. The sterile hospital scent hung in the air, but it was overpowered by the overwhelming sense of relief and gratitude. She'd seemed so far gone when he'd laid her down in the boat. Now that he had his family back, truly back with him, he was damned if he would let anyone come between them.

Beside him, Matt sat quietly. Jason couldn't fathom

the thoughts scrolling through his son's head. He'd been through more than anyone his age was expected to endure. And the threat remained as long as Porras was at large. They couldn't protect him from that fact. Keeping the danger hidden from Fiona for so many years never protected her, but made her too complacent. She'd let her guard down at the house because she had no idea such an evil man was headed in her direction. How Jason could make Matt understand the seriousness of the Porras cartel, without destroying what was left of his teenage years, he had no idea.

The exhaustion in Fiona's eyes was undeniable, but all her attention was now on protecting them. Jason had always respected her strength and determination, but he'd never seen her as some savage defender. She'd not only killed someone in cold blood, but she'd never stopped to process it. Instead, she carried on to the next task of saving Meaghan. Someday he'd get the answers he wanted, maybe even deserved, although he couldn't claim any righteousness in the matter of hidden lives.

He leaned in closer to her, and he gently squeezed her hand. "Do you need some rest?"

She shook her head. "Where's the rest of the team? I think they should come to my room so we can make a plan."

"Steve, Meaghan and Sam went to the cafeteria. I can text them to come up."

"Please." She reached back out to Matt. "Stay in this room. No matter what. I don't trust the security in this place."

"We're safe, Fiona," Jason reassured her. "We've

taken all the necessary precautions. There's even an armed guard at the door."

"That won't stop him," she whispered. "I saw the despair in his face when he pointed the gun at me. It's like he will never be forgiven for his son's death until he places the blame on you. It's like the revenge gods will give him absolution on his own bad decision by sending someone else to the grave, only he won't get his son back. That's something that he'll have to just endure for the rest of his life."

"Which makes it even more important that we get the hell out of here." Jason paused and watched as Fiona nodded in agreement. He leaned down to gently kiss her forehead. "We'll find a way to get through this. I don't know what it will be, but we'll find a way."

Fiona smiled for a moment, and then her smile disappeared, and her attention went back inside, scheming, planning and finding a way.

# *Chapter 23*

Fiona lay on the sterile hospital bed, her body throbbing with pain though she concealed it as best she could. The harsh fluorescent lights above cast an unforgiving pallor on the room, adding to her anxiety. She knew she had to keep her mind clear, no matter how intense the pain. She wished she could fade into a drug-induced sleep and wake up when the danger was gone and her leg was healed, but that wasn't an option so she had to let it go. She focused on the small cup of pain medication hidden under her pillow. She'd deliberately kept it out of sight, determined to maintain her mental clarity. In this life-and-death situation, any lapse in judgment could be fatal. Porras was out there, a relentless threat to her and her son Matt, and there was no room for weakness.

Beside her, Jason clutched his right arm. His shirt and whatever he'd tied around it as a makeshift bandage was stained with blood. She could see him slowing because of the pain. His stubbornness kept him from seeking medical attention.

She pressed the button for assistance. When the nurse arrived, Fiona asked to see the doctor. Dr. Gwen Ramirez, an old friend of Steve's from his days at Providence College, had taken over Fiona's care after a personal request from Steve. The head of the emergency department, she could keep an eye on anyone coming and going in the ER.

"Fiona, how are you feeling?" the doctor asked.

"I could be better."

Dr. Ramirez nodded and checked her vitals and the wound.

While she was busy, Meaghan and Sam walked in looking as though they'd both been hit by an eighteen wheeler. Fiona owed them and Noah for helping save her family.

Steve arrived a minute later, carrying a tray of food.

"Gwen, thanks for all of your assistance," he said as he placed the tray on the table next to Fiona.

"No problem. Are you hungry?" She glanced at the decadent tray piled with three slices of pizza, a few brownies, cookies and a doughnut.

"Just feeding the troops."

Jason reached for a slice of the pizza, but Fiona placed a hand on his to stop him. "Did you want the veggie slice?" he asked.

"I want you to get your arm looked at," she said.

"I'm not leaving this room. Not while you're here."

Dr. Ramirez must have understood Fiona's stared request, because she walked over to him and pointed at the blood leeching through his shirt. "Jason, you really should let me take a look at that arm. It's bleeding quite a bit."

Jason hesitated, glancing at Fiona and then Matt. "I'm okay." Typical idiot. He'd pass out in the name of protecting Fiona and Matt.

"You're not okay." Fiona recognized the struggle in his eyes and made the decision for him. "You can't help me if you're injured too. Let her take care of it."

Dr. Ramirez nodded in agreement. "Let me at least look at it. If it's not serious, I can treat it in here so you don't have to leave Fiona's side."

Reluctantly, he agreed. She carefully pulled the clothing from his arm and examined him. Fiona could see him straining to hide his suffering.

Once the doctor was done, she spoke only to Jason. "The scratch on your arm is deep enough to cause some nasty bleeding but not severe enough to warrant more than a stitch or two. Let me call my assistant and we can have it fixed in a few minutes."

"I don't think it's necessary."

"Don't be a baby," Meaghan said, which made Fiona smile. Jason hated being challenged.

"Fine," Jason relented. "If we can remain here while we figure out a few things."

Dr. Ramirez agreed. She called for a physician assistant to bring her what she needed. They worked efficiently, cleaning the wound and stitching Jason up.

As they finished, the doctor offered Jason a reassuring smile. "All done. Just keep it clean and change the dressing regularly. You'll be all right, but try not to get shot again." She looked at Fiona. "You too."

"I'll do my best," Fiona replied, knowing she'd step in front of a gun again if someone she cared about needed her help.

Jason nodded to the doctor. "Thanks. I probably would have left it to fester if I had to leave Fiona alone."

Dr. Ramirez looked over at Meaghan, Sam and Steve.

"I think she would have been in adequate hands either way." As she left the room, she waved to Steve.

"Thanks, Gwen. If you ever need anything, I've got your back," Steve called out to her.

"I don't want to think about what trouble I'd be in to require your assistance." Then she disappeared down the hall.

Don, the physician assistant, remained behind to finish wrapping a bandage around Jason's wound.

Meaghan stepped closer to Fiona. "We're on borrowed time. News crews had caught word of the arrests by the Coast Guard. If Porras doesn't know where we are, he'll know soon enough." She pointed out the window toward several news crews setting up cameras near the hospital entrance.

Fiona glanced over at Matt, who was playing a game on the phone and trying to avoid any eye contact with his mother or father. "We need a plan."

Steve received a phone call and stepped toward the edge of the room to speak with someone. He agreed with whoever was on the phone and only gave one-word answers that showed no indication of the topic of conversation. Then he took a huge inhale and spit out, "Shit. Okay, we'll be prepared."

Everyone's attention turned to him as he ended the call.

"What?" Jason asked.

Fiona somehow knew what was coming. She prepared for the worst, but held her breath until Steve spoke in case it wasn't as bad as she imagined.

"Porras was seen on camera stealing a car in Cotuit. He's headed in this direction."

"What are the police doing about it?" Fiona asked.

"They found the car about ten miles away from where it was stolen. They have no idea where he's disappeared to, but he's within two miles of the Falmouth Hospital."

"We couldn't exactly blast our way out of this hospital without a serious amount of people getting hurt or worse, killed," Fiona said. "It would be better to meet him somewhere less populated. Does he have backup?"

Steve shook his head. "The Coast Guard have both his team and family in custody. Depending on the evidence they have, they could arrest or deport the whole group of them back to Colombia. If they're arrested here, they stand a much lower chance of being able to bribe or threaten the judges. He has nothing to lose if he carries out his plan alone."

Even without his team, Porras remained a relentless threat, and they couldn't afford to lower their guard for a moment. Fiona wished she had more energy. Her thoughts cycled from fear to fury as the pain from her leg sent her mood spiraling and fogged her brain almost as much as pain medications would.

With the armed police officer stationed outside their room, the small group gathered around Fiona's hospital bed.

Steve cleared his throat, his brow furrowed with concern. "I agree with Fiona. We can't stay in this hospital indefinitely. It's only a matter of time before Porras tracks us down. Hell, he could already be here."

"We can't let him find us here," Jason said.

When Don finished with Jason's arm, he joined the conversation. "I could get you discharged, and maybe we can have you leave through the service elevator. Somewhere he wouldn't expect." He stood at the door, not leaving, as though he were more part of the team than a member of the hospital staff.

Sam pulled out his phone. "I'll contact the local police and give them a description of Porras. They can be on the lookout and provide extra security here. If they've been tracking him, we might gain a head start."

"We have a safe house in the area," Meaghan said. "We can get you there discreetly, and it'll be a secure place to hide out."

"Like the last safe house that went down in flames only a day ago?" Fiona asked.

"You may be right. Our security might be compromised."

Fiona looked over at Don. She didn't know anything about him. He could be working for Porras for all she knew, and although that was far-fetched, they needed to keep their plans under wraps in front of him.

"We've arranged a police presence at your residence, Fiona. But it's not safe to go back there," Steve said.

"I agree. I'd prefer to go somewhere no one can connect us to." She glanced at Don, who was now scratching notes on his iPad.

Jason followed the direction of her gaze to Don and nodded. Steve motioned that he understood what she was saying as well.

Jason patted Don on the shoulder. "Thank you. We appreciate your help."

Fiona received a text message from Steve to her and the rest of the team. "'My brother has a cabin up in the mountains, far away from here. It's secluded and secure. We could take you and Matt there until we're sure it's safe,'" she said, reading the text aloud.

Meaghan and Sam both agreed with a thumbs-up emoji. Jason gave a real thumbs-up.

As the group continued to brainstorm and finalize their plans via cell phone, Fiona couldn't help but feel a glimmer of hope amid the uncertainty. They had a fighting chance to outsmart Porras and keep their family safe.

She tried to sit up and nearly fell over with pain. Jason rushed to her side. "If you're not ready…"

"If I'm not ready, I'm dead. We have to get out of here." She winced through the agony of movement and sat up. She pointed to her clothes, but paused as her ears strained to catch the distant echoes of chaos that filtered through the hospital corridor. Shouts, running footsteps and urgent voices signaled the approaching danger. She didn't have the time or energy to battle into a pair of pants.

She turned to Matt, who sat on the edge of her hospital bed, somehow as aware of the danger approaching as she was. "Matt," she whispered, "I need you to hide behind the recliner. Stay quiet, and don't come out until one of us says it's safe."

The fear in Matt's eyes mirrored her own, but he nodded and slid beneath the bed without hesitation. He sadly had experience in hiding now. Fiona reached out to give his hand a reassuring squeeze before returning her attention to the unfolding crisis.

Steve, Meaghan and Sam leaped into action, taking up defensive positions around the small hospital room. Meaghan was by the door, her hand on the handle, ready to bar it if necessary. Sam crouched by the window, his trained eyes scanning the exterior for any sign of trouble.

Jason moved to the side table and pulled a compact, concealed weapon from his back pocket.

"Jason, what are you doing with that?" Fiona asked, with more appreciation than anger.

He smiled. "I thought it might come in handy."

Fiona couldn't argue with the logic, but the sight of the weapon in his hands sent a shiver down her spine. It was a chilling reminder of just how far they had been pushed. He had been told by the Coast Guard to keep a small profile.

Meaghan's voice cut through the tension. "Something is getting closer. We need to be prepared."

Fiona took a deep breath, rallying her resolve. It was difficult turning fierce when her leg felt like a deadweight and her ass hung out of her hospital gown. "Matt, stay behind the recliner," she said. "Sam and Steve, move the bed. We'll put it in front of the door."

Sam nodded and joined Steve in sliding the heavy hospital bed across the room, positioning it as a makeshift barricade. It wasn't much, but it was the best they could do with the limited resources at hand.

Don, who had turned from a spy wannabe into a trembling mess, finally found his voice. "What should I do?"

Meaghan, as always, cool and collected under pressure, directed him to a corner of the room by the window, where he would be shielded from the door. "Don, you'll be in charge of calling security to get us additional protection on this floor. Keep your voice low."

With Don settled into his new role, the room was as fortified as it could be. Fiona took a deep breath, her mind racing, her heart pounding, as the sounds of chaos outside the room grew louder, drawing nearer with each passing second. They were ready, but they were defending a fishbowl and had to take into account all the innocent souls around them. And then a loud boom sent the entire room into confusion.

Jason stood near the barricaded hospital room door, his heart pounding as his nemesis arrived like a tornado. The deafening explosion rattled the corridor. He wanted to rush out of the room and put a stop to this once and for all, but Porras could be expecting that. It could all be a trap. Or maybe law enforcement had arrived and had finally subdued him.

He exchanged a glance with Fiona, and their unspoken agreement was palpable. She held her space as though nothing had changed. There was not an ounce of optimism in her expression, but instead a steadfast focus on protecting everyone around them. She had a better mindset. Thinking about being saved would only weaken their position. Innocent lives might already have been taken. At least Matt was safely hidden. Meaghan, Sam and Steve stood beside him, as focused as Fiona. They were ready to confront Porras.

When a loud bang came down on the door, Porras's voice, cold and menacing, punched up the tension. "Open this door or I'll start taking hostages. You have one minute."

Time was of the essence. They needed to make a decision. Fiona appeared both immobile and indestructible sitting up on the bed, her eyes lasered on the door.

"Jason," she whispered, "if he wants us, he can't be focused on anyone else."

He nodded, his mind racing as he contemplated their

limited options. So much for a peaceful stay at a cabin in the woods. This would be the final showdown. "I agree."

Jason signaled to Steve, Meaghan and Sam. "Steve, create a diversion—throw something loud on the floor. Meaghan and Sam, be prepared to act."

Don, the physician assistant, was still relaying information to hospital security. He lowered the phone from his ear and shrank into the corner.

Jason knew this was not the most straightforward defense, but they had few other options. If Porras started shooting through the door, any or all of them could get killed.

While the others prepared to act, Jason addressed Porras through the door. "Let's talk. We don't want anyone else to get hurt."

There was a tense silence, broken by more disruptions outside the door. A woman screamed as though someone had hurt her.

Porras's voice, filled with malicious intent, once again pierced through the door. "Time's up, Stirling. Open the door."

Jason took a deep breath and then nodded at Steve, Meaghan and Sam. Sam pushed the bed back and threw open the door, revealing a hallway filled with a faint haze of smoke. Porras stood in the doorway, holding an AK-15. Steve, tucked into the edge of the room just out of sight of Porras, hurled the food tray to the floor. The clattering noise echoed down the hallway, diverting their attacker's attention. At that same moment, Jason saw his chance and rushed him, while Meaghan and Sam lunged at him from different sides.

The room filled with shouts, grunts and the harsh

clatter of a firearm hitting the floor. Steve rushed forward to help.

"Jason, look out!" Meaghan yelled as Porras slammed his fist into Jason's face.

The blow rocked him to the side, nearly crashing him into the wall. Jason shifted and kicked Porras's legs out from under him. He went down easily. As Meaghan went to hold Porras down, he swung at her, sending her onto the floor. Porras then moved toward Sam, but Sam kicked him in the face, sending his head back into the wall. Fiona called out, pulling everyone's attention for a moment.

Steve stayed out of the brawl, but got hold of the weapon. He pointed it carefully toward Porras, who had had the fight knocked out of him.

With one final push, Meaghan and Sam managed to overpower Porras, pinning him to the ground. Jason and Steve stood over him.

Fiona tossed Jason a white cord. He didn't stop to ask what she'd unplugged to obtain it. He wanted to use it to strangle the bastard, but Fiona was right. An eye for an eye wasn't worth it. Instead, he pulled back Porras's arms and tied him up. In the process, his elbow might have slipped and broken Porras's nose. He wouldn't, however, kill the man.

Breathing heavily, Meaghan picked up Don's cell phone, which was still connected to hospital security. "We need immediate law enforcement in Room 215. Subject is currently unarmed and subdued."

Jason returned to Fiona's side. She'd remained on the bed, almost as though she made herself the most visible person available when Porras came inside. The thought that she'd put herself out there as a target scared the hell out of him, but made perfect sense. She was protecting Matt and Jason and the whole team.

The police arrived, a full-on SWAT unit. According to the officer in charge, Porras had gotten hold of a doctor's white coat and hid his weapon underneath. No one stopped him from entering and by the time he learned the location of Fiona, he was already on the second floor and taking out anyone who tried to slow his approach. Two people were injured, but luckily, no one was killed.

Fiona wanted to leave the hospital immediately after the police left. Dr. Ramirez thought she could move to another room and spend the evening there. They had moved the other patients from the second floor to different rooms and in some cases, different hospitals.

"No, thank you. I'd feel safer at home." She had somehow managed to sneak into the bathroom and get dressed, pulling her bad leg though some large blue scrub pants. Matt assisted her to a wheelchair and they waited until she received an official discharge.

Dr. Ramirez shrugged, knowing she wasn't going to convince Fiona to remain there after so much had happened. "Promise me you'll be back in three days so I can check on the wound?"

Fiona smiled. "I promise." She raised her hand up like a scout.

"Very well. Will there be anyone there to check on you?"

Meaghan nodded. "I'll spend the night on the couch. If she does anything to jeopardize her healing, she'll suffer the consequences."

Fiona burst out laughing and Jason appreciated the humor.

He wasn't sure if he was invited back to the house as well, so he stayed silent for a few minutes. After everything they'd been through, he certainly didn't want to crash her peace.

"Ready?" Fiona asked him, putting her hand out for him to hold.

"Ready for what?" he responded, taking her hand and loving the warmth from the touch of her skin against his.

"To go home."

"I'd thought you'd never ask." And he finally breathed again.

# Chapter 24

For four beautiful, perfect, dream-like days, Fiona lived in a bubble with her once dead husband and their son. Jason couldn't stop complimenting the decor of the house, the food on the table, and her flexibility, which was better than it had been when they'd both been younger. Fiona supplied him with just as many compliments. In the years they'd been apart, he'd learned to cook, clean and take care of a place. A far cry from the man-child who held her with the strength of a soldier and loved her every night, but couldn't pick up his socks from the floor or find the dishwasher. He still knew exactly how to turn his wife on in the bedroom, and he made a fabulous chocolate cheesecake. Despite their injuries, they found plenty of ways to reignite their romance. She'd missed being with someone who could take off some of the burden that had been crushing her. She'd missed those strong arms and the way he bit her lip when they kissed good-night, an invitation to so much more. She couldn't wait to spend the rest of their hopefully long lives together.

He and Matt took the time to know each other again. Matt quizzed him on his military service, and Jason was surprisingly open with where he'd been deployed early in his career and many of his assignments later in his career. At least the assignments that weren't still classified. Matt seemed in awe of his father, and Fiona had never been happier.

When Matt returned to school with a bodyguard shadowing him for the time being, Fiona and Jason had time to enjoy one fabulous cup of coffee together before the doorbell rang.

She put down her mug and frowned. The thought of someone breaking up this perfect moment with Jason annoyed her.

"I'll get it," Jason said, strolling to the door with a calm focus and alertness.

Fiona stood up and slipped a perfectly weighted paring knife into her hand. Just in case.

When Jason opened the door, a very tall, middle-aged white man in a navy suit was standing with a forced ease. Fiona knew before the man opened his mouth exactly who he was. CIA. Not field, but an analyst.

He put out his hand toward Jason. "Phil Mayers. I'm looking for Fiona Stirling."

"Why?" Jason did not release his hand and seemed to hold it more securely.

The man tried not to wince, but Jason seemed intent on creating an uncomfortable moment.

Fiona waited for his answer out of his view.

"I'd like to discuss it privately with her."

"I'm here," Fiona said, rushing forward before Jason broke the man's fingers.

Jason looked over his shoulder at her. He had that adorable protective look that had made her fall in love

with him so many years ago. But this wasn't his battle
to fight. "You can discuss anything in front of my husband." She hoped the man would tell Jason all her secrets.

"Actually, I can't, ma'am."

Jason backed up and allowed Fiona to get closer to Mr.
Mayers. "If you need anything..." He slipped the knife
out from behind her back as he headed to the kitchen.

Fiona stepped outside with Mayers. "What can I do
for you?"

"Director Downes wants to see you."

"Right now?"

"He's waiting at the Four Seasons."

"He still has expensive taste," she said.

"I wouldn't know, ma'am." Decades in a cubicle must
have scrubbed the humor right out of this guy.

"When?"

"Now."

It was no use trying to have a normal conversation,
so she stuck to the facts. "What room?"

"In the restaurant."

"That's new." She didn't have a choice. If she didn't
comply with this demand, she'd receive a less hospita-
ble invitation. "I'm taking my own car. I'll be there in
under an hour."

He didn't seem excited about her response, but went
back to his car and sat. He'd be following her into the
city to make sure she arrived on time.

Jason was standing at the sink cleaning the coffeepot
when she returned. "Everything okay?"

"I have to go out."

"Want me to come?"

"Yes, but you weren't invited."

There was a silence between them, but from the look in his eyes, he understood. "I'll head into the office. Want to meet me there when you get out?"

"That would be great." She wrapped her arms around his neck and kissed him.

He pulled her closer to him, pressing his lips harder into hers. The scratch of his chin made her want to stay there in his arms and ignore everyone else in the world. It was Jason who pulled away first. "Stay safe." His finger traced the curve of her jaw, and he pulled her back for one more kiss.

She walked away from him breathless.

Arriving in the hotel restaurant forty minutes later, Fiona strolled inside in a red wrap dress, her hair styled to perfection. Despite the lift in her chin, she felt a deep sense of unease settling over her. Fiona now found herself in the more unsettling presence of a familiar figure from her past.

CIA Director Ron Downes sat at a table in the back of the restaurant. Private, but it provided a perfect view of the room. He held a lowball glass in his hand, most likely containing a Manhattan. He couldn't resist that drink, even at eleven in the morning. His imposing stature contrasted sharply with his controlled demeanor. Ron was renowned for his acute observation skills and his uncanny ability to make swift, precise decisions. Fiona had never been comfortable working under his command in the clandestine force, and she had hoped to leave those days behind. He made kill orders seem as though he were ordering out for coffee. Each success she had had ripped a bit of her soul away from her.

"Mrs. Stirling," he greeted her, his voice as cold and unforgiving as steel. "I've missed having you on my crew."

Fiona shook her head, her expression tainted with suspicion. "After this week, I remember why I chose not to work with you anymore."

Ron leaned forward, his penetrating gaze locked onto hers. "You and your husband have created quite the mess. Gun and murder charges looming over everyone on Jason's team, not to mention the myriad antics from this past week and the years before. They've skirted the law just enough to stay one step ahead of the authorities for several years now."

Familiarity with Ron led Fiona to the unsettling realization that he hadn't convened this meeting merely for a new attempt to recruit her back into service. There was a deeper purpose, an ulterior motive that filled her with trepidation. And it would involve more than just her.

"I'm done, retired, my aim is off, my heart isn't in it anymore, my soul isn't corrupt enough to carry on."

Ron ignored her speech. "You just proved how valuable you still are to your country. I want your skills back in service, Fiona, and occasionally, the skills of your team as well. You're all highly valuable assets to the government."

Fiona hesitated, her mind racing through the potential consequences. "Jason and I have no working relationship. He's not linked to me at all."

"I think he's very much linked to you. You don't give yourself enough credit. He'll do anything for you. And without you, the whole group of them might lose their business license and all spend a bit of time in jail as an example to the good citizens of Massachusetts."

The prospect of working once more with Ron sent her mind reeling back in time to when she'd do anything to keep her family free from her past actions. Blackmail was Ron's favorite game and he never lost. He wouldn't lose this time either, because Fiona would never sacrifice her husband and friends, as he knew.

In their world, the boundaries between right and wrong, legal and illegal, were often blurred. The events of the past week had underscored that reality, and they'd teetered on the brink of catastrophe more times than she could count. If accepting Ron's terms meant safeguarding Jason's team's well-being and protecting her family, then Fiona knew she had no choice but to consider the proposition. Porras could have his team follow up and take out Jason, Matt or her, even from a federal prison. Having Ron's protection would prove useful in the future.

With a heavy sigh, she finally nodded. "I'd have to talk to Jason and Steve. It's not my business. We'd also need guarantees. Not that I don't trust you, Ron, but really, should I trust anyone in my life?"

"Absolutely not. Everyone has a breaking point. Although I've found you to be a particularly difficult person to crack."

"I learned from the best."

Ron smiled at the compliment. "Welcome back to the game."

She drove straight to Jason's office, once a sanctuary, now marred by the events of the past week. With Porras in custody and his main cartel officers behind bars, the immediate threat had been neutralized. Jason's team had returned, their mission accomplished, yet the scars of their recent ordeal still lingered.

Fiona located Jason first. He was at his desk. He jumped out of his seat when he saw her.

"Well?"

"Grab Steve and let's meet in the conference room. We need to talk."

"Both of us?"

She nodded, then turned back to the conference room. She didn't want to delay and she wasn't going to explain this twice. She stood by the window when they both arrived.

Steve, wearing a golf shirt and khakis like an accountant nearing retirement, strolled in and sat at the table. Jason followed, but he didn't sit. He stayed on the opposite side of Fiona and propped one hip on the table.

Fiona couldn't bring herself to speak directly about her shadowy past and the director's demands. Not yet. She steered the conversation toward safer ground. "It seems you guys are doing a great job of building this business. And it's not my place to step in and offer suggestions on how to add more depth to your services."

"But?" Steve asked, his eyes never leaving Fiona's face.

"Have you ever thought of branching out into some more profitable areas of security?" she asked.

"Such as?" Jason moved closer to her, his expression far more hostile than Steve's.

"Maybe adding the government as a client, a silent partner."

"Fi, you've always been so guarded about your past

work. What aren't you telling me? Not that I don't have an idea. I have a very vivid idea."

She hesitated, her gaze locking onto his. "There are things in my past I'm not proud of. Things not even my therapist knows, but I've changed. Yet, there are advantages to going into business with this kind of underground government entity."

Steve leaned forward. "I have got to hear the advantages, because most of our employees are not exactly fans of working for the military or any police force."

"For one thing, the charges about to be brought down on you, Jason, Meaghan and Sam will be dropped."

"Charges? We didn't break any laws." Steve jumped to his feet.

Jason shook his head. "We may have skirted a few things, but we've never had an issue before."

"It wouldn't matter if you broke every law on the books or not. Evidence will materialize, gun permits will disappear from the government database, and there would be prison time." They understood how this worked—they'd both worked in highly classified levels of the government, although most of their work involved assignments on the up-and-up. Ron preferred to work in the total dark. "So anyway, I agreed to their terms."

"Son of a bitch." Steve clenched his fist. "Can we inform the team?"

"Probably not right away."

"So what about you? How are you a part of this?"

"You use me when you need me. Otherwise, I keep my head down in my laptop and write for a living."

After Steve departed, still swearing under his breath,

Fiona walked over to Jason and rested her head in his chest. He kissed the top of her head.

"You retired from a job you hated, didn't you?" He wrapped her in his arms tight.

"I tried."

"And this fiasco brought you back into their sight."

"Sort of. Although they were waiting for a chance to bring me back in."

"You did save Matt by diving off a ship in the middle of the ocean."

"Any parent would have done that for their child."

"Then you snuck back on the boat and saved my life."

"We're married." She looked up into his beautiful eyes. "I'd already lost you once. I couldn't let you die again without a fight."

"Had I known you were such a badass, I definitely would have put my dishes in the dishwasher when we first married."

"You made up for your lack of domestic skills with outstanding bedroom abilities. I'm glad to know you're still so very—" she kissed his lips "—very capable there."

They kissed in a slow, easy way that gave Fiona comfort while also heating up her need for him. He pulled her over to the couch where they stayed wrapped in each other's arms.

"I'm sorry you got dragged into this. I should have made this all go away years ago," he said.

"But it brought you back to me. The price was high, but I have expensive taste." She leaned into his arms and closed her eyes.

"Perhaps we can use our new silent partner to secure better pay for everyone and improve our security systems. This opportunity could keep you in a lifestyle that you deserve." Jason tried to be positive, which Fiona appreciated.

"Or get us killed." She didn't want to live like this forever, always looking over her shoulder, always worried about her family and friends. No amount of money was worth that, but keeping everyone out of prison—that was worth it.

"Do you think they could protect us? We still have to fend off Porras and his cartel members. There were over fifty people involved in his operation at the time of his arrest."

"Downes will send us resources that we'd never be able to acquire as civilians, so there's that. In exchange, we're going to have to handle problems that will make our war against Porras seem like dodgeball." Fiona didn't want to think about the future anymore. It would arrive sooner than she wanted.

Director Ron Downes's proposition loomed over them, and Porras was still very much alive and still intent upon revenge for the death of his son and now the arrest of not only himself, but his wife, his other son and several key members of his entourage. Perhaps they would never find peace.

# Chapter 25

*One Month Later*

Fiona Stirling twirled around like Ginger Rogers in a bright blue chiffon tea-length gown, off the shoulder so her curled blond hair could rest on her bare shoulders. She swirled around again and smiled.

"Beautiful," Meaghan said from across the room. When Fiona had first learned about Meaghan's assignment protecting her, it had felt like a punch to the face. That she'd opened up her heart to this woman who was being paid to remain at her side hurt more than anything. Yet, Meaghan had both taken her job seriously and valued Fiona's friendship. Fiona thought long and hard about that and realized it was possible to do both at once. Her friend looked elegant in a short white dress that revealed annoyingly long legs. With her hair pulled up in a French twist, she seemed every bit the fashionista.

Fiona's mother would be rolling over in her grave at her daughter's refusal to wear white when walking down the aisle again. But Fiona never prioritized other people's insecurities over her own need to be herself. Although she and Jason wanted something a bit different from their first wedding where she wore black, white felt as though she was going backward. So she opted for the pale blue dress and he opted for a light gray suit with a tie matching her dress. The invited guests were asked to wear black or white.

Perhaps Fiona was being a bit superstitious, but she had ended up a widow after she'd worn black to her first wedding. A mourning color wasn't the perfect shade, but at the time she cared more about rebelling against her mother's social demands. For this wedding, she was embracing color and life and fun. Having the wedding at her favorite restaurant, The Oceanside Grill, made the day even more special. The view of the harbor provided an elegant backdrop to the ceremony and dinner.

Matt arrived with his friend Sarah. Both dressed all in black. They looked good together. After everything he'd gone through, it was great he had a person he trusted in his life. He'd changed since his kidnapping. He'd hardened, taking every risk seriously. Sarah, with her sense of humor and ability to roll through life without too much worry, made for a perfect complement to Matt's more serious nature. Fiona hoped he'd get through the adversity with minimal emotional damage, but she was realistic and had already arranged for him to meet with a therapist to air his thoughts about the torture they'd put him through—having his father resurrected and living with a constant threat on his shoulders.

"You nervous, Mom?" he asked as he gave her a hug.

"Nervous? Not a chance. I'm so very happy and excited about starting the rest of my life with your dad."

"He's pretty nervous."

"Is he?" That made Fiona's heart burst with a whole flutter of butterflies.

"He's pulling at his tie and looks like he's biting down on a bullet."

"Good to know."

She called over the waitress who had just arrived with a tray of champagne and asked if she would bring Jason some scotch in a champagne flute. The server thought that would be a great idea.

When she left, Meaghan laughed. "That'll loosen him up."

"Maybe. He's too in control of everything in his life—at least he thinks he is."

"That is a definite personality flaw, although he did hire you, and you're his most unpredictable hire yet." She tipped her glass toward Fiona. "I'm glad he and Steve added you to the roster. Now that there are two women on the ground, we have more standing. And thank you for making sure I had a very generous pay raise."

"You deserve it. The same bullets are flying at you as are flying at the men."

"True. Although I'm better at avoiding them." She shifted back and forth like a character in *The Matrix*.

"Which means, in reality, you should make more than the men on the team. Bullets take a lot of time off to heal." She thought of the intensive physical therapy Noah had done to return to good enough shape to get back into the office, but not yet back into the field. Fiona and Jason had also suffered through weeks of rehabilitation. She told herself she'd start back in small roles at the security agency.

Meaghan's continued friendship made the idea of

working with Jason and the team easier to swallow, although she preferred a life of writing to anything that involved bullets and blood. Ron Downes had made it clear that she would be placed back in service at his discretion. He tended to deal with the assignments that carried the highest risk.

Meaghan tweaked the clip in Fiona's hair, lifting a section just over her ear and twisting it behind in an elegant curl. After they both decided she was perfect, they walked toward the outside deck where the guests and Jason waited for the exchange of vows. They had no officiant and no best man, maid of honor or anyone except them. Instead, they gave all thirty people an intimate role in their public declaration of love toward each other.

Meaghan handed Fiona a simple bouquet of blue irises, before leaving her side and heading to her seat. Fiona walked down the aisle toward her husband, past, present and future. His smile widened as he caught sight of her. And a bit of something else, a devilishness that assured her that they would not only remain together for a long, long time, but they'd each enjoy life so much more with the other by their side. Their relationship had so many new angles and corners and curves in it, but they weren't the same people who had married years ago and they didn't want the same relationship. They wanted something more.

When she arrived at the end of the aisle, she kissed Jason as though a minister had just announced the groom could kiss the bride. Deep, sensuous, a claiming, a promise and an oath between them.

"I owe you my life, all of my love and everything I

own. My purpose on earth is being your partner. I love you, Fi."

She kissed him again, never getting enough of his lips. "Each minute we're together makes my life sweeter and happier. You're my phoenix and I hope this is your final rising."

The crowd clapped and lifted a glass to toast them.

The dinner featured roasted sea bream and beef tenderloin finished with a three-tiered cake that included a layer of Fiona's favorite carrot cake, Jason's favorite chocolate truffle cake and Matt's favorite red velvet.

Janet, Fiona's agent, had flown in from New York City dressed in a Ralph Lauren long black skirt with a white silk blouse. She oozed money, much of it from the profit of Fiona's book. As she sipped champagne, she tried to convince some of Jason's colleagues that they each had a story to tell and she was the person to represent them. None of them took the bait. They preferred a life in the shadows, away from the spotlight. With their new collaboration with the government, they would get their wish.

Barbara also attended with news. She'd received notice from the Justice Department that Montana and her son were deported back to Colombia. Porras and his men weren't so fortunate. They'd been charged with federal racketeering, murder and drug distribution. If found guilty, Porras wasn't going anywhere for a long time.

The risk still lingered, but as Fiona and Jason stepped out into the beautiful day, they both felt unshackled and able to be free.

Until Ron called.

* * * * *

*Look for the next thrilling story in*
*Veronica Forand's Fresh Pond Security miniseries,*
*coming March 2025 from*
*Harlequin Romantic Suspense!*